HOME FIRES IN FRANCE

By

DOROTHY CANFIELD

Author of "The Bent Twig," "The Squirrel-Cage,"
"Hillsboro People," etc.

NEW YORK

HENRY HOLT AND COMPANY

1918

PRINTED IN THE U. S. A.

THE QUINN & BODEN CO. PRESS
RAHWAY, N. J.

DEDICATED
TO
GENERAL PERSHING

PUBLISHER'S NOTE

This book is fiction written in France out of a life-long familiarity with the French and two years' intense experience in war work in France. It is a true setting-forth of personalities and experiences, French and American, under the influence of war. It tells what the war has done to the French people at home. In a recent letter, the author said, "What I write is about such very well-known conditions to us that it is hard to remember it may be fresh to you, but it is so far short of the actual conditions that it seems pretty pale, after all."

CONTENTS

HOME FIRES IN FRANCE

NOTES FROM A FRENCH VILLAGE IN THE WAR ZONE

PERHAPS the first thing which brought our boys to a halt, and a long, long look around them, was the age of the place. Apparently it has—the statement is hardly exaggerated—always been there. As a matter of historical fact it has been there for more than a thousand years. On hearing that, the American boys always gasped. They were used to the conception of the great age of "historical" spots, by which they meant cities in which great events have occurred—Paris, Rome, Stratford-on-Avon, Granada. But that an inconsiderable settlement of a thousand inhabitants, where nothing in particular ever happened beyond the birth, life, and death of its people, should have kept its identity through a thousand years gave them, so they said, "a queer feeling." As they stood in the quiet gray street, looking up and down, and taking in the significance of the fact, one could almost visibly see their minds turning away from the text-book idea of the Past as an unreal, sparsely settled period with violent historical characters in doublet and ruff or chain mail thrusting broadswords into one an-

other or signing treaties which condemned all succeeding
college students to a new feat of memory; you could
almost see their brilliant, shadowless, New World youth
deepened and sobered by a momentary perception of the
Past as a very long and startlingly real phenomenon,
full, scaringly full of real people, entirely like ourselves,
going about the business of getting born, being married
and dying, with as little conscious regard as we for
historical movements and tendencies. They were never
done marveling that the sun should have fallen across
Crouy streets at the same angle before Columbus discovered America as to-day; that at the time of the French
Revolution just as now, the big boys and sturdy men
of Crouy should have left the same fields which now lie
golden in the sun and have gone out to repel the invader;
that people looked up from drawing water at the same
fountain which now sparkles under the sycamore trees
and saw Catherine de Medici pass on her way north as
now they see the gray American Ambulance rattle
by. . . . " And I bet it was over these same cussed hard-
heads! " cried the boy from Ohio, trying vainly to ease
his car over the knobby paving-stones.

" No, oh no," answered the town notary reasonably.
" The streets of Crouy were paved in comparatively recent times, not earlier than 1620."

" Oh, the Pilgrim Fathers! " cried the boy from Connecticut.

" And nothing ever happened here all that time?"
queried the boy from California incredulously.

" Nothing," said the notary, " except a great deal of human life."

" Gee! what a lot o' that! " murmured the thoughtful boy from Virginia, his eyes widening imaginatively.

After the fact that it had been there so long, they were astonished by the fact that it was there at all, existing, as far as they could see, with no visible means of support beyond a casual sawmill or two. " How do all these people earn their living? " they always asked, putting the question in the same breath with the other inevitable one: " *Where* do the people live who care for all this splendid farming country? We see them working in the fields, these superb wheat-fields, or harvesting the oats, but you can drive your car for mile after mile and never see a human habitation. We thought Europe was a thickly populated place! "

Of course you know the obvious answer. The people who till the fields all live in the villages. If you inhabit such a settlement you hear every morning, very, very early, the slow, heavy tread of the big farm-horses and the rumble of the huge two-wheeled carts going out to work, and one of the picturesque sights of the sunset hour is the procession of the powerful Percherons, their drivers sitting sideways on their broad backs, plodding into the village, both horses and farmers with an inimitable air of leisurely philosophy; of having done a good day's work and letting it go at that; of attempting no last nervous whack at the accumulated pile of things to be done which always lies before every one; with an unembittered acceptance of the facts that there are but twenty-four hours in every day and that it is good to spend part of them eating savory hot soup with one's family. According to temperament, this appearance, only possible, apparently, when you have lived a thousand years in the same place, enormously reposes or enormously exasperates the American observer.

You do not see the cows going out to pasture, or coming back at night through the village streets, because those farmers who have a dairy live on the outskirts of the town, with their big square courtyards adjacent to the fields. The biggest farmhouse of this sort in Crouy is lodged in the remnants of the medieval castle of the old seigneurs (symbol of modern France!) where at night the cows ramble in peaceably through the old gate where once the portcullis hung, and stand chewing their cud about the great courtyards whence marauding knights in armor once clattered out to rob.

Of course this arrangement whereby country folk all live in villages turns inside out and upside down most of those conditions which seem to us inevitable accompaniments of country life; for instance, the isolation and loneliness of the women and children. There is no isolation possible here, when, to shake hands with the woman of the next farm, you have only to lean out of your front window and have her lean out of hers, when your children go to get water from the fountain along with all the other children of the region, when you are less than five minutes' walk from church and the grocery-

rabbit-hutches with carefully made lattice gates and cement floors, before which visitors always stopped to gaze at the endlessly twitching pink noses and vacuous faces of the little beasts. I hastened to explain that they were not at all for the children to play with, but that they form a serious part of the activities of every country family in the region, supplying for many people the only meat they ever eat beyond the very occasional fowl in the pot for a fête-day. They take the place, as far as I could see, of the American farm family's hog, and are to my mind a great improvement on him. Their flesh is much better food than the hog's, and since the animal is so small and so prolific, he provides a steady succession all the year round of fresh meat, palatable and savory, not smoked and salted into indigestibility like most of our country pork. In addition, he costs practically nothing to raise. This is, under the usual conditions of the French countryside, almost literally true. They are given those scraps from the kitchen and garden which hens will not touch, the potato and vegetable parings, the carrot-tops, the pea-vines after they have stopped bearing, the outer leaves of the cabbages, and, above all, herbage of all sorts which otherwise would be lost. Every afternoon, the old women of the town, armed with gunny sacks and sickles, go out for an hour or so of fresh air and exercise. The phrase is that they *va à l'herbe* (go for the grass). It is often a lively expedition, with the children skipping and shouting beside their grandmother, or one of the bigger boys pushing the wheelbarrow, cherished and indispensable accessory of French country life. They take what with us would be a "walk in the country," and as they pass they levy toll on every sod beside the road, or in a corner of a wall; on the fresh green leaves and twigs of neglected thickets; on brambles and weeds—rabbits adore weeds!—on underbrush and vines. Since seeing these patient, ruddy, vigorous, white-capped old women at their work I have made another guess at the cause of the miraculously neat and ordered aspect of French landscapes. It is an effect not wholly due to the esthetic sense of the nation. Toward twilight, the procession of old women and children, red-cheeked and hungry, turns back to the village, with wheelbarrows loaded and sacks bursting with food which otherwise would have served no human purpose. No need to give the rabbit, as we do the hog, expensive golden corn, fit for our own food, and which takes the heart out of the soil which produces it. The rabbit lives, and lives well, on the unconsidered and unmissed crumbs from Mother Nature's table.

The rabbit-hutches being near the kitchen, we usually went next into that red-and-white-tiled room, with the tiny coal-range (concession to the twentieth century) with the immense open hearth (heritage of the past) and the portable charcoal-stove, primitive, universal implement.

"But you can't bake your bread in such a play-stove as that," commented the American.

And with that we were launched into a new phase of

Crouy life, the close-knit communal organization of a French settlement. Since all these country people live side by side, they discovered long ago that there is no need to duplicate, over and over, in each house, labors which are better done in centralized activity. Instead of four hundred cook-stoves being heated to the baking-point, with a vast waste of fuel and effort, one big fire in the village *boulangerie* bakes the bread for all the community. These French country women no more bake their own bread than they make their own shoes. In fact, if they tried to they could not produce anything half so appetizing and nourishing as the crusty, well-baked loaves turned out by that expert specialist, the village bakeress; and they buy those loaves for less than it would cost to produce them in each kitchen.

In addition to the *boulangerie* where you buy your bread, there is in Crouy (and in all other French towns of that size) another shop kept by a specially good cook among the housewives, where you can always buy certain cooked foods which are hard to prepare at home in small quantities. Ham, for instance. In American towns too small to have a delicatessen shop, how many of us quail before the hours of continuous heat needed to boil a ham, and the still more formidable enterprise of getting it all eaten up afterward without a too dreary monotony! I have known American villages where people said the real reason for church suppers was that they might taste boiled ham once in a while. In Crouy, backward, primitive, drainageless community that it is, they

cater to the prime necessity of variety in diet with a
competence like that with which the problem of good
bread is solved all over France. Every Wednesday morning you know that Madame Beaugard has a ham freshly
boiled. You may buy one slice, just enough to garnish a
cold salad, or ten slices to serve in a hot sauce for dinner.
On Saturdays she has a big roast of beef, hot and smoking out of her oven at a quarter of twelve, and a family
or two may thus enjoy this luxury without paying the
usual Anglo-Saxon penalty of eating cold or hashed beef
for many days thereafter. On another day she has beans,
the dry beans which are such a bother to prepare in small
quantities and such an admirable and savory food. She
is the village fruit-seller, and when you go to buy your
fruit in her little shop, which is rothing more or less
than her front parlor transformed, you are sure to find
something else appetizing and tempting. Note that this
regular service not only adds greatly to the variety and
tastefulness of the diet of the village, but enables Madame Beaugard to earn her living more amply.

In another big operation of housekeeping the simplest
French country community puts its resources together,
instead of scattering them. On wash days there is no
arduous lifting and emptying out of water, no penetrating odor of soapsuds throughout all the house, no waste
of fuel under hundreds of individual wash-boilers, no
solitary drudging over the washtubs. The French country housekeeper who does her own washing brings around
to the street door her faithful steed, the wheelbarrow,

and loads it up; first the big galvanized boiler full of soiled clothes, then a wooden box open at one side, filled with clean straw, then the soap, a flat, short-handled wooden paddle, and a stiff scrubbing-brush. Leaving the children not yet at school in the charge of a neighbor— for whom she will perform the same service another day of the week—her head done up in a kerchief, her skirts kilted high to let her step free, she sets off down the road for the *lavoir*. I use the French word because the institution does not exist in English.

This is usually a low stone building, with an open place in the roof, either covered with glass or open to the air. In the center is a big pool of water, constantly renewed, which gushes in clean and eddies out soapy, carrying with it the impurities of the village linen. Here our housewife finds an assortment of her friends and neighbors, and here she kneels in the open air, in her straw-filled box, and soaps, and beats, and rinses, and scrubs at the spots with her scrubbing-brush (they never use a rubbing-board), and at the same time hears all the talk of the town, gets whatever news from the outer world is going the rounds, jokes and scolds, sympathizes and laughs, sorrows with and quarrels with her neighbors,— gets, in short, the same refreshing and entire change from the inevitable monotony of the home routine which an American housewife of a more prosperous class gets in her club meeting, and which the American housewife of the same class gets, alas! almost never.

And, yes, the clothes are clean! I know it runs coun-

ter to all our fixed ideas and what we are taught in do-
mestic-science classes. I don't pretend to explain it but
the fact remains that clothes soaped and beaten and
rinsed in cold water, boiled in a boiler over the open fire
and dried on the grass, are of the most dazzling whiteness. It is just another wholesome reminder that there
are all kinds of ways to kill a cat, and that our own,
natural and inevitable as it seems to us, may not even be
the most orthodox.

Another such reminder is the fashion in which they
manage baths in Crouy. There are not (you can hear,
can't you, the supercilious Anglo-Saxon tourist saying,
" *Of course there are not* "?) any bathrooms in the
houses, nor in the one little inn. And yet the people
take plenty of baths, and in big porcelain bathtubs too,
bigger and deeper and fuller of hot water than those we
have in our houses.

Among the many curious little industries of the place
is the *établissement des bains*. As you go down the
main street of a morning you stop in and fill up a little
printed card stating that you wish a hot (or cold) plain
(or perfumed or sulphur or starch or what not) bath, at
such and such an hour. The little old woman in charge
(note that this is another way for a little old woman
to earn an honest living) notes your hour, and stokes
up her stove according to the schedule of the day. When
you arrive you are shown into an immaculately clean tiled
bathroom, with an enormous tub, lined with a clean sheet
(it has been definitely decided by doctors that this pre-

caution obviates any possibility of contagion) and filled with clear, sparkling hot water. You can rent your towels for two cents apiece, and buy a bit of soap for three cents, or you may bring them from home, if you prefer. Of course, being unused to this particular way of killing the cat, you feel rather foolish and queer to be taking a bath in a community bathtub instead of in your own. But the bath is a fine one; with a cold rub-down at the end, there is no danger of taking cold; and as you dress, glowing and refreshed, you cannot put out of your mind some such colloquy as this:

" Yes, of course I prefer a bathtub in my own house. Everybody would. But suppose I haven't money enough to have one? At home, in a town like this, you can only get a bath, or give it to your children, if you have capital enough to buy, install, and keep up a bathroom of your own. Here you can have an even better one, any time you can spare fifteen cents in cash. Which method produces the bigger area of clean skin in a given community? "

You usually end your colloquy by quoting to yourself, laughingly, the grandly American-minded remark of the boy from Illinois, whose reaction to the various eye-openers about him was thus formulated:

" Do you know, the thing we want to do at home is to keep all the good ways of doing this we've got already, and then add all the French ones too."

We laughed over the youthful self-confidence of that ambition, but, as the boy from Illinois would say, "Honestly, do you know, there is something in it."

In one of the few large, handsome houses in Crouy there is something else I wish we might import into America. Very simply, with no brass band of a formal organization, secretaries, or reports, the younger girls of the town are brought together to learn how to sew and cook and keep their household accounts. The splendid park which looks so lordly with its noble trees is only the playground for the little girls in gingham aprons in the intervals of their study; and the fine, high-ceilinged, spacious old *salon,* a veritable Henry James room, is employed in anything but a Henry James manner as the workroom where all the children from the poorer houses round about sit in the sunshine, setting beautiful fine stitches and chattering like magpies.

A large room at the side has been fitted up—oh, so long before domestic science "struck" America—as a kitchen, and here the little girls daily prepare their own luncheons, after having, turn by turn, done the marketing and made up their small acounts under the supervision of an expert teacher. Their rosy cheeks and bright eyes testify to the good training which their own mothers received in this very room, in these very essentials of life.

The gracious, gray-haired owner of the beautiful home has always been so busy with her school and workroom that she almost never runs into Paris, although she is not more than a couple of hours away.

"I've only been there five or six times in my life," she says, shaking her head in mocking contrition, and turning superb old rings around on her soft, wrinkled hands. She adds, with a pretty whimsical smile: " To tell the truth, it bores me awfully when I do go. I have so much to see to here, that I'm uneasy to be away."

You are to remember that this has been going on for at least two generations. The quiet-eyed *châtelaine* of the manor mentions, in passing, that she is but continuing the work of her aunt who lived there before her, and who for fifty years gave all her life and property for her neighbors' children in quite the same way. When you leave you try to murmur something about what two such lives must have meant to the community, but this entirely unmodern, unradical, unread provincial Frenchwoman cuts you short by saying in a matter-of-fact tone, with the most transparent simplicity of manner:

" Oh, but of course property is only a trust, after all, isn't it? "

Will some one please tell me what are the appropriate sentiments for good Socialists to feel about such people?

There is another *ouvroir* (sewing-room) in Crouy of another sort, where the older girls, instead of being forced to go away from home, as in most American villages, to work in factories or shops, may earn an excellent living doing expert embroidery or fine sewing. They are well paid, and the enterprise is successful commercially because the long-headed philanthropist at the head of the organization manages to sell direct to consumers —as will always be done as a matter-of-course in the twenty-first century—instead of passing the product through the acquisitive hands of many middlemen. But there is so much to report in detail about this wholly admirable and modern undertaking that I must make another story of it. It is really curious how often, in this little, backward, drainageless French village, an American is brought to a halt, a long, scrutinizing inspection, and much profitable meditation.

So far you have seen Crouy as it was before the war, and as it is now in the brief intervals between the departure of a regiment going back to the front and the arrival of another with the trench mud still on its boots. You have seen the long, gray, stony street filled morning and evening with horses and laborers going out to work or returning, and in the meantime dozing somnolent in the sun, with only a cat or dog to cross it, an old woman going out for the grass, or a long, gray American Ford Ambulance banging along over the paving, the square-jawed, clean-shaven boy from the States zigzagging desperately with the vain idea that the other side of the street cannot be so rough as the one he is on. You have seen the big open square, sleeping under the airy shadow of the great sycamores, only the occasional chatter of children drawing water at the fountain breaking the silence. You have seen the beautiful old church, echoing and empty save for an old, poor man, his ax or his spade beside him, as he kneels for a moment to pray for his grandsons at the front; or for a woman in black, rigid and silent before a shrine, at whose white face you dare not glance as you pass. You have seen the plain, bare walls of the old houses, turning an almost blank face to the street, with closely shuttered or thickly curtained windows.

But one morning, very early, before you are dressed, you hear suddenly, close at hand, that clear, ringing challenge of the bugle which bids all human hearts to rise and triumph, and the vehement whirring rhythm of the drums, like a violent new pulse beating in your own body. The house begins to shake as though with thunder, not the far-off roar of the great cannon of the horizon which you hear every day, but a definite vibration of the earth under your feet. You rush to your street window, throw open the shutters, and, leaning from the sill, see that all Crouy is leaning with you and looking up the street.

There, at the turn, where the road leaves the yellow wheat-fields to enter the village, the flag is coming, the torn, ragged, dingy, sacred tricolor. Back of it the trumpets, gleaming in the sun, proclaim its honor. They are here, the poilus, advancing with their quick, swinging step, so bravely light for all the cruel heavy sacks on their backs and the rifles on their shoulders. Their four-ranked file fills our street from side to side, as their trumpets fill our ears, as the fatigue and courage of their faces fill our hearts. They are here, the splendid, splendid soldiers who are the French poilus. Everybody's brother, cousin, husband, friend, son, is there.

All Crouy leans from its windows to welcome them back from death—one more respite. They glance up at the windows as they pass; the younger ones smile at the girls' faces; the older ones, fathers certainly, look wistfully at the children's bright heads. There are certain ones who look at nothing, staring straight ahead at immaterial sights which will not leave their eyes.

One detachment has passed; the rumbling has increased till your windows shake as though in an earthquake. The camions and guns are going by, an endless defile of monster trucks, ending with the rolling kitchen, lumbering forward, smoking from all its pipes and caldrons, with the regimental cook springing up to inspect the progress of his savory ragoût.

After the formless tumult of the wheels, the stony street resounds again to the age-old rhythm of marching men. Another detachment. . . .

You dress quickly, seize the big box of cigarettes kept ready for this time, and, taking the children by the hand, go out to help welcome the newcomers as they settle down for their three weeks' rest.

I have told you that Crouy has a thousand inhabitants. There are twelve hundred men in a regiment. Perhaps you can imagine that when the troops are there men seem to ooze from every pore of the town. There are no great barracks erected for them, you understand. Somehow Crouy people make themselves small, move over to the edge, and make the necessary room. There are seventy soldiers sleeping on straw in the big hall which was before the war used for a concert-room or for amateur theatricals; two hundred are housed in what is left of the old *salles de garde* of the ruined castle, old guard-rooms which after five hundred years see themselves again filled with French fighting-men; every barn-loft is filled with them; every empty shed has a thick layer of straw on the ground and twenty to thirty men encamped; every empty stable has been carefully cleaned and prepared for them; every empty room harbors one or more officers; every attic has ten or fifteen men. One unused shop is transformed into the regimental infirmary, and hangs out the Red Cross flag; another sees the quartermaster and his secretaries installed at desks improvised from pine boards; a sentry stands before the Town Hall where the colonel has his headquarters, and another guards the fine old house which has the honor of sheltering the regimental flag.

The street, our quiet, sleepy street, is like an artery pulsing with rapid vibrations; despatch-riders dash up and down; camions rumble by; a staff-car full of officers looking seriously at maps halts for a moment and passes on; from out the courtyard where a regimental kitchen is installed a file of soldiers issues, walking on eggs as they carry their hot stew across the street to the lodging where they eat it. Our green-vegetable woman, that supreme flower of a race of consummate gardeners, arrives at the house, breathless and smiling, with only an onion and a handful of potatoes in her usually well-garnished donkey-cart.

" *Que voulez-vous, madame?* " she apologizes, sure of your sympathy. " The instant I leave the garden, they set upon me. You can't refuse your own soldiers, can you! With my Jacques at the front?"

Everywhere, everywhere where there is a scrap of cover from the sky, are huddled horses, mules, guns, wagons, and camions. Every spreading chestnut-tree harbors, not a blacksmith, but a dozen army mules tied close to the trunk. Near the station the ground under the close-set double line of trees in the long mall is covered to its last inch with munition-wagons and camions, and to reach the post-office on the other side of the little shady square you must pick your way back of lines of guns, set end to end, without an inch to spare. The aviators, whose machines wheel ceaselessly over the town, can see no change in its aspect, unless perhaps the streets and courtyards send up to the sky a gray-blue reflection like its own color. Not another trace of twelve hundred men with all their impedimenta betrays to the occasional German airman that Crouy's life is transformed.

Three times a week, in the late afternoon, just before sunset, the regimental band gives a concert, in our big open square under the sycamores, where, in the softer passages of the music, the sound of splashing water mingles with the flutes. All Crouy puts on its Sunday best and comes out to join itself to the horizon-blue throngs, and the colonel and his staff stand under the greatest of the sycamores, listening soberly to the music and receiving paternally the salutes of the men who saunter near him.

Once during their stay there is a *prise-d'armes*, on the square, when the men who have especially distinguished themselves are decorated with the *croix de guerre*. All Crouy goes to see that, too—all Crouy means now, you must remember, old men, women, little children, and babies—and stands respectfully, with tear-wet eyes, watching the white-haired colonel go down the line, pinning on each man's breast the sign of honor, taking his hand in a comrade's clasp and giving him on both cheeks a brother's kiss. That is a sight the children there will not forget, those two, bronzed, grave soldiers' faces, meeting under their steel casques in the salutation of blood-kin.

And once there is a mass said for the regimental dead in the old, old church. All Crouy goes there too, all Crouy lost in the crowd of soldiers who kneel in close ranks on the worn stones, the sonorous chant of whose deep voices fills the church to the last vaulting of the arches which echoed to the voices of those other Crusaders, praying there for their dead, six hundred years ago. The acolytes at the altar are soldiers in their shabby honorable uniforms; the priest is a soldier; the choir is filled with them singing the responses; in an interval of the service up rise two of them near the organ, violin in hand, and the French church rings with the angel's voice of whom but old Johann Sebastian Bach—oh, generous-hearted, wise poilu musicians, who hate only what is hateful!

At the end, suddenly, the regimental music is there, wood-wind, trumpets, and all. The service comes to a close in one great surging chant, upborne on the throbbing waves of the organ notes. The church rings to the pealing brass, thrilling violins, the men's deep voices. . . .

Ah, when will it resound to the song of thanksgiving at the end?

THE PERMISSIONAIRE

"What was in the ground, alive, they could not kill."

Two weeks after the German retreat from the Aisne was rumored, five days after the newspapers were printing censored descriptions of the ravaged country they had left, and the very moment the official bulletin confirmed the news, Pierre Nidart presented himself to his lieutenant to ask for a furlough, the long-delayed furlough, due for more than two years now, which he had never been willing to take. His lieutenant frowned uneasily, and did not answer. After a moment's silence he said, gently, "You know, my old fellow, the Boches have left very little up there."

(Nidart was not an old fellow at all, being but thirty-four, and the father of two young children. His lieutenant used the phrase as a term of endearment, because he had a high opinion of his silent sergeant.) Nidart made no answer to his officer's remark. The lieutenant took it that he persisted in wanting his furlough. As he had at least three furloughs due him, it was hard to refuse. There was a long silence. Finally, fingering the papers on the dry-goods box which served him as desk, the lieutenant said: "Your wife is young. They say the Germans carried back to work in Germany all

27

women under forty-five, or those who hadn't children under three."

Nidart swallowed hard, looked sick, and obstinately said nothing. His lieutenant turned with a sigh and motioned the *fourrier* to start the red tape for the authorization for the furlough. "All right, I think I can manage a three weeks' 'permission' for you. They're allowing that, I hear, to men from the invaded regions who haven't taken any furloughs since the beginning of the war."

"Yes, *mon Lieutenant.* Thank you, *mon Lieutenant.*" Nidart saluted and went back to his squad.

His lieutenant shook his head, murmuring to the *fourrier:* "Those north-country men! There is no use saying a word to them. They won't believe that *their* homes and families aren't there, till they see with their own eyes . . . and when they do see. . . . I've heard that some of the men in these first regiments that followed up the Boche retreat across the devastated regions went crazy when they found their own villages . . . Nidart has just one idea in his head, poor devil!—to go straight before him, like a homing pigeon, till . . ." He stopped, his face darkening.

"Oh, damn the Boches!" the *fourrier* finished the sentence fervently.

"You see, Nidart is a master-mason by trade, and he built their own little house. He carries around a snapshot of it, with his wife and a baby out in front."

" Oh, damn the Boches! " responded the *fourrier* on a deeper note.

" And like all those village workmen, they got half their living out of their garden and a field or two. And you've read what the Boches did to the gardens and fruit-trees."

" Isn't there anything else we can talk about? " said the *fourrier*.

Nidart passed through Paris on his way (those being before the days of strictly one-destination furloughs) and, extracting some very old bills from the lining of his shoe, he spent the five hours between his trains in hasty purchasing. At the hardware shop, where he bought an ax, a hammer, some nails, and a saw, the saleswoman's vivacious curiosity got the better of his taciturnity, and she screwed from him the information that he was going back to his home in the devastated regions.

At once the group of Parisian working-people and bourgeois who happened to be in the shop closed in on him sympathetically, commenting, advising, dissuading, offering their opinions with that city-bred, glib-tongued clatter which Nidart's country soul scorned and detested.

" No, no, my friend, it's useless to try to go back. The Germans have made a desert of it. My cousin's wife has a relative who was in the regiment that first followed the Germans after their retreat from Noyon, and he said . . ."

" The Government is going to issue a statement, say-

ing that land will be given in other parts of France to
people from those regions, because it's of no use to try
to rebuild from under the ruins."

"No, not the Government, it's a society for the Protection of the People in the Invaded Regions; and they
are Americans, millionaires, every one.   And it's in
America they are offering land, near New York."

"No, near Buenos Aires."

"The Americans want the regions left as a monu-
ment, as a place to see.   You'll make much more money
as a guide to tourists than trying to . . ."

"Your family won't be there, you know.   The Boches
took all the able-bodied women back with them; and the
children were sent to . . ."

"*Give me my change, won't you!*" said Nidart with
sudden fierceness, to the saleswoman.   He turned his
back roughly on the chattering group and went out.
They shrugged their shoulders.   "These country-people.
Nothing on earth for them but their little hole of a village!"

Down the street, Nidart, quickening to an angry stride
his soldierly gait, hurried along to a seed-store.

That evening when he got into the battered, dingy,
third-class compartment of the train going north, he
could hardly be seen for the innumerable packages slung
about his person.   He pulled out from one bulging pocket
a square piece of bread, from another a piece of cheese,
and proceeded to dine, bent forward with the weight of
his burdens and his thoughts, gazing out through the

dirty windows at the flat farming country jerking by him in the moonlight. It was so soon after the retreat that the train went no further north than Noyon, and Nidart had lived far beyond Noyon. About midnight, he rolled off the train, readjusted his packages and his knapsack, and, after showing his perfectly regular *sauf-conduit* to five or six sentries along the way, finally got out of town.

He found himself on the long, white road leading north. It was the road down which they had driven once a week, on market-days. Of all the double line of noble poplar-trees, not one was standing. The utterly changed aspect of the familiar road startled him. Ahead of him as he tramped rapidly forward, was what had been a cross-roads, now a gaping hole. Nidart, used to gaping holes in roads, walked down into this, and out on the other side. He was panting a little, but he walked forward steadily and strongly. . . .

The moon shone full on the place where the first village had stood, the one where his married sister had lived, where he and his wife and the children used to come for Sunday dinners once in a while. He stood suddenly before a low, confused huddle of broken bricks and splintered beams, and looked about him uncomprehending. The silence was intense. In the instant before he understood what he was seeing, he heard and felt a rapid vibration, his own heart knocking loudly. Then he understood.

A moment later, mechanically, he began to move about, clambering up and down, aimlessly, over the heaps of rubble. Although he did not know it, he was looking for the place where his sister's house had stood. Presently his knees gave way under him. He sat down suddenly on a tree-stump. The lopped-off trunk beside it showed it to have been an old cherry-tree. Yes, his sister's big cherry-tree, the pride of her garden. A long strip of paper, one end buried in a heap of bits of plaster, fluttered in the night-wind. It beat against his leg like some one calling feebly for help. The moon emerged from a cloud and showed it to be a strip of wall-paper; he recognized the pattern; he had helped his brother-in-law put it on the bedroom of the house. His sister's four children had been born within the walls of that bedroom. He tried to fix his mind on those children, not to think of any other children, not to remember his own, not to . . .

The paper beat insistently and rhythmically against his leg like a recurrent thought of madness—he sprang up with the gesture of a man terrified, and stumbling wildly among the formless ruins sought for the road again.

He walked heavily after this, lifting his feet with an effort. Several miles further, at the heap of débris which had been Falquières, where his wife's family had lived, he made a wide detour through the fields to avoid passing closer to the ruins. At the next, Bondry, where he had been born and brought up, he tried to turn aside, but against his will his feet carried him straight to the center of the chaos. When the first livid light of dawn showed him the two stumps of the big apple-trees before the door, which his grandfather had planted, he stopped short. Of the house, of the old walled garden, not a trace beyond the shapeless heap of stones and plaster. He stood there a long time, staring silently. The light gradually brightened, until across the level fields a ray of yellow sunshine struck ironically through the prone branches of the murdered trees upon the gray face of the man.

At this he turned and, walking slowly, dragging his feet, his head hanging, his shoulders bent, he followed the road which led like a white tape laid straight across the plain, towards—towards . . . The road had been mined at regular intervals, deep and broad craters stretching across it, enough to stop a convoy of camions, not enough to stop a single soldier, even though he stumbled along so wearily, his cumbersome packages beating against his legs and arms, even though he walked so slowly, more and more slowly as he came in sight of the next heaped and tumbled mound of débris. The sun rose higher. . . .

Presently it shone, with April clarity, on Nidart lying, face downwards, upon a heap of broken bricks.

For a long hour it showed nothing but that,—the ruins, the prostrate trees, the man, like them stricken and laid low.

Then it showed, poor and miserable under that pale-gold light, a wretched ant-like procession issuing from

holes in the ground and defiling slowly along the scarred
road towards the ruins; women, a few old men, a little
band of pale and silent children.　They approached the
ruins and dispersed.　One of the women, leading three
children, picked her way wearily among the heaps of
stone, the charred and twisted beams . . . stopped
short, both hands at her heart.

And then the sun reeled in the sky to a sound which
rang as strangely from that silent desolation as a burst
of song out of hell, scream after scream of joy, ringing
up to the very heavens, frantic, incredulous, magnificent
joy.

There they stood, the man and wife, clasped in each
others' arms in the ruins of their home, with red, swollen
eyes, smiling with quivering lips, silent.　Now that the
first wild cries had gone rocket-like to the sky and fallen
back in a torrent of tears, they had no words, no words
at all.　They clasped each other and the children, and
wept, constantly wiping the tears from their white cheeks,
to see each other.　The two older children, a little shy of
this father whom they had almost forgotten, drew away
constrained, hanging their heads, looking up bashfully
under their bent brows.　Nidart sat down on a heap
of stone and drew the little girl to him, stroking her
hair.　He tried to speak, but no voice issued from his
lips.　His wife sat down beside him, laying her head on
his shoulder, spent with the excess of her relief.　They
were all silent a long time, their hearts beginning to beat

in the old rhythm, a sweet, pale peace dropping down upon them.

After a time, the youngest child, cowering under the woman's skirts, surprised at the long silence, thrust out a little pale face from his shelter. The man looked down on him and smiled. "That's a Dupré," he said in his normal voice, with conviction, all his village lore coming back to him. "I know by the Dupré look of his nose. He looks the way my cousin Jacques Dupré used to, when he was little."

These were the first articulate words spoken. With them, he turned his back on the unfriendly, unknowable immensity of the world in which he had lived, exiled, for three years, and returned into the close familiar community of neighbors and kin where he had lived for thirty-four years,—where he had lived for hundreds of years. The pulverized wreck of this community lay all about him, but he opened its impalpable doors and stepped once more into its warm humanity. He looked at the little child whom he had never seen before and knew him for kin.

His wife nodded. "Yes, it's Louise and Jacques' baby. Louise was expecting him, you know, when the mobilization . . . he was born just after Jacques went away, in August. We heard Jacques was killed . . . we have heard everything . . . that Paris was taken, that London was burned. . . . I have heard twice that you were killed. Louise believed it, and never got out of bed at all after the baby came. She just turned over and let herself die. I took the baby. Somebody had to. That's the reason I'm here now. ' They ' carried off all the women my age unless they had children under three. They thought the baby was mine."

" But Jacques isn't killed," said Nidart; " he's wounded, with one wooden leg, frantic to see Louise and the baby. . . ." He made a gesture of blame. " Louise always was a fool! Anybody's a fool to give up!" He looked down at the baby and held out his hand. " Come here, little Jeannot."

The child shrank away silently, burrowing deeper into his foster-mother's skirts.

" He's afraid," she explained. " We've had to make the children afraid so they would keep out of sight, and not break rules. There were so many rules, so many to salute and to bow to, the children couldn't remember; and when they forgot, they were so dreadfully cuffed, or their parents fined such big fines . . ."

" *I* never saluted! " said the boy of ten, wagging his head proudly. " You have to have something on your head to salute, they won't let you do it bareheaded. So I threw my cap in the fire."

" Yes, he's gone bareheaded since the first days, summer and winter, rain and shine," said his mother.

" Here, Jean-Pierre," said his father, wrestling with one of his packages, " I've got a hat for you. I've been saving it for you, lugged it all over because I wanted my boy to have it." He extracted from its brown canvas bag a German helmet with the spike, which he held out.

"And I've got something for my little Berthe, too."
He fumbled in an inner pocket. "I made it myself, near
Verdun. The fellows all thought I was crazy to work
over it so, when I didn't know if I'd ever see my little
girl again; but I was pretty sure Maman would know
how to take care of you, all right." He drew out from
a nest of soft rags a roughly carved aluminum ring and
slipped it on the child's forefinger.

As the children drew off a little, to compare and ex-
amine, their parents looked into each other's eyes, the
deep, united, serious look of man and wife before a common problem.

"*Eh bien,* Paulette," said the man, "what shall we
do? Give up? Move away?"

"Oh, Pierre!" cried his wife. "You *wouldn't?*"

For answer, he shook himself free of his packages and
began to undo them, the ax, the hammer, the big package of nails, the saw, the trowel, the paper bags of seeds,
the pickax. He spread them out on the clutter of broken
bricks, plaster, splintered wood, and looked up at his
wife. "That's what I bought on the way here."

His wife nodded. "But have you had your breakfast?
You'd better eat something before you begin."

While he ate his bread and munched his cheese, she
told him, speaking with a tired dullness, something of
what had happened during the years of captivity. It
came out just as she thought of it, without sequence,
one detail obscuring another. "There wasn't much left

inside the house when they finally blew it up. They'd
been taking everything little by little. No, they weren't
bad to women; they were horrid and rough and they
stole everything they could, but they didn't mistreat us,
only some of the foolish girls. You know that good-for-
nothing family of Boirats, how they'd run after any
man. Well, they took to going with the Boches; but any
decent woman that kept out of sight as much as she
could, no, I wasn't afraid of them much that way, unless
they were drunk. Their officers were awfully hard on
them about everything—*hard!* They treated them like
dogs. *We were sorry for them sometimes.*"

Yes, this ignorant woman, white and thin and ragged,
sitting on the wreck of her home, said this.

"Did you hear how they took every single thing in
copper or brass—Grandfather's candlesticks, the andi-
rons, the handles of the clothes-press, the door-knobs,
and all, *every one* of my saucepans and kettles?" Her
voice trembled at this item. "The summer after that, it
was everything in linen. I had just the chemise I had
on my back . . . even what was on the clothes-line, drying, they took. The American Committee distributed
some cotton material and I made a couple for me and
Berthe, and some drawers for Jean-Pierre and the baby.
That was when we could still get thread. The winter
after that, it was woolen they took, everything, especially
mattresses. Their officers made them get every single
mattress in town, except the straw ones. Alice Bernard's
mother, they jerked her mattress right out from under

her, and left her lying on the bed-ropes. And M. le Curé, he was sick with pneumonia and they took his, that way, and he died. But the Boches didn't dare not to. Their officers would have shot them if they hadn't."

"I can make beds for you," he said. "There must be trenches somewhere, near,"—she nodded,—"they'll have left some wire-netting in an *abri*. You make a square of wood, and put four legs to it, and stretch the wire-netting over it and put straw on that. But we had some wire-netting of our own that was around the chicken-yard."

"Oh, they took that," she explained,—"that, and the doors of the chicken-house, and they pried off our window-cases and door-jambs and carried those off the last days, too . . . but there was one thing they wouldn't do, no, not even the Boches, and that was *this* dirty work!" She waved her hand over the destruction about her, and pointed to the trees across the road in the field, all felled accurately at the same angle. "We couldn't understand much of what happened when they were getting ready to leave, but some of them had learned enough French to tell us they wouldn't 'do it'—we didn't know what. They told us they would go away and different troops would come. And Georges Duvalet's boy said they told *him* that the troops who were to come to 'do it' were criminals out of the prisons that the officers had let out if they would 'do it'—all this time we didn't know what, and somebody said it was to pour oil on us and burn us, the way they did the people in the barn at Vermadderville. But there wasn't anything we

could do to prevent it. We couldn't run away. So we
stayed, and took care of the children. All the men who
could work at all and all the women too, unless they
had very little children, were marched away, off north,
to Germany, with just what few extra things they could
put in a big handkerchief. Annette Cagnon, she was
eighteen, and had to go, but her mother stayed with
the younger children—her mother has been sort of
crazy ever since. She had such a long fainting turn
when Annette went by, with a German soldier, we
thought we never could bring her to life. . . ." The
rough, tired voice shook a moment, the woman rested
her head again on her husband's arm, holding to him
tightly. " Pierre, oh Pierre, *if we had known what was
to come*,—no, we couldn't have lived through it, not any
of us!" He put his great, workingman's hand on her
rough hair, gently.

She went on: " And then the troops who had been
here did go away and the others came, and they made
the few of us who were left go down into the cellars
of those old houses down the road. They told us to stay
there three days, and if we went out before we'd get shot.
We waited for two whole days. The water they had
given us was all gone, and then old Granny Arnoux said
she was all alone in the world, so it wouldn't make any
difference if she did get shot. She wanted to make sure
that her house was all right. You know what she thought
of her house! So she came up and we waited. And in
half an hour we heard her crutches coming back on the

road, and she was shrieking out. We ran up to see. She had fallen down in a heap. She hasn't known anything since; shakes all the time as if she were in a chill. She was the first one; she was all alone, when she saw what they had done . . . and *you* know . . ."

Nidart turned very white, and stood up. "God! yes, I know! *I* was alone!"

"Since then, ten days ago, the French soldiers came through. We didn't know them for sure, we were expecting to see the red trousers. I asked everybody about you, but nobody knew. There are so *many* soldiers in an army. Then Americans came in cars and brought us bread, and blankets and some shoes, but they have leather soles and I make the children keep them for best, they wear out so. And since then the Government has let the camions that go through to the front, leave bread and meat and once a bag of potatoes for us. The préfet came around and asked if we wanted to be sent to a refugee home in Paris or stay here, and of course I said stay here. The children and I have come every day to work. We've got the plaster and bricks cleared out from the corner of the fireplace, and I cook there, though there isn't any chimney of course, but I think the tiles of the kitchen floor are mostly all there still. And oh, Pierre, we have one corner of the garden almost cleared, *and the asparagus is coming up!* Come and see! They cut down everything they could see, even the lilac bushes, but what was in the ground, alive, they couldn't kill."

Nidart put the shovel in his wife's hand, and took up

the pickax. "Time spent in traveling isn't counted on furloughs," he said, "so we have twenty-one days, counting to-day. The garden first, so's to get in the seeds."

They clambered over the infernal disorder of the ruins of the house, and picked their way down and back into what had been the garden. A few sections of the wall were still standing, its thick solidity resisting even dynamite petards.

"Oh, see, almost all of the pleached trees are saved!" cried Nidart, astonished, "that part of the wall didn't fall."

"I'm not sure I pruned those right," said his wife doubtfully, glancing at them. "I couldn't remember whether you left two or four buds on the peaches, and I just gave up on the big grapevine. It grew so, it got all ahead of me!"

"Did they bear well?" asked the man, looking across the trash heap at the well-remembered trees and vines. "We'd better leave those till some odd time, they won't need much care. I can do them between other things some time when I'm too tired to do anything else. Here is where the big job is." He looked the ground over with a calculating eye and announced his plan of campaign.

"We won't try to carry the rubbish out. It's too heavy for you, and my time has got to go as far as it can for the important things. We'll just pile it all up in a line along the line where the walls used to stand. All of us know that line! I'll use the pickax, and Maman the shovel. Jean-Pierre will throw the bigger pieces over on the line, and Berthe will go after and pick up the littler ones."

They set to work, silently, intensely. When they reached the currant-bushes, all laid low, Pierre gave a growl of wrath and scorn, but none of them slackened their efforts. About eleven the big convoy of camions on the way to the front came through, lurching along the improvised road laid out across the fields. The workers, lifting their eyes for the first time from their labors, saw at a distance on the main road the advance guard of the road-menders already there, elderly soldiers, gray-haired territorials, with rakes and shovels, and back of them, shuttle-like, the big trucks with road-metal coming and going.

Reluctantly leaving her work, Paulette went to get the supplies for dinner, and started an open-air fire in the cleared-out corner of the chimney. Over this she hung a big pot, and leaving it to boil she hurried back to her shovel. " The soup-kettle and the flat-irons," she told her husband, " they were too hard to break and too heavy to carry away, and they are about all that's left of what was in the house."

" No, I found an iron fork," said Berthe, " but it was all twisted. Jean-Pierre said he thought he could . . ."

" Don't talk," said their father firmly,—" you don't work so fast when you talk."

At noon they went back to the fire burning under the open sky, in the blackened corner of the fireplace where

it had cooked the food during the years past. The man
looked at it strangely, and turned his eyes away.

"Now where is your fork, little Berthe?" he said.
"I'll straighten it for you. With that and my kit . . ."

"I have my jackknife too," said Jean-Pierre.

They ate thus, dipping up the stew in the soldier's
gamelle, using his knife and fork and spoon and the
straightened iron fork. The baby was fed on bread
soaked in the gravy, and on bits of potato given him from
the end of a whittled stick. In the twenty minutes' rest
which their captain allowed the little force after the
meal, he and Jean-Pierre whittled out two wooden forks,
two-tined, from willow twigs. "That's one apiece now,"
said Nidart, "and the asparagus bed is all cleared off.
We have made a beginning."

They went back to work, stooping, straining, heaving,
blinded with the flying plaster, wounded with the sharp
edges of the shattered stones. The sun shone down on
them with heavenly friendliness, the light, sparkling air
lifted the hair from their hot foreheads. After a time,
Nidart, stopping for an instant to wipe away the sweat
which ran down into his eyes, said: "The air has a different feel to it here. And the sun looks different. It
looks like home."

At four they stopped to munch the piece of bread
which is the supplementary meal of French working-
people at that hour. Nidart embellished it with a slice of
cheese for each, which made the meal a feast. They
talked as they ate; they began to try to bridge over the

gap between them. But they lacked words to tell what lay back of them; only the dry facts came out.

" Yes, I've been wounded, there's a place on my thigh, here, put your hand and feel, where there isn't any flesh over the bone, just skin. It doesn't bother me much, except when I try to climb a ladder. Something about that position I can't manage . . . and for a mason . . ."

" I'll climb the ladders," said Jean-Pierre.

" Yes, I was pretty sick. It got gangrene some. They thought I wouldn't live. I was first in a big hospital near the front, and then in a convalescent hospital in Paris. It was awfully dull when I got better. They thought if I had made an application to be *réformé* and retired I could be like Jacques Dupré with his wooden leg. But with you and the children here . . . what could I have done with myself? So I didn't say anything, and when my time was up in the hospital I went back to the trenches. That was a year ago last winter."

" Berthe and Jean-Pierre had the mumps that winter," said their mother. " The baby didn't get it. I kept him away from them. The Boches shut us up as though we had the smallpox. They were terribly strict about any sickness. The Boche regimental doctor came every day. He took very good care of them."

" He wanted to give me a doll because I didn't cry when he looked in my throat," said Berthe.

" Of course she didn't take it," said Jean-Pierre. " I told her I'd break it all to pieces if she did."

" But she cried afterwards."

"Come," said the father, "we've finished our bread. Back to work."

That night, after the children were asleep on straw in the cellar down the road, their parents came back to wander about in the moonlight over their ravaged little kingdom. The wife said little, drawing her breath irregularly, keeping a strained grasp on her husband's arm. For the most part he succeeded in speaking in a steady voice of material plans for the future,—how he could get some galvanized roofing out of the nearest trench *abri;* how he could use the trunks of the felled trees to strengthen his hastily constructed brick walls, and for roof-beams; what they could plant in the garden and the field—things which she and the children could cultivate after he had gone back.

At this reminder of the inevitable farewell again before them, the wife broke out in loud wailings, shivering, clutching at him wildly. He drew her down on a pile of rubbish, put his arms around her, and said in a peremptory tone: "Paulette! Listen! *You are letting the Boches beat you!*" He used to her the tone he used for his squad, his new soldier's voice which the war had taught him, the tone which carried the laggards up over the top. At the steel-like ring of it his wife was silent.

He went on: "There's nothing any of us *can* do but to go on. The only thing to do is to go on without making a fuss. That's the motto in the army, you know.

Don't make a fuss." He lifted his head and looked around at his home dismantled, annihilated. *"Not to give up,*—that and the flatirons are about all the Boches have left us, don't you see?"

He was silent a moment and went on with his constructive planning. "Perhaps I can get enough lime sent on from Noyon to really rebuild the chimney. With that, and a roof, and the garden, and the allocation from the Government . . ."

"Yes, Pierre," said his wife in a trembling voice. She did not weep again.

He himself, however, was not always at this pitch of stoicism. There were times when he looked up suddenly and felt, as though for the first time, the downfall and destruction of all that had been his life. At such moments the wind of madness blew near him. The night after they had moved from the cellar into the half-roofed, half-walled hut, to sleep there on the makeshift beds, he lay all night awake, crushed with the immensity of the effort they would need to put forth and with the insignificance of any progress made. There came before him the long catalogue of what they had lost, the little decencies and comforts they had earned and paid for and owned. He sickened at the squalid expedients of their present life. They were living like savages; never again would they attain the self-respecting order which had been ravished from them, which the ravishers still enjoyed. With all his conscious self he longed to give up the struggle, but something more than his conscious self was at work. The tree had been cut down, but something was in the ground, alive.

At dawn he found himself getting out of bed, purposefully. To his wife's question he answered: "I'm going to Noyon to buy the seed for the field. We haven't half enough corn. And I can get young cabbage plants there, too, they say. I can make it in six hours if I hurry."

He was back by ten o'clock, exhausted, but aroused from his waking nightmare—for that time! But it came again and again.

On the day he began to spade up the field he noticed that two of his murdered fruit-trees, attached by a rag of bark to the stumps, were breaking out into leaf. The sight turned him sick with sorrow, as though one of his children had smiled at him from her deathbed. He bent over the tree, his eyes burning, and saw that all the buds were opening trustfully. His heart was suffocating. He said to himself: "They have been killed! They are dead! But they do not know they are dead, and they try to go on living. *Are we like that?*"

In an instant all his efforts to reanimate his assassinated life seemed pitiful, childish, doomed to failure. He looked across the field at the shapeless, roughly laid brick wall he had begun, and felt a shamed rage. He was half-minded to rush and kick it down.

"Papa, come! The peonies have begun to come up in the night. The whole row of them, where we were raking yesterday."

The man found his wife already there, bending over the sturdy, reddish, rounded sprouts pushing strongly through the loosened earth. She looked up at him with shining eyes. When they were betrothed lovers, they had together planted those peonies, pieces of old roots from her mother's garden. "You see," she said again; "I told you what was in the ground alive they couldn't kill!"

The man went back to his spading silently, and, as he labored there, a breath of sovereign healing came up to him from that soil which was his. The burning in his eyes, the taste of gall in his mouth, he had forgotten when, two hours later, he called across to his wife that the ground for the beans was all spaded and that she and Jean-Pierre could come now with their rakes, while he went back to building the house-wall.

But that quick scorching passage through fire was nothing compared with the hour which waited for him in his garden beside the wall on which the branches of his pleached trees and vines still spread out their carefully symmetrical patterns. He had put off caring for them till some odd moment. He and his wife, glancing at them from time to time, had made estimates of the amount of fruit they would yield, "and for *us* this time —we haven't had a single peach or apple from them. The Boche officers sent their soldiers to get them always."

"Queer they should have left those unharmed," said his wife once, and he had answered: "Perhaps the man they sent to kill them was a gardener like us. I know I couldn't cut down a fruit-tree in full bearing, not if it were in hell and belonged to the Kaiser. Anybody who's ever grown things knows what it is!"

One gray day of spring rains and pearly mists, the fire would not burn in the only half-constructed chimney. Paulette crouched beside it, blowing with all her might, and thinking of the big leathern bellows which had been carried away to Germany with all the rest. Jean-Pierre shaved off bits from a dry stick and Berthe fed them under the pot, but the flame would not brighten. Pierre, coming down, cold and hungry, from the top of the wall where he had been struggling with a section of roof, felt physically incapable of going on with that work until he had eaten, and decided to use the spare half-hour for pruning the pleached trees and vines. Almost at the end of his strength after the long-continued strained effort to accomplish the utmost in every moment and every hour, he shivered from the cold of his wet garments as he stood for a moment, fumbling to reach the pruning-shears. But he did not give himself the time to warm his hands at the fire, setting out directly again into the rain. He had been working at top speed ever since the breakfast, six hours before, of black coffee and dry bread.

Sodden with fatigue and a little light-headed from lack of food, he walked along the wall and picked out the grapevine as the least tiring to begin on. He knew it so well he could have pruned it in the dark. He had planted it the year before his marriage, when he had been building the house and beginning the garden. It had not been an especially fine specimen, but something about the situation and the soil had exactly suited it, and it had thriven miraculously. Every spring, with the first approach of warm weather, he had walked out, in the evening after his day's work, along the wall to catch the first red bud springing amazingly to life out of the brown, woody stems which looked so dead. During the summers as he had sprayed the leaves, and manured the soil and watered the roots and lifted with an appraising hand the great purple clusters, heavier day by day, he had come to know every turn of every branch. In the trenches, during the long periods of silent inaction, when the men stare before them at sights from their past lives, sometimes Nidart had looked back at his wife and children, sometimes at his garden on an early morning in June, sometimes at his family about the dinner-table in the evening, and sometimes at his great grapevine, breaking into bud in the spring, or, all luxuriant curving lines, rich with leafage, green and purple in the splendor of its September maturity.

It was another home-coming to approach it now, and his sunken, bloodshot eyes found rest and comfort in dwelling on its well-remembered articulations. He noticed that the days of sunshine, and now the soft spring rain, had started it into budding. He laid his hand on the tough, knotted, fibrous brown stem.

It stirred oddly, with a disquieting lightness in his hand. The sensation was almost as though one of his own bones turned gratingly on nothing. The sweat broke out on his forehead. He knelt down and took hold of the stem lower down. The weight of his hand displaced it. It swung free. It had been severed from the root by a fine saw. The sap was oozing from the stump.

The man knelt there in the rain, staring at this, as though he were paralyzed. He did not know what he was looking at, for a moment, conscious of nothing but a cold sickness. He got up heavily to his feet, then, and made his way to the next vine. Its stem gave way also, swinging loose with the horrible limpness of a broken limb.

He went to the next, a peach-tree, and to the next, a fine pleached pear. Everything, everything, peach-trees, apple-trees, grapevines, everything had been neatly and dextrously murdered, and their corpses left hanging on the wall as a practical joke.

The man who had been sent to do that had been a gardener indeed, and had known where to strike to reach the very heart of this other gardener who now, his hands over his face, staggered forward and leaned his body against the wall, against the dead vine which had been so harmless, so alive. He felt something like an inward bleeding, as though that neat, fine saw had severed an artery in his own body.

His wife stepped out in the rain and called him. He

heard nothing but the fine, thin voice of a small saw, eating its way to the heart of living wood.

His wife seeing him stand so still, his face against the wall, came out towards him with an anxious face. "Pierre, Pierre!" she said. She looked down, saw the severed vine-stem and gave a cry of dismay. "Pierre, they haven't . . . they haven't . . .!"

She ran along the wall, touching them one by one, all the well-known, carefully tended stems. Her anger, her sorrow, her disgust burst from her in a flood of outcries, of storming, furious words.

Her husband did not move. A deathlike cold crept over him. He heard nothing but the venomous, fine voice of the saw, cutting one by one the tissues which had taken so long to grow, which had needed so much sun and rain and heat and cold, and twelve years out of a man's life. He was sick, sick of it all, mourning not for the lost trees but for his lost idea of life. That was what people were like, could be like, what one man could do in cold blood to another—no heat of battle here, no delirium of excitement, cold, calculated intention! He would give up the effort to resist, to go on. The killing had been too thoroughly done.

His wife fell silent, frightened by his stillness. She forgot her own anger, her grief, she forgot the dead trees. They were as nothing. A strong, valiant tenderness came into her haggard face. She went up to him, close, stepping into his silent misery with the secure confidence only a wife can have in a husband. "Come,

Pierre," she said gently, putting her red, work-scarred hand in his. She drew him away from the wall, his arms hanging listlessly. She drew him into the sheltered corner of the room he had half finished. She set hot food before him and made him eat and drink.

The rain poured down in a gray wall close before them. The heaped-up ruins were all around them. Inside the shelter the children ate greedily, heartily, talking, laughing, quarreling, playing. The fire, now thoroughly ablaze, flamed brightly beside them. The kettle steamed.

After a time Nidart's body began slowly to warm. He began to hear the children's voices, to see his wife dimly. The horror was an hour behind him. The blessed, blurring passage of the moments clouded thick between him and the sound of that neat small saw, the sight of that deft-handed man, coolly and smilingly murdering . . .

He looked at his wife attentively, as she tried to set in order their little corner saved from chaos. She was putting back on the two shelves he had made her the wooden forks and spoons which she had cleaned to a scrupulous whiteness; she was arranging neatly the wretched outfit of tin cans, receptacles, and formless paper packages which replaced the shining completeness of her lost kitchen; she was smoothing out the blankets on their rough camp-beds; she was washing the faces and hands of the children, of their own children and the little foster-son, the child of the woman who had given up, who had let herself be beaten, who had let herself be killed, who had abandoned her baby to be cared for by another, braver woman.

A shamed courage began slowly to filter back into his drained and emptied heart. With an immense effort he got up from the tree-stump which served for chair and went towards his wife, who was kneeling before the little child she had saved. He would begin again.

" Paulette," he said heavily, " I believe that if we could get some grafting wax at once, we might save those. Why couldn't we cover the stumps with wax to keep the roots from bleeding to death, till the tops make real buds, and then graft them on to the stumps? It's too late to do it properly with dormant scions, but perhaps we might succeed. It would be quicker than starting all over again. The roots are there, still."

He raged as he thought of this poor substitute for his splendid trees, but he set his teeth. " I could go to Noyon. They must have wax and resin there in the shops by this time, enough for those few stumps."

The little boy presented himself imploringly. " Oh, let me go! I could do it, all right. And you could get on faster with the roof. There aren't but ten days left, now."

He set off in the rain, a small brave spot of energy in the midst of death. His father went back to his house-building.

The roads were mended now, the convoys of camions rumbled along day after day, raising clouds of dust;

staff-cars flashed by; once in a while a non-militarized automobile came through, sometimes with officials of the Government on inspection tours, who distributed miscellaneous lots of seeds, and once brought Paulette some lengths of cotton stuff for sheets; sometimes with reporters from the Paris newspapers; once with some American reporters who took photographs, and gave some bars of chocolate to the children. Several times people stopped, foreigners, Americans, English, sometimes women in uniforms, who asked a great many questions and noted down the answers. Pierre wondered why those able-bodied young men were not in some army. He had thought all the able-bodied men in the world were in some army.

For the most part he found all these people rather futile and uninteresting, as he had always found city people, and paid little attention to them, never interrupting his work to talk to them, his work, his sacred work, for which there remained, only too well known, a small and smaller number of hours. He took to laboring at night whenever possible.

The roof was all on the one tiny room before the date for his return. The chimney was rebuilt, the garden spaded, raked, and planted. But the field was not finished. It takes a long time to spade up a whole field. Pierre worked on it late at night, the moonlight permitting. When his wife came out to protest, he told her that it was no harder than to march all night, with knapsack and blanket-roll and gun. She took up the rake and began to work beside him. Under their tan they were both very white and drawn, during these last days.

The day before the last came, and they worked all day in the field, never lifting their eyes from the soil. But their task was not finished when night came. Pierre had never been so exacting about the condition of the ground. It must be fine, fine, without a single clod left to impede the growth of a single precious seed. This was not work which, like spading, could be done at night in an uncertain light. When their eyes, straining through the thickening twilight, could no longer distinguish the lumps of earth, he gave it up, with a long breath, and, his rake on his shoulder, little Berthe's hand in his, he crossed the mended road to the uncomely little shelter which was home.

Paulette was bending over the fire. She looked up, and he saw that she had been crying. But she said nothing. Nor did he, going to lean his rake against the reconstructed wall. He relinquished the implement reluctantly, and all through the meal kept the feel of it in his hand.

They were awake when the first glimmer of gray dawn shone through the empty square which was their window. Pierre dressed hurriedly and taking his rake went across the road to the field. Paulette blew alive the coals of last night's fire, and made coffee and carried it across to her husband with a lump of bread. He stopped work

to drink and eat. It was in the hour before the sunrise.
A gray, thin mist clung to the earth. Through it they
looked at each other's pale faces, soberly.

"You must get the seed in as soon as you can, after
I'm gone," said the husband.

"Yes," she promised, "we won't lose a minute."

"And I think you and Jean-Pierre can manage to
nail in the window-frame when it comes. I thought I'd
be able to do that myself."

"Yes, Jean-Pierre and I can do it."

"You'd better get my kit and everything ready for
me to leave," he said, drinking the last of the coffee
and setting his hand again to the rake.

They had reckoned that he would need to leave the
house at ten o'clock if he were to make the long tramp
to Noyon in time for the train. At a quarter of ten he
stopped, and, the rake still tightly held in his hand,
crossed the road. His knapsack, blanket-roll, all the various brown bags and *musettes* were waiting for him
on the bench hewn from a tree-trunk before the door.
He passed them, went around the little hut, and stepped
into the garden.

Between the heaped-up lines of rubble, the big
rectangle of well-tilled earth lay clean and brown and
level. And on it, up and down, were four, long, straight
lines of pale green. The peas were up. He was to see
that before he went back.

He stooped over them. Some of them were still
bowed double with the effort of thrusting themselves up

against the encumbering earth. He felt their effort in the muscles of his own back. But others, only a few hours older, were already straightening themselves blithely to reach up to the sun and warmth. This also he felt—in his heart. Under the intent gaze of the gardener, the vigorous little plants seemed to be vibrating with life. His eyes were filled with it. He turned away and went back to the open door of the hut. His wife, very pale, stood there, silent. He heaved up his knapsack, adjusted his blanket-roll and *musettes,* and drew a long breath.

" Good-bye, Paulette," he said, kissing her on both cheeks, the dreadful long kiss which may be the last.

" I will—I will take care of things here," she said, her voice dying away in her throat.

He kissed his children, he stooped low to kiss the little foster-child. He looked once more across at the field, not yet seeded. Then he started back to the trenches.

He had gone but a few steps when he stopped short and came back hurriedly. The rake was still in his hand. He had forgotten his gun.

VIGNETTES FROM LIFE AT THE REAR

I

I was tucking the children into bed after their bath, my rosy, romping, noisy children, when " le soldat Deschamps " was announced. Deschamps is the man from the north of France, who had been a coal-miner before the war, the man whose wife and little boy are still " up there," the man who has not seen his family since he kissed them the fourth of August three years ago.

A veil seemed to drop between me and the faces of my rosy, romping, noisy children. . . .

I went slowly along the hall to our living-room. Yes there he was, poor Deschamps, the big, powerfully built fellow, a little thinner, a little more gaunt, a little whiter than when I had seen him last, although that was only a week ago. He rose up, very tall in his worn gray-blue uniform, not so neatly brushed as it had been, and put out a flaccid hand. " Bonsoir, madame . . . excuse me for coming again so soon. I know I ought not to take your time. But when we are allowed to go out . . . where shall I go? I know so few people in Paris " . . . as though one would not be willing to give time when there is so tragically nothing else to give him!

I say something cordial, take up my sewing, and settle myself for what I know is coming.   Poor Deschamps!
He needs only a word or two of sympathy when out he
pours it all in a rush, the heartsick desolation of the up-
rooted exile, the disintegrating misery of the home-loving
man without a home.   Of late, alas! it does not come out
very coherently.   " You see, madame, we were so well
off there.   What could a man ask for more?   My day
in the mine began at four in the morning, but I was free
at two in the afternoon, and I am very strong, as you
see, so that I could go on working out of doors as long
as the daylight lasted.   We had our own house paid for,
our own!   And a big, big garden.   I earned ten francs a
day cash in the mines, and we almost lived out of our
garden, so we were saving all the time.   Our boy was
to have a good schooling.   Perhaps, we thought, he
might be like Pasteur.   You know his father was a
simple tanner.   My wife never had to work for others,
never!   She could stay there and have everything clean
and pleasant and take care of the boy.   We were so
happy and always well. . . .   We both worked in the
garden, and people who garden are never sick.   And always contented.   And our garden . . . you ought to
see it . . . all the potatoes we could eat I raised there,
and early ones too!   And all the cabbages and some to
sell.   The coal company sold us cheap all the manure we
wanted from their stables, and I could make the land as
rich, as rich!   Such early vegetables!   Better than any
you can buy in the towns.   And the winter ones . . .

you should see how we protect our cabbages in the winter. . . ."

The monologue has carried the big fellow out of his chair now. He is grasping an imaginary spade, a heap of imaginary cabbages by his side. " So . . . we sprinkle sand first, and then cabbages all laid so . . . you understand. . . ." The voice goes on and on, almost the voice of a person hypnotized.

I lose my perception of what he is saying as I gaze at his sunken eyes fixed on homely, much-loved scenes I cannot see.

" The best place for the carrots was the sloping bit of ground near the big oak. . . ." He sees it, his big oak, there before him. He makes me see it, and what it meant to him. This was the man whom the twentieth century forced to march away, to kill, and be killed.

". . . And little Raoul used to help; yes, with his little hands he would pat down the sand and laugh to see his finger-marks."

The voice stops abruptly. In the resultant silence I move uneasily . . . I find Deschamps' talk heartbreaking enough, but his silences terrify me. I try to arouse him from his bleak brooding reverie. . . .

" You had hares too, didn't you, and hens, and a pig . . . ? That must have helped out with the living."

He comes to himself with a start. " Oh, it was my wife who kept the animals. She has such a hand for making them thrive. They were like her other children. Those little chicks, they never died, always prospered, grew so fat. We always had one or two to sell when she went to town to market. Angèle used to dress them herself, so that we could have the feathers. Then she put them in one of the neat baskets she made from the willow sprouts on the side of our little stream, with a clean white cloth over them, as clean as her neckerchief. Angèle is as neat as a nun, always. Our house shone with cleanness . . ." He breaks off abruptly. " I have shown you the photograph of Angèle and Raoul, haven't I, madame? "

I hold out my hand and gaze again, as I have so many times before, into the quiet eyes of the young peasant woman with the sturdy little boy at her side. " She is very pretty, your wife," I say, "and your little boy looks so strong and vigorous."

" I hear," he said with a great heave of his broad chest, now so sunken, " that the Boches have taken all the livestock away from the owners, all the hens and pigs and hares, and sent them to Germany. Perhaps Raoul and Angèle have not enough to eat . . . perhaps there is even no house there now . . . a cousin of mine saw a refugee from his own region . . . who had seen the place where his house had been! . . . it had been shelled, there was . . ." His mouth sets hard in an angry line of horror.

I bestir myself. This is the sort of talk Deschamps must not be allowed.

" M. Deschamps," I say, " I shall be writing soon to that group of American friends who gave the money for your articulated arm. Have you any message to send them? I think they are planning to send some more money to help you. . . ."

He waves it away with a great gesture. " Money can't do anything for me," he says bitterly, adding quickly: " Not of course that I am not very, very grateful for the so-costly artificial arm. It means I can earn their living again, if ever Angèle . . ."

I break in once more: " But I promised them a statement of all your case, you know, the dates and places and everything. Could you just run over them again . . . ? "

But I do not listen as he goes wearily over the old story as familiar to me now as to him: mobilized the first day, was in the Battle of the Marne, advanced to B————, was wounded there in the leg, taken to a hospital in an American ambulance, cured, returned to the trenches; wounded in the shoulder, taken to the hospital, cured, returned to the trenches . . . all this time with no news whatever from his family, knowing that his region was occupied by the invaders, hearing stories of how the women and children were treated. . . . Fought during the winter of 1914-15, wounded in three places in June, 1915, taken to the hospital where his arm was amputated. While there, heard indirectly that his wife and child were still alive. As soon as the articulated arm (paid for out of my blessed fund of American money) allowed him to work, he had begun to learn the tinner's trade, since a one-armed man could no longer be a miner.

Now he had passed his apprenticeship and could soon be ready to earn his living.

I knew all this laborious, heroic, commonplace story already, and looked through it at the hospital pallor on the haggard face, at the dreadful soft whiteness of the hands so obviously meant to be hard and brown, at the slack looseness of the great frame, at a man on the point of losing his desire to live. . . .

"What use is it to earn money when not a cent can I send to them up there, when I can hear nothing from Angèle beyond that line on a post-card once in three months? Madame, you have education, *why* will they not allow a wife to write to her husband?"

I have only the old answer to the old question: "We suppose they are afraid of spies, of people sending information to France."

"But why do they *keep* Angèle there? Why don't they let women go to their husbands? What harm can that do? Why do they make it a hell on earth for them and then refuse to let them go?"

I had for this only the usual murmur: "A few *are* allowed to come away."

He struck his hands together. "So few! When they last said they would allow some women and children to come to France, only a fifteenth part of those who asked for leave were allowed to come. Why? Why? What has Angèle to do with the war?"

He gets up for the restless pacing about our little living-room which always ends his visits. "I think I

shall go mad, madame. I am there in the hospital, two
hundred of us in one great room . . . oh, they are
kind enough to us, we have enough to eat. But we are
not children. It is not enough to have food and a roof.
Two hundred men there . . . what a life . . . for
fourteen months! Nothing to work for, nothing to live
for, no home, no family, not even a chance to go back to
the trenches. The other men drink as much as they can
get money for. I never drank in my life. Madame, do
you suppose it would make me sleep to drink? "

"See here, M. Deschamps," I say, moving to my desk,
"I will write again to the Spanish Embassy. I will tell
them again about Angèle and Raoul, they will send the
request to the German authorities in your town . . .
perhaps *this* time . . ." It is a perilous stimulant to
administer to a sick heart, but what other have I? So I
sit, swallowing the lump in my throat, and once more
make out the application which never has any result.

"There," I say, putting it into an envelope with hands
that are not very steady—"there, my friend, you mail
that. And now you must go, or the night-nurse will
scold you for being late."

He reaches for his cap, his old shabby cap with the
bullet hole through it, and stands fumbling with it, his
head hanging. He towers above me, gaunt, powerful,
as pitiably defenseless as any little child. I wink back the
tears which threaten to come, shake his hand hard, and
tell him to be sure to come again the next time he has
the "*cafard.*" He nods absently and shuffles to the door.

"You will pardon me, madame . . . but when I think that my little Raoul has perhaps not enough to eat, and I am not . . ."

He has gone his lonely way to the hospital bed which is all he has for home. I go back to the cool dark bedroom and look down at my sleeping children.

There is no reason for it . . . why should I feel guilty to see them rosy and safe?

II

When I come in from the street, very tired, after a talk with a war-widow about ways and means for taking care of her children, I find him in the living-room, the hearty, broad-faced fellow, smiling, giving me his great, farm-laborer's hand, thanking me for the last package of goodies . . . as though he had not just come through the inferno of the attack at M———. "The package never arrived at a better moment," he said gaily. "We had been on awfully short rations for three days . . . in a shell-hole, you know." I know that I do not know it all, but it is futile to try to draw fine distinctions with Groissard, cheeriest and simplest of "permission-naires," always the same, always open-faced and clear-eyed, always emanating quiet confidence and always seeing it about him. If there are any tired or disheartened or apprehensive or perplexed soldiers in the army, they pass unperceived of Groissard's honest eyes. His companions are all . . . to hear him talk . . . as brave, as untroubled, as single-hearted as he. They never complain—that is, if Groissard's account of them is accurate: they think as little as possible about anything but food and packages from the rear and jokes. And when they do think, it is always only to be sure that everybody must hold hard and stick it out quite to the end. As long as "they" are on French soil, of course there is nothing else for an honest Frenchman to do. And they are all honest Frenchmen around Groissard.

"Oh yes, madame," he says simply, balancing my little boy on his knee, "the spirit of the army is excellent. Why shouldn't it be? We're going to get them, you know. And you ought to see our regimental fireless cookers now. They're great! The cooks fill them up at the kitchen at the rear, quite out of range, you know, where there's no danger of a shell upsetting the pots, and then the men bring the big fireless cookers up on mitrailleuse carriages that can go anywhere. They worm their way clear up to us in the first-line trenches, and our ragoût is piping hot. It's like sitting down to the table at the farm at home. There's nothing so good for the spirit of an army as hot *rasta*. And your packages, the packages madame sends with the money from her American friends . . . why, the days when they come it's like being a kid again, and having a birthday! And then we get two days out of five for rest at the rear, you know, except when there is a *very* big attack going on. We're not so badly off at all!"

"During those big attacks aren't you sometimes cut off from food supplies?" I ask.

"Oh, not so often. The longest one was three days and four nights, and we had our emergency rations for half that time." He tosses my fat little son up in the air and catches him deftly in his great farm laborer's hands, butcher's hands. The children adore Groissard, and his furloughs are festivals for them. As for me, I have an endless curiosity about him. I can never be done with questioning him, with trying to find out what is underneath his good-natured acceptance of the present insane scheme of the universe; I sometimes descend to banalities, the foolish questions schoolgirls ask. I lower my voice: "Groissard, did you ever—have you ever had to . . . I don't mean firing off your rifle at a distant crowd, I mean in close quarters . . . ? "

"Have I killed many Boches, you mean, madame?" he breaks through my mincing, twentieth-century false-modesty about naming a fact I accept . . . since I accept Groissard! "Oh yes, a good many. We fought all over Mort-Homme, you know; and we were in the last attack on Hill 304. There was a good deal of hand-to-hand work there, of course." He turns the delighted baby upside down and right-side up, and smiles sunnily at the resultant shrieks of mirth.

I try again: "Do you see many prisoners, Groissard?" He is always ready to answer questions, although he cannot understand my interest in such commonplace details.

"Yes indeed, madame, ever so many. Just the day before this 'permission' began, day before yesterday it

was, we brought in a squad of twenty from a short
section of trench we had taken. I'm not likely to forget
them for *one* while! Our cook, who is from the South
and loses his head easily, went and cooked up for them
at three o'clock in the afternoon every last beefsteak we
were going to have for dinner that night. We didn't
have a thing but beans left! But we didn't grumble very
much, either. They were the coldest, hungriest-looking
lot you ever saw. It did your heart good to see the way
they got around those beefsteaks!"

I gaze at him baffled. "But, Groissard, you kill them.
You are there to kill them! What can you care whether
they have beefsteaks or not."

He stops playing with the baby to look at me, round-
eyed with astonishment. "I'm not there to kill *prisoners!*" he says, with an unanswerable simplicity. And
I lose myself again in a maze of conjecture and specu-
lation.

III

"Oh, it's got to stop, that's all; it's too sickening, too
imbecile, too monstrous!"

It is the *brancardier* talking, the one who had been a
prosperous sugar-broker before the war, and who has
been a first-line stretcher-carrier since the beginning of
the war. If you think you have any idea what it has
meant to be first-line stretcher-carrier for three years,
you have only to hear Paul Arbagnan talk for five minutes to guess at the extent of your ignorance. He is

just back from the front, on a twenty-four hours' furlough, granted after a terrible fortnight under incessant
fire. He sits in the midst of our family group, beside
his older brother, the despatch-carrier, also here " *en
permission.*" The brother was before the war a professor of political economy. From the worn blue
uniforms of both brothers swings the *croix de guerre*
gloriously. The younger one's face is thin and very
brown, his blue eyes look out at us with an irritable
flicker. The mud dried on his clumsy boots crumbles
off in great flakes on my polished floor. His hard, grimy
hand with broken nails (which had been so fine and
well-kept before the war) teases and pulls at his close-
clipped hair, now as grizzled with silver as that of a man
twenty years his senior.

A harmless elderly relative murmurs something sentimental about the mud on the floor being sacred earth, like
that the Crusaders brought back from Jerusalem, and the
inevitable explosion takes place. " Oh, you people at the
rear, your silly chatter about heroism and holy causes!
You don't know what you are talking about. There
ought to be a law to make all the civilian population keep
silence about the war. You have no idea, not the faintest
glimmering of a notion of what life is at the front! If
you *had* . . .! My *croix de guerre!* Don't you suppose I would give it back ten times over if I could forget
what I feel deliberately to leave a mortally wounded man
to die because I have orders to select (if my stretcher
has not room enough for all) only those who may get

well enough to go back and fight again. Without having
known what it is, you've no right to say a word, to have
an opinion or a thought about it, you safe, clean, soft,
gossiping people at the rear! The dirt . . .! Why,
the bath I had this morning here in Paris was the first
time I have taken my clothes off, except to hunt for
vermin, for twenty-two days. Do you know what your
body is like, what your clothes are like, what your socks
are like, when you have lived and cooked and sweat and
slept and bled in them for twenty-two days? Of course
you don't. No civilized being does. And until you do,
less talk from you about the heroism of the soldier!
Filth, that's what war is, and dirty diseases lying in
wait for decent men. And cold, cold day and night, cold
that brutalizes, that degenerates you till you would sell
your soul, your mother's soul to be warm again. And
mud, not clean country mud, but filth, and up to your eyes
and beyond, horrible infected mud splashing upon the
emergency bandage you are trying to put on a wound.
And the wounded . . . see here, when the newspapers
speak complacently of the superb artillery preparation
which after three days of cannon-duel silences the
enemy's batteries, do you know what that means to me?
It means I am squatting all day in an underground
shelter, with twenty wounded, the German shells falling
one a minute over my head, my supplies of bandages
gone, my anæsthetics gone, no cotton, not even a cup of
water left. To see them die there, begging for help,
calling for their mothers . . . to crouch there helpless,

all day long, hearing the shells falling, and wondering which one will come through the roof—oh, you have plenty of time to think the whole proposition over, the business you're in. You have time, let me tell you, to have your own opinion of the imbecility of setting one highly civilized man down in filth and degradation to shoot at others. When some idiot of a journalist, reporting the war, speaks of the warlike ardor of the men, how it is difficult to restrain them until the order to charge is given . . . when we read such paragraphs in the papers . . . if you could hear the snarl that goes up! We ' charge ' when the word of command is given, yes, because we know nothing better to do, but . . ."

The sentimental aunt breaks in resolutely: " Of course, it's very noble of you, Paul; the fact is simply that you don't or won't recognize your own courage."

" Courage, nonsense! A rat in a hole, surrounded by other rats putrefying . . . that's what I am in my underground shelter! What else can I do? What else can we any of us do? We can't get away! There wouldn't be anywhere to go if we did! But when I think of the people at the rear, how they don't know, will never know, the sickening hours the troops live through. See here! No sensitive, civilized being can forget it if he has only *once* been wholly filthy, wholly bestial . . . and we have been that, time without number. When I come back to Paris on furlough and look at the crowds in the Paris streets, the old men with white collars, and clean skins, the women with curled hair and silk stockings, I could *kill* them, when I think that they will have a voice in the future, will affect what will be done hereafter about war . . ."

"Time for your train, Paul," warns the elder brother soberly.

The man who had been reviling the life of a soldier springs instantly to his feet and looks anxiously at his watch. He claps on his blue steel casque.

We try to give a light touch to the last of his stay. "How medieval those helmets make you look!"

He is not to be distracted. "Put it further back, stone-age, cannibalistic," he cries bitterly, marching out hurriedly so that he may be promptly at his task.

The elder brother comes back from the door, a dim, patient smile on his lips. "Oh, Paul, poor boy! He takes it hard! He takes it hard!" he murmurs. "Who would think to hear him that he is accounted the best *brancardier* in his section? He is the one always sent out to do the impossible, and he always goes, silently, and does it. After this last engagement, he had shown such *bravoure,* they wanted to have him cited again, to give him the palms to wear above his *croix*. But he said he had had his share, that others had done as much as he, and he persuaded them to give the *croix* to one of the other *brancardiers,* a stevedore from Marseilles who can't read or write. You are perhaps not surprised to know that he is adored by his comrades."

"But is it *true* . . . all he says?" I ask, shivering a little.

"Oh yes, true enough, and more than he says or any one can ever say. But, but . . ." He searches for a metaphor and finds it with a smile. "See, Paul is like a man with a fearful toothache! He can't think of anything else. But that doesn't mean there isn't anything else."

I ask him: "But you, who have been through all that Paul sees, what do *you* find, besides?" He hesitates, smiling no longer, and finally brings out in a low tone: "When a mother gives birth to a child, she suffers, suffers horribly. Perhaps all the world is now trying to give birth to a new idea, which we have talked of, but never *felt* before; the idea that all of us, each of us, is responsible for what happens to all, to each, that we must stick together for good . . ." He picks up his steel helmet, and looks at us with his dim, patient, indomitable smile. "It is like a little new baby in more ways than one, that new idea. It has cost us such agony; and it is so small, so weak, so needing all our protection . . . and then also, because . . ." his sunken eyes are prophetic, "because it is *alive,* because it will grow!"

IV

I glance at my calendar in dismay. Is it possible that three months have gone, and that it is time for Amieux to have another "permission"? How long the week of his furlough always seems, how the three months between race away! Of course we have the greatest regard for Amieux. We feel that his uniform alone (he is a *chasseur alpin* who has been a first-line fighter since the Battle of the Marne) would entitle him to our services, but more than that, his personality commands our respect, sound, steady, quiet Amieux whose sturdy body is wounded in one place after another, who is repaired hastily in the nearest hospital and uncomplainingly goes back to the trenches, his sleeve decorated with another one of the V-shaped marks which denote wounds. The only trouble with Amieux as a household hero is a total dearth of subjects of conversation. You see, he is a glass-blower by profession. We often feel that if we were not as ignorant of glass-blowing as Amieux is of everything else, we could get on famously with him. As it is . . .

" *Oh bon jour,* M. Amieux," I say, jumping to my feet, " welcome back to the rear! All well? "

" Yes, madame," he says with as ponderous an emphasis on the full-stop as that of any taciturn New England farmer.

" Well, has it been hard, the last three months? " I ask.

" No, madame."

I draw a long breath.

" Do the packages we send, the chocolate, the cigarettes, the soap—do they reach you promptly? "

" Yes, madame. Thank you, madame."

The full-stop is more overpowering with each answer.

I resort to more chatter, anything to fill that resounding silence. "Here we have been so busy! So many more American volunteers are coming over for the Ambulance service, my husband has not a free moment. The children never see him. My little daughter is doing well in school. She begins to read French now. Of course the little son doesn't go to school, but he is learning to speak French like a French baby. It has been so cold here. There has been so little coal. You must have heard, the long lines waiting to get coal . . ." I stop with almost a shrug of exasperation. As well talk to a basalt statue as to Amieux, impassive, his rough red hands on his knees, his *musette* swollen with all the miscellaneous junk the poilu stuffs into that nondescript receptacle, his cap still firmly on his head . . . formal manners are not specialties of Amieux. And then I notice that one leg is thrust out, very stiff and straight, and has a big bulbous swelling which speaks of a bandage under the puttees.

I glance at it. "Rheumatism? Too much water in the trenches?"

He looks down at it without a flicker on his face. "No, madame, a wound."

"Really? How did it happen this time?"

He looks faintly bored. They always hate to tell how they were wounded. "Oh, no particular way. A shell had smashed up an *abri*, and while I was trying to pull my captain out from under the timbers another shell exploded near by."

"Did you save the captain?"

"Oh yes. He was banged up around the head. He's all right now."

"Were you there with him? How did it happen you weren't buried under the wreck too?"

"I wasn't there. I was in a trench. But I saw. I knew he was there."

I am so used to Amieux's conversational style that I manage even through this arid narration to see what had happened. "Do you mean to say that you left the trench and went out under shell-fire to rescue your captain! And they didn't give you a decoration! It's outrageous not recognizing such bravery!"

He shuffles his feet and looks foolish. "The captain wanted to have me cited all right. He's a *chic type,* but I said he'd better not."

"Don't you want the *croix de guerre?*" I cry, astounded at such apathy even from Amieux.

"Oh, I wouldn't mind. It's my mother."

"Don't you suppose your mother would *love* to have her son decorated?" I feel there must be some absurd misunderstanding between us, the man seems to be talking such nonsense.

"Well, you see, my mother . . . my only brother was killed last winter. *Maman* worries a good deal about me, and I told her, just so she could sleep quietly, you know, I have told her my company isn't near the front at all. I said we were guarding a munitions depot at the rear."

"Well . . ." I am still at a loss.

"Well, don't you see, if I get the *croix de guerre* for being under fire, *maman* would get to worrying again. So I told my captain I'd rather he'd give it to one of the other fellows."

V

I had just come from several hours spent with one of the war-blind, one of those among the educated, unresigned war-blind, who see too clearly with the eyes of their intelligence what has happened to them. I had been with him, looking into his sightless face, pitting my strength against the bitterness of his voice; and I was tired, tired to the marrow of my bones, to the tip of every nerve.

But the children had not been out for their walk and the day was that rare thing in a Paris March, a sunshiny one, not to be wasted. "Come, dears," I told them as I entered the apartment, "get on your wraps. We'll all go out for a play while the sun is still high."

I walked along the street between them, my little daughter and my little son, their warm soft hands in mine. The sparrows chattered in the bare trees above us, the sparrows who even in this keen air felt the coming of spring which was foretold by the greening of the grass in the public squares. My children chattered incessantly, like the sparrows. Perhaps they felt the spring too. *I* did not want to feel the spring. We turned away from the Seine and walked on one side of the open square before Notre Dame.

"Mother, I caught my ball twenty-three times to-day without missing."

"Muvver, I see a white horse, a *big* white horsie!"

"Mother, do you like arithmetic as well as history? *I* don't."

"Muvver, I have a little p'tend doggie here, trotting after me, a little brown p'tend doggie."

"Mother, O *mother,* let me tell you what happened at school to-day, during recess!"

Through the half-heard ripple of clear little voices, there came upon me one of those thunder-claps of realization which, since the beginning of the war, have brought wiser and stronger people than I to the brink of insanity —realization for an instant (longer than an instant would carry any one over the brink) that the war is really going on, realization of what the war really means, one glimpse of the black abyss. I felt very sick, and stood still for an instant, because my knees shook under me. . . .

But those wiser and stronger ones had not little children of their own to draw them away from that black gulf. . . . I was pulled at by impatient little hands, lucid, ineffably pure eyes were turned up to mine, the clear little voices grew louder, "Muvver, muvver, I'm losing my mitten!"

"Mother, why are you standing still? *This* isn't a good place to play! There! A little nearer the big church is some sand. And a bench for you."

How could I go on this everyday commonplace life, eating, drinking, sleeping, caring for the children, cheer-

ing them . . . in such a wicked and imbecile world!
I looked up and down the bare, sun-flooded square. All
about me were other women, caring for little children.
And for the most part, those other women were in
mourning. But they were there under that cruel, careless
sunshine, caring for their children, cheering them. . . .

I put the little mitten on; I walked forward to the
bench, the little singing voices died away to a ripple
again. "Oh, this is fine! See, little brother, here is a
cave already. Let me have that stick!" "No, me!
Me!"

That was what was sounding in my ears. But what
I heard was a muffled voice saying scornfully: "Re-
education . . . courage, taking up our lives again
. . . oh yes, whatever you please to imagine to distract
our attention! But we are finished men, done for . . .
lost!"

My children played before me in the sunshine, but
what I saw were the scarred, mutilated, sightless faces
of young men in their prime, with long lives of darkness
before them. And as I sat there, then, that instant, other
young men in their prime were being blinded, were being
mutilated for life.

My fatigue deepened till it was like lead upon me.
Under it I was cold. The sun did not warm me. It fell
like a mockery upon a race gone mad, upon a world
bankrupt in hope. Yes, what we suffered was not the
worst, not even what *they* suffered, the men at the front;
what was worst was the fact that the meaning of it all

was hopelessness, was the end, a black end to all we had looked forward to, striven for . . . paralysis, death in life. And an indifferent sun shining down on it, as it had on our illusions.

After a time the children tired of sand. " Mother, mayn't we go in the big church? You never have taken us inside. What does it look like?"

Their restless upspringing life thrust my paralysis aside as an upspringing young tree cleaves the boulder which would hamper it. We pushed open the heavy leather door and stepped into the huge cavern, our eyes so full of the glare of the sunshine that, as we walked forward up the nave, we could see nothing but velvety darkness, faintly scented with mold and incense.

The silence was so intense that I could hear my sore, angry heart beating furiously in my breast. . . .

Further along before us, where rich-colored patches lay, on the stone pavement, there was the light from the great rose-windows. . . . We stood there now, our eyes slowly clearing, the blackness slowly fading out into twilight, to a sweet, clear translucent dimness which hid nothing.

Silence, long, shadowy veiled aisles, hushed immensity. . . .

A great calm hand seemed laid on my shoulder, so that my fever sank, my pulses were quieted. I stood motionless, feeling slowly pulsating through me a vaster rhythm than the throbbing irregularity of my own doubting heart.   A great soundless benediction was breathed upon me out of the man-wrought beauty around and above me.

Up, up, up, I raised my eyes, following the soaring of the many-columned pillars, and something in my heart burst its leaden bonds and soared up out of my breast. . . .

Yes, here was beauty, here was that beauty I had forgotten and denied . . . *and men had made it!* It had nothing to do with the glare of the indifferent sun, with the callous face of our calamity.   Men had made this beauty, imperfect, warring, doubting, suffering, sinning men had upreared this perfect creation.   They had created this beauty out of their faith in righteousness, and they would again create other beauty, out of other manifestations of righteousness, long after this war was a forgotten nightmare. . . .

"What is that shining on your face, mother?"

I put my hand up.   My cheeks are wet.   "Tears, dear."

"O mother, why do you cry?"

"Because I am very happy, my darling."

A FAIR EXCHANGE

THE energetic, well-dressed man who walked so quickly in spite of his gray hair was quite out of breath from the unusual experience of mounting stairs on foot, when he stepped into the anteroom. There he looked about him with a keenly observant eye. The room had obviously not been intended as the entrance to modern offices. Its dingy, paneled walls and darkened carved ceiling dated at least from the time when the ancestors of the newcomer were hunting Indians in the untracked forests of Massachusetts. It was a forlorn cheerless apology for a convenient, well-equipped business waiting-room. And yet the intelligent, keen eyes now looking at it saw in it . . . what? Something he could not analyze, something he tried to express. "What the devil is it about their little old holes . . . ?" he asked himself with the fresh vivid curiosity which was his habit about phenomena new to him.

A one-armed young soldier, in a worn blue uniform, with a patch over one eye, rose up from the cane-bottomed chair, took from the white-pine table a small pad of paper and held it out to the newcomer sketching a bow. The older man looked the other way sedulously. He was a very tender-hearted person (except of course for his business competitors) and the constant sight of the maimed wreckage of young manhood made him sick.

On the pad of paper was printed " Nom du Visiteur," with a blank following it, and, underneath, " Objet de la visite." Mr. Hale's French was limited, but he made out that he was to write down who he was and what his business was, and generously he admired the little detail of office administration which he had never happened to see in an American business office. " That beats sending in a message by the office-boy, all right!" he thought to himself as he wrote. " They are funny people! Just when you get absolute proof that they can't do business any more than a sick cat, you run into something that makes you wonder."

He had written on the pad " Randolph Metcalf Hale, President of the Illinois Association of Druggists," and, underneath that, " On business connected with closer commercial relations of France and the United States." As he handed the slip of paper back to the young soldier he thought, " I might about as well get a rubber stamp for that last, and save writing it over so often."

The uniformed messenger limped out of the room. " Oh Lord! and a wooden leg, along with only one eye and one arm," thought Mr. Hale, wincing at the too familiar sound of the halting gait. He thrust his hands deep into his pockets and stood meditatively looking down at his own vigorous, well-clad legs.

The soldier came back and motioned the visitor to follow him. They went along a narrow corridor with occasional steps up and other steps down, with large old windows looking out through time-dimmed panes upon a stone-paved court with an old gray stone fountain. The American shook his head. "Never anything new! Always cutting their clothes out of their grandfather's left-overs and sewing them up by hand; that's it, everything hand-made!"

He was ushered into an office where a man of about his own age, with a black beard, streaked with white, rose up and came towards him with outstretched hand.

"Ninth to-day," noted the American mentally. He amused himself by keeping statistics on the fabulous amount of handshaking accomplished in French business life.

Then he explained his presence. Partly because he accounted it a crime to take longer than necessary to state your business, and partly because he had stated it so many times, he packed a succinct account of himself into comparatively few phrases.

"Like almost everybody else in America, Monsieur Portier, I want to help make up to France for the way she's been having the rough end of all this war. But everybody does best at his own sort of help; and I didn't come over for reconstructing villages or taking care of refugees. That sort of work's got to be done, of course, but there are a lot of our own folks at that already. Anyhow, not knowing your language, or your folks, I'd make a poor job of trying to fix up their personal lives. That's not my specialty. But I *have* a specialty, and that's the American toilet preparations business. And it occurred to me out there in Evanston that perhaps getting American business along my line joined up closer with French business would be as good a turn as I could do for France. After all, though it does give you the horrors to see the poor boys with their legs and arms shot off, that doesn't last but one generation. But *business* now . . . all the future is there!" His eye kindled. He had evidently pronounced his *credo*. The attentive Frenchman behind the desk nodded, acquiescing in carefully accurate English: " Precisely, Mr. Hale. You had the very same idea which induced my Government to organize this committee of which I am secretary. I am more than at your disposition."

" I know it," said the American without further expression of gratitude than this recognition, " and that's why I'm here. I've got to a place where I need some help. It's this way. I've done a lot of straight business, I mean paying business. And I've managed that all right. I've got the rails laid for our sending over drug specialties you don't have here and for shipping to the States the toilet preparations specialties I find here. But now I'm here I want to do *more* than just regular business. Now that I *see* your country and take in what the war's been, and think what you've been up against . . . well, Monsieur Portier, I tell you I want to *do* something for France!"

He said this with a simple, heartfelt sincerity which moved the Frenchman to lean from his chair and give him a silent handshake of appreciation. The American forgot to add this to his total for the day, going on earnestly with his story: " And so, I keep my eyes open all the time for little good turns I can do. I don't mean charity . . . honestly, I think that does about as much harm as good, though of course we have to go through the motions in a time like this. I mean business good turns, such as I'd like to have anybody do me, look at my concern with a fresh eye and tell me how I could make it better, or else tell me where I could find a bigger market. You understand? Like that. Now I've been doing business with a big chemical factory out in the country near Paris. The nearest place to it, for me, is Versailles . . . maybe you happen to know Versailles?"

The Frenchman nodded gravely. Yes, he had a married sister living in Versailles. " Well, there's a little drug-store out there, one of these peaceful, sleepy-looking, home-and-mother French drug-stores, with a big cat dozing in the window, and somebody in a white apron putting up pills behind the counter, and so far as anybody from *my* part of the world can see, not enough business doing from one week's end to another, to buy a postage-stamp."

The Frenchman laughed. " Oh, it's a very good business in France being a *pharmacien.*"

" That's what everybody tells me, and that's what gets me. *One* of the things that gets me! In *our* country when there is any business being done you hear the wheels going 'round.' I can't get used to this smooth European way of doing it and not letting on. Well, my main interest in life being the toilet preparations business I hardly ever go by one without stopping in. You never know when you're going to run onto something worthwhile. Well, out there in Versailles, I certainly did. I ran onto a genius. Yes, sir, that's not too much to say; a genius! Any man who can make a cold cream like that . . ."

He interrupted himself to ask: " You don't happen to be up on cold cream? No? It's a pity, because you can't appreciate what that man is doing. By George, I never saw anything like it, and I've dealt in cold creams for thirty years! It's got anything in America beaten a mile! The two great faults of cold cream, you see, are being greasy and being crumbly. This isn't either. And it keeps! He showed me some he'd had for four years in a pot, with just a flat earthenware lid laid on top, and you wouldn't believe it, Monsieur Portier, but it hadn't changed an atom, not an *atom!* And the fineness of it! The least little pinch between your fingers, and it just sinks right into your pores before your eyes! It's *like* cream, thick, rich cream off a three-days-set pan of milk, and yet it don't run! And the perfume! Monsieur Portier, I give you my word for it, and I know what I'm talking about, the perfume that little old druggist out in his dinky little old shop has got into his cold cream is the only *refined* cold cream perfume I ever smelled! It makes all the others smell like a third-rate actress. It's

got a . . . it's got a . . ." He hesitated, searching for
exactly the right word and brought it out with enthusi-
asm, " it's got a *clean* smell, if you get me, like a nice
girl after a bath! I've got daughters of my own," he
added in whimsical justification of his metaphor.

The Frenchman had been watching him with appre-
ciative eyes. " Mr. Hale, I see that, like so many of
your countrymen, you are a real artist in your line, and
you have the artist's flavor."

The American was disconcerted by this characterization. " Who? Me? I know a good thing when I see
it, that's all, and that's *business*, that's not art."

The Frenchman smiled with the amused, respectful
sympathy which men of his race so often feel for their
American contemporaries. " Well, and what did you
do when you discovered this miraculous cold cream ? "

Mr. Hale laughed, a young, vigorous laugh which
made his gray hair seem a paradox. " Well, you've
guessed it. I threw a fit, first of all. I was taken off
my feet, and I wouldn't be surprised if I acted like a cat
over catnip. So I decided I'd better go away and cool
off before I did anything rash. I bought a couple of pots
and went back to the hotel to sleep on it. That's something I always try to do, Monsieur Portier, before I let
myself in for a *big* proposition; and I meant this to be
big, all right. I wanted to see if that cold cream seemed
as good after twenty-four hours as it did at first. Well,
it did, and *then* some! So I got the Swede porter at my
hotel, who can talk some English, to go back with me.

And I started in to ask the old fellow all about it. Right there I struck a difference. After the way I'd gone on, an American, when I went back the next day, would have been wondering what I was trying to take away from him; but my old friend was just as pleased as a mother is when you tell her she's got a pretty baby. In fact he reminded me of that, the way he talked. So glad to tell me all about it. I got the impression before he got through that it was a member of the family. I don't mean, of course, that he told me how he made it. I wouldn't have let him if he'd started to. But he told me everything else. To begin with, he told me that his folks have been pharmacists right there for more than a hundred years! *A hundred years* in that little shop in that little street in that little town! I tell you, Monsieur Portier, I never can get used to the way your people stay put."

The Frenchman looked grave. " Perhaps too much so, Mr. Hale."

" Anyhow, he said they had the recipe, the first recipe for that cold cream in his great-grandfather's handwriting. He said there'd been some talk always in the family about its having come from his great-grandfather's father, who had sold toilet specialties to Marie Antoinette, the queen, you know. He said he himself didn't take much stock in that story because everybody in France, more or less, claimed to have a great-grandfather who'd had dealings with Marie Antoinette, but I just thought to myself what a good smart advertisement agency could do with that item . . . you could see it on every billboard between New York and San Francisco . . . 'Marie Antoinette's own cold cream, rediscovered recipe.' If you've been in America, you can imagine."

"Yes," said the Frenchman, "I can imagine."

"He said, of course, they had not stuck absolutely to that recipe just as it stood. His grandfather had made some changes, experimented with it all his life, and his father had changed the proportions, just little shadings, with years in between, to think them over and to be sure they were right. But he himself had changed it the most, because modern chemistry had let him substitute for one ingredient that had never been just right, something else that exactly filled the bill. Do you know, Monsieur Portier, as he stood there telling me how, for a hundred years, three generations of his folks had concentrated on that, I said to myself: 'By George, there's a *reason!* No wonder it's better than any of our get-there-quick products. They've certainly got us beat.'"

To this handsome tribute the Frenchman replied dubiously: "It is very generous, Mr. Hale, to say such a thing. But since taking over the work on this committee I have had periods of great depression when it has seemed to me that no power on earth, not even American energy from which I hope a great deal, could ever move our trades-people from their century-old habits of business inertia and lack of enterprise."

"Well, I understand that, too," agreed the American sympathetically; "I certainly do, because that's just what

I've come to see you about. We went on with our con-
fab, my old friend and I, and he showed me his books
to show how the sale of the cold cream had grown
since they began on it. It seems they've had quite a lot
of their customers for sixty or seventy years. Not Versailles people at all, you know, people from all over,
people who had tried it once and never would have
another, and I don't blame them. He's got quite a lot
of aristocrats on his list. He showed me names on his
account book that made it look like a history of France.
Well, the sum-total of it came to this. His grandfather
sold on an average three hundred pots a year, which was
good for those days; in his father's time it went up, so
he said, astonishingly, to fifteen hundred pots a year;
but he had done even better, and in his little factory-
laboratory that he'd had to enlarge, he made four thousand pots a year and sold them all. 'More than *ten
times* what his grandfather had done.'"

In repeating these statistics he reproduced with an
ironical exactness the tone of self-congratulation of the
pharmacist. The man before him fell into the little trap,
remarking innocently: "That is indeed making a remarkable enlargement."

The American sat up straight in his chair so suddenly
that he gave the effect of having leaped to his feet.
"*Remarkable!* Why, it was all I could do to keep from
sitting right down and crying. Remarkable! Why,
with the article he has there, the family ought to
have been millionaires a generation ago! Anybody with

a particle of business imagination would have put it on the bathroom shelf of every family in Christendom." He went on, more quietly: " I said something of that to the old fellow and I tried, through that hotel porter, to make him understand what my proposition was, to take up his cold cream. To take it up strong. I outlined my plan for the advertising campaign, I told him some of the figures of our toilet preparations market, and I told him I'd guarantee him in less than six months' time to have a demand for fifteen hundred gross pots and by the end of the first year it would pass the four thousand gross mark. I told him just how I could get him credit on the easiest terms for the enlargement of his plant . . . one of our Merchants' Associations is prepared to give credit to French and Belgian firms, and I was just starting in to explain how it wouldn't be any risk for him at all, and absolute certain big profits for him and his son . . . he's got a son at the front now who's passed his pharmacist's examination and is ready to go on with his father's business. . . ."

He stopped short for a moment, staring into space as though recalling the scene.

" Well," prompted the French listener, " what did he say? "

" He said, as near as I could make out from what the hotel porter told me, he said *he didn't want to*," replied the American, in the carefully restrained voice of one who recounts an enormity so patent that there is no need for emphasis to bring out its monstrousness. " Yes, from what the hotel porter said, I took it that he said he didn't want to! It wasn't that he was afraid of losing money, or that he suspected a skin deal . . . at least that was what he *said* . . . nor that he doubted a single thing I said, it was just that he guessed he didn't feel like it to-day, thank you."

He reached for his hat and stood up. "There, Monsieur Portier, there's where I am. I started to argue, of course. I tried to get at what in hell was the matter anyhow. But I soon saw I was up against something too big for that hotel porter to manage. So I came to see if you would go back with me, or send somebody who's got good sense and business experience, and help me make that proposition all over again. It must be of course that that hotel porter got the thing all balled up, the way he put it. I ought to have known better than to trust it to a Swede, anyhow."

Monsieur Portier looked at the calendar on his desk. "Yes, I shall be glad to go out with you. Let me see, to-day is Monday, next Thursday afternoon."

The visitor's face dropped. "Not till *Thursday!*" he cried, as though that date were in the next century. "I was hoping you could go right back with me now. I've got a taxi waiting downstairs."

The Frenchman's face wore for an instant a look of consternation which changed into a rather curious, strained expression. Then he said with the accent of heroism, laughing a little, "Yes, Mr. Hale, there is really no valid reason for my not going with you now, *at this instant,* and I will!" He seemed to regard the resolution as an extraordinary one, adding whimsically, as he put on his overcoat, "Ah, you can never, never understand, my dear Mr. Hale, the awful effort of will it costs a European to do something the moment it is suggested instead of putting it off till the next week."

"No," said the American heartily, "that's something I never will understand."

As they approached the shining windows of the pharmacy, where as a matter of fact a big, beautifully cared-for cat was sleeping in the sun, the Frenchman exclaimed: "Oh, it's Monsieur Réquine's pharmacy! I've known him for years, ever since my sister came to live in Versailles. I didn't think it could be he because you spoke of him always as old."

"Isn't he?" asked the American.

"Fifty-two. Is that old? I hope not."

"Fifty-two! I'm fifty-four myself! That's one on me!"

"What made you think him old? His hair isn't white. He hasn't any wrinkles. Really, I'm curious to know."

The American stopped on the curbstone, pondering, his alert mind interested by the little problem in self-analysis. "What *did* make me, I wonder?" He glanced in through the open door and said: "Well, just look at him as he stands there, his hands clasped over his stomach,—you can see for yourself. It's a kind of

settled-down-to-stay look that I'm not used to seeing unless a man is so old that he can't move on any more."

The Frenchman looked at the druggist and then at
the man beside him. "Yes, I see what you mean," he
admitted. He said it with a sigh.

They entered the shop. The druggist came forward
with a smile, and shook hands heartily with them both.
"Eleven," noted the American mentally.

"Monsieur Réquine," said the French visitor, "can't
we go through into your salon, or perhaps out into your
garden for a little talk?" Mr. Réquine glowed with
hospitality. "Yes, yes, delighted. I'll just ask my wife
to step here to mind the shop."

"*His wife!*" asked the American, "to wait on customers?"

A well-dressed, tall, full-bosomed woman of forty-
odd, with elaborately dressed black hair and a much
powdered, intelligent face came in answer to the call
and installed herself back of the counter with her knitting.

"Yes, and she knows as much about the business end
as he does, you may be sure," said the Frenchman as they
went through a door at the back of the shop, emerging,
not, as the American expected, into a storeroom, but
into an attractive parlor. They passed through the salon,
into an exquisitely kept little dining-room and out into
a walled garden which made the American pass his hand
over his eyes and look again. While their host was
installing them at the little round green iron table under

a trellis overgrown by a magnificent grapevine, Mr. Hale's eyes traveled from one point to another of the small paradise before him. It could not have been more than a hundred feet wide and three hundred long, but like a fabled spot in the "Arabian Nights" it shone resplendent with incredible riches. The stone walls, ten feet high, were carpeted to the top with a mantle of glistening green leaves, among which hung peaches and pears, glorious to the view, rank on rank, such fruit as the American had never thought could exist. On each side of the graveled path down the center were flowering plants, like great bouquets each. Back of them were more fruit-trees, none more than eight feet tall, bearing each a dozen or more amazing apples, as brightly colored as the flowers. Around the trees were vegetables, carrots, salads, cabbages, every specimen as floridly full-leafed and perfect as the incredible pictures Mr. Hale had seen, and disbelieved in, on the front of seed catalogues.

From the other end of the garden, drenched in sunshine, came the humming of bees. Above their heads a climbing rose covering the end of the house sent down a clear, delicate perfume from its hundred flowers.

The American's eyes came back from their inspection of all this and rested with a new expression on his rather snuffy, rather stout and undistinguished host. "Will you please tell Monsieur Réquine from me," he said to his companion, "that I never saw such a garden in my life?"

Monsieur Réquine waved the tribute away with sincere humility. "Oh, it's nothing compared to those all about me. I can't give it the time I would like to. Later on, when I am retired, and my son has the business . . ." his gesture seemed to indicate wider horizons of horticultural excellence before which the American's imagination recoiled breathless.

The straw-colored liqueur had been poured out into the glasses, which were, so Mr. Hale noticed, of extremely fine and delicate workmanship . . . "and his wife tending shop!" The two Frenchmen drank with ceremonious bowings and murmured salutations. Mr. Hale consumed his fiery draught silently but with a not ungraceful self-possession. He was at his ease with all kinds of ways of taking a drink.

Then, drawing a long breath, taking off his hat and putting his elbows on the table, he began to expound and the French official with him to translate. The bees hummed a queer, unsuitable accompaniment to his resonant, forceful staccato.

He talked a long time. The patches of sunlight which fell through the vines over their heads had shifted their places perceptibly when he stopped, his head high, his gray eagle's eyes flashing.

The elderly Frenchman opposite him had listened intently, his fat, wrinkled hands crossed on his waistcoat, an expression of thoughtful consideration on his broad face and in his small, very intelligent brown eyes. When the American finished speaking, he bent his head courteously and said: " Mr. Hale, you have spoken with great eloquence. But you have forgotten to touch on one matter, and that is the reason for my doing all that you outline so enthusiastically. Why *should* I?" It was evidently a genuine and not a rhetorical question, for he paused for a reply, awaiting it with sincere curiosity on his face. He received none, however, the fluent American being totally at a loss. " Why *should* you?" he said blankly. " I don't believe I understand you." The two exchanged a long puzzled look across the little table, centuries and worlds apart.

" Why, I mean," Monsieur Réquine went on finally, " I don't see any possible reason for embarking in such a terrifyingly vast enterprise as you outline; no reason for, and many against. To speak of nothing else, I am absolutely, morally certain that my cold cream " (he spoke of it with respect and affection) " would immediately deteriorate if it were manufactured on such an inhuman scale of immensity as you plan, with factories here and factories there, run by mercenary superintendents who had no personal interest in its excellence, with miscellaneous workmen picked up out of the street haphazard. Why, Mr. Hale, you have no idea of the difficulties I have, as it is, to get and train and keep serious, conscientious work-people. I should be lost without the little nucleus of old helpers who have been with our family for two generations and who set the tone of our small factory. They have the reputation and fine quality of our cold cream at heart as much as we of the family.

They help us in the selection of the newer, younger workers whom we need to fill the ranks, they help us to train them in the traditions and methods of our work, and with patience teach them, one by one, year by year, the innumerable little fine secrets of manipulation which have been worked out since my grandfather began the manufacture there in that room back of you in 1836. Our recipe is much of course, it is all important; but it is not all. Oh no, Mr. Hale, it is not all. We put into our cold cream beside the recipe, patience, conscience, and pride, and that deftness of hand that only comes after years of training. You cannot buy those qualities on the market, not for any price. To think of my recipe put into the hands of money-making factory superintendents and a rabble horde of riffraff workmen! . . . Mr. Hale, you must excuse me for saying that I am astonished at your proposing it, you who have shown by your generous appreciation of its qualities that you are so worthy a member of our guild."

He paused, stirred from his usual equable calm and waited for an answer. But he still received none. The American was staring at him across an unfathomable chasm of differences.

Monsieur Réquine continued: " And as for me personally, I am almost as astonished that you propose it. For nothing in all the world would I enter upon such a life as you depict, owing great sums of money to begin with, for no matter how ' easy ' your business credit may be made in the modern world, the fact remains that I should lie down at night and rise up in the morning conscious that thousands of men had intrusted their money to me, that I might easily, by one false step or piece of bad judgment, lose forever money which means life to poor women or old men. Such a fiery trial would shrivel me up. It would be my death, I who have never owed a penny in my life. And then what? Even with the utmost success which you hold out, I should have a life which, compared with what I now have, would be infernal; rushing to and fro over the face of the earth, away from home, my wife, my children, homeless for half the time, constantly employed in the most momentous and important decisions where in order to succeed I must give all of myself, all, *all,* my brain, my personality, my will power, my soul . . . what would be left of me for leisure moments? Nothing! I should be an empty husk, drained of everything that makes me a living and a human being. But of course there would not be any leisure moments. . . . I see from what you so eloquently say that I would have become the slave and not the master of that invention which has come down to me from my fathers; that instead of its furnishing me and my work-people with a quiet, orderly, contented life, I should only exist to furnish it means for a wild, fantastic growth, like something in a nightmare, because a real growth is never like that, never!

" Mr. Hale, do you know what I do of an evening, in the summer? I leave the shop at half-past five or six, and I step into my garden, where I work till half-past seven, when I am most exquisitely hungry. We dine here under this vine, my wife, my daughters, and my son (he who is now at the front). Afterwards we sit and chat and exchange impressions of the day, as the moon comes up or the stars come out. Perhaps some of the young friends of the children drop in for a game of cards. My wife and I sit down at the other end of the garden on the stone bench where we sat when she came here as a bride, where my father and mother sat when they were bride and groom. The stars come out. I smoke my pipe and watch them. Mr. Hale, it is very surprising, the things which come into your head, if you sit quietly and watch the stars come out. I would not miss thinking them for anything in the world. We talk a little, my wife knits. We meditate a great deal. We hear the gay voices of our children coming to us mingled with the breath of the roses. We have finished another day, and we are very glad to be there, alive, with each other, in our garden. When we come in, my wife makes me a cup of tisane and while I sip that I read, sometimes a little of Montaigne, sometimes a little of Horace, sometimes something modern. And all that while, Mr. Hale, there is in our home, in our hearts, the most precious distillation of peace, the . . ."

For some moments the American had been surging inwardly, and he now boiled over with a great wave of words. "Will you just let me tell you what you've been describing to me, Monsieur Réquine? The life of an old, old man . . . and you're younger than I am!

And will you let me tell you what I'd call your ' peace '?
I'd call it laziness! Why, that's the kind of life that
would suit an oyster right down to the ground! And,
by George, that's the kind of life that gave the Boches
their strangle-hold on French commerce before the war.
They *weren't* afraid of good credit when it was held out
to them! They had it *too* easy, with nobody to stand up
against them but able-bodied men willing to sit down in
their gardens in the evenings and meditate on the stars,
instead of thinking how to enlarge their business! I'll
bet they didn't read Horace instead of a good technical
magazine that would keep them up to date. Why, Monsieur Réquine, I give you my word, I have never looked
inside my Horace since the day I took the final exam in
it! I wouldn't *dream* of doing it! What would business
come to if everybody sagged back like that? You don't
seem to realize what business is, modern business. It's
not just soulless materialistic money-making, it's the
great, big, wide road that leads human beings to progress!
It's what lets humanity get a chance to satisfy its wants,
and get more wants, and satisfy them, and get more,
and conquer the world from pole to pole. It's what gives
men, grown men, with big muscles, obstacles of their
size to get through. It gives them problems that take
all their strength and brain power to solve, that keeps
them fit and pink and tiptoe with ambition and zip, and
prevents them from lying down and giving up when they
see a hard proposition coming their way, such as chang-
ing a small factory into a big one and keeping the prod-

uct up to standard. Business, modern business keeps a man *alive* so that when he sees a problem like that he doesn't give a groan and go and prune his roses, he just tears right in and *does* it!"

Monsieur Réquine listened to the translation of this impassioned *credo* with the expression of judicial consideration which was evidently the habitual one upon his face. At the end he stroked his beard meditatively and looked into space for a time before answering. When he spoke, it was with a mildness and quiet which made him indeed seem much the older of the two, a certain patient good humor which would have been impossible to the other man. "Mr. Hale, you say that my conception of life looks like laziness to you. Do you know how yours looks to me? Like a circle of frenzied worshipers around a fiery Moloch, into whose maw they cast everything that makes life sweet and livable, leisure, love, affection, appreciation of things rare and fine. My friend, humanity as a whole will never be worth more than the lives of its individuals are worth, and it takes many, many things to make individual lives worth while. It takes a mixture, and it needs, among other elements, some quiet, some peace, some leisure, some occupation with things of pure beauty like my roses, some fellowship with great minds of the past. . . ." His eyes took on a dreamy deepening glow. "Sometimes as I dig the earth among my fruit-trees, the old, old earth, a sentence from Epictetus, or from Montaigne comes into my head, all at once luminous as I never saw it before. I have a vision of things very wide, very free, very fine. Almost, for a moment, Mr. Hale, almost for a moment I feel that I understand life."

The American stood up to go with a gesture of finality. He put his hat firmly on his head and said in pitying valedictory: "Monsieur Réquine, you're on the wrong track. Take it from me that nobody can understand life. The best thing to do with life is to live it!"

The Frenchman, still seated, still philosophic, made a humorous gesture. "Ah, there are as many different opinions as there are men about what that means, to 'live life'!"

In the cab going back to Paris the American said little. Once he remarked almost to himself, "The thing I can't get over is that his damned cream *is* better than anything we make."

The French official emerged from a thoughtful silence of his own to comment: "Mr. Hale, the generosity of that remark is only equaled by its perspicacity! It makes me more than ever concerned for the future of French commerce."

That evening Monsieur Réquine was stooping over a dwarf-apple tree, string in one hand, pruning shears in the other. He was clipping away all except one of the vigorous young shoots. That one he then laid along a wire, strung about a foot from the ground and tied it

fast at several points so that in growing it would follow the exact line traced by the horizontal wire. When
he finished he gathered up all the clipped shoots, put
them under his arm, and stood looking at the severely
disciplined little tree, which did not look in the least like
a tree any more. The sight apparently suggested an
analogy to his mind, for he said in the tone of one who
makes an admission: "It's true one does it for apple-
trees and vines." After considering this for a moment,
he shook his head with decision, "But not for human
beings, no."

And yet his brow was far from clear as he betook himself to the stone bench at the end of the garden.

When his wife went out later to join him, she missed
the glow of his pipe and inquired, a little troubled,
"Why, René, you've forgotten to light your pipe!
what's the matter?"

"Adèle, do you remember, just before the order for
mobilization came, how Robert wanted to travel a year
in America to study American business and to see something of other conditions? Perhaps I was wrong not to
consent. I've been sitting here thinking it over. Perhaps when he comes back [they always forced themselves
to say "when" and never "if"] perhaps we would better
let him go, before he settles down to take my place."
He took her hand and held it for a moment. "Do you
know, Adèle, after all, the world changes, perhaps more
than we realize, here in Versailles."

That evening Mr. Hale sat in his hotel bedroom with all the electric lights blazing, and filled sheet after sheet with elaborate calculations. He was concerned with an important detail of transatlantic transportation to which he did not believe half enough attention had been paid: the question as to what form of carrier is the best for certain breakable objects which he was arranging to send in large quantities into the States. The quantities were so large that if he could effect a small saving of space, with no increase of the breakage per cent., the sum-total would be considerable.

He figured out the relative cubic contents in boxes of a given dimension and in barrels, having always had a leaning towards barrels himself. He looked up technical tables as to the relative weight of sawdust, powdered cork, and excelsior, together with the statistics as to the relative amount of breakage with each sort of packing. His days were so filled with " seeing people " that he often thought the evenings were the only times he had to do " real work," the careful, minute, infinitely patient, and long-headed calculations which had made him the wealthy man he was.

The room was very hot and close, with all its windows and shutters closed and its curtains drawn to keep the light from showing in the street, a recent air-raid having tightened up the regulations about lights. The American's face was flushed, his eyes hot and smarting, his collar first wilted, and then laid aside. But he was accustomed to pay small heed to discomforts when there was work to be done, and continued obstinately struggling with the problems of cubic feet contained in a compartment of a ship's hold of given dimensions with given curves to the sides. The curve of the sides gave him a great deal of trouble, as he had quite forgotten the formulæ of abstract mathematics which would have solved the question, never having concerned himself with abstract mathematics since the day he had taken the final examination in that subject.

He sat up, wiping his forehead, rubbing his eyes. Behind the lids, for an instant shut, there swam before his eyes the garden in which he had sat that afternoon, green and hidden and golden. The perfume from the roses floated again about him.

He opened his eyes on the gaudy, banal hotel bedroom, cruelly lighted with the hard gaze of the unveiled electric bulbs. He felt very tired.

" I've half a notion to call that enough for to-night," he said to himself, standing up from the table.

He snapped off the electric lights and opened the shutters. A clear, cool breath of outdoor air came in silently, filling the room and his lungs. The moonlight lay in a wide pool at his feet and on the balcony before his window. He hesitated a moment, glanced out at the sky, and pulled an armchair out on the balcony.

There was a long silence while he puffed at a cigar and while the moon dropped lower. At first he went on thinking of cubic feet and relative weights, but presently his cigar began to glow less redly. After a time it went out unheeded. The hand which held it dropped on the arm of the chair, loosely.

The man stirred, relaxed all his muscles, and stretched himself out in the chair, tipping his head back to see the stars.

He sat thus for a long, long time, while the constellations wheeled slowly over his head. Once he murmured meditatively, " Maybe we *do* hit it up a little too fast."

He continued looking up at the stars, and presently drew from the contemplation of those vast spaces another remark. It was one which had often casually passed his lips before, but never with the accent of conviction. For never before had he believed it. He said it earnestly, now, in the tone of one who states with respect a profound and pregnant truth: " Well, it takes all kinds of people to make a world."

THE REFUGEE

When we had seen her last, just before the war, she could have stood for the very type and symbol of the intelligent, modern woman; an energetic leader for good in her native town (a bustling industrial center in the north of France); unsentimental, beneficent; looking at life with clear, brightly observant, disillusioned eyes; rather quick to laugh at old-fashioned narrowness; a little inclined to scoff at too fervently expressed enthusiasms, such as patriotism; very broad in her sympathies, very catholic in her tastes, tolerant as to the beliefs of others, radical as to her own, above all, a thoroughgoing internationalist; physically in the prime of her life, with a splendid, bold vigor in all her movements.

Now, after less than three years of separation, she sat before us, white-haired, gaunt, shabby, her thin face of a curious grayish brown which none of us had ever seen before, her thin hands tightly clasped, her eyes burning and dry—the only dry eyes in the room as she talked.

Much of what she told us I may not repeat, for she said, with a quick gesture of terror, dreadful to see in one who for forty years had faced life so indomitably: " No, no, don't publish what I say—or at least be very careful; choose only those things that can't hurt the people who are up there, still in ' their ' power."

" Why not publish what you say? " I asked her, rather challengingly. " I don't think people in general understand half enough what the life of the invaded provinces is. One never sees any really detailed descriptions of it."

She answered bitterly, " Doesn't the reason for that silence occur to you? "

" No, it doesn't. I never have understood why so little is given to the public about the sufferings of the invaded populations."

She looked at me strangely, the half-exasperated, half-patient look one gives to a child who asks a foolish, ignorant question, and explained wearily: " If those who escape tell what they have seen up there, those who are left suffer even worse torments. ' They ' have spies everywhere, you know; no, that's not melodramatic nonsense, as I would have thought it three years ago, it's a literal fact. Very probably that little messenger-boy who brought the letter in here a moment ago is one. Very probably your baker is one. Anywhere in the world whatever is printed about what ' they ' do to our people in their power is instantly read by some German eyes, and is instantly sent to German headquarters in the invaded regions. And it's the same with our poor, little, persistent attempts to express a little bit of what we feel for France. For instance, one of my friends who escaped at the risk of her life told about how we tried in our orphan asylum to keep the children mindful of

France, how after closing hours, when the doors were shut, we took out the French flag from its hiding-place and told the children about France and whatever news of the war we had managed to hear. That article appeared, a half-column, in an obscure provincial newspaper with no indication as to which town was meant. In less than two weeks, from German headquarters in Brussels, went out a sweeping order to search to the last corner of the cellar every orphan asylum in the invaded regions. It was two o'clock in the morning when the searching squad in our town knocked at the doors. The flag was found, and our little collection of patriotic French recitations; and before dawn the superintendent, a splendid woman of fifty-seven, the salt of the earth, had disappeared. She was sent to a prison camp in Germany. Three months later we heard she was dead. Do you understand now why you must not repeat most of what I tell you, must give no clue as to how we hide our letters, how we get news from France; above all, say nothing that could give any idea of who I am? 'They' would do such dreadful things to Marguerite and little Julien and old Uncle Henri if 'they' knew that I have talked of the life there, of what 'they' have done to our people."

No, until the world turns over and we have awakened from the hideous nightmare no one may speak aloud of certain matters up there in Belgium and in the invaded provinces of France. But there are some things she told us which I may pass on to you, and I think you ought to know them. I think we all ought to know more than we do of what life is to the people who are awaiting deliverance at our hands. There are certain portions of her narration, certain detached pictures, brief dialogues and scenes, which may be set down in her own words. Your imagination must fill in the gaps.

" The first months were the worst—and the best. The worst because we could not believe at first that war was there, the stupid, imbecile anachronism we had thought buried with astrology and feudalism. For me it was like an unimaginably huge roller advancing slowly, heavily, steadily, to crush out our lives. During the day, as I worked with the wounded, I threw all my will power into the effort to disbelieve in that inexorable advance. I said to myself: ' No, it's not possible! They *can't* have invaded Belgium after their promises! Modern peoples don't do that sort of thing. No, it's not possible that Louvain is burned! Wild rumors are always afloat in such times. I must keep my head and not be credulous. The Germans are a highly civilized people who would not dream of such infamies as those they are being accused of.' All that I said to myself, naïvely, by day. At night, every hour, every half-hour, I started up from sleep, drenched in cold sweat, dreaming that the crushing roller was about to pass over us. Then it came, it passed, it crushed.

" But there were other, better things about those first months. For one thing, we had hope still. We hoped constantly for deliverance. Every morning I said to the girl who brought the milk, 'Are they here yet?' 'They' meant the French troops coming to deliver us. Yes, at first we expected them from one day to the next. Then from one week to the next, then from one month to the next. Finally, now, we have no strength left for anything but silent endurance. Besides that hope, which kept us alive those first months, we were not yet in that windowless prison which 'they' have succeeded in making our own country to us. We had news of France and of the outside world through the French and English prisoners. They were brought into our improvised hospital to have their wounds dressed before they were put on the train to be sent forward to their German prisons. As we cared for them we could get news of the battles; sometimes we heard through them of the men of our families; always they were a link with the world outside. We did not know what a priceless boon that was.

" But even this slight contact was soon forbidden us. We showed too openly the comfort it brought us. Free people, as we had always been, we were not then trained, as tyranny since has trained us, to the wretched arts of secrecy. We did too much for those prisoners. The people in the streets crowded about them too eagerly, showed them too many kindnesses. 'They' decided that our one link with the outside world must be broken. Fewer and fewer prisoners were sent; finally we saw none—for weeks and weeks none at all. We knew nothing but what 'they' told us, saw no other world, were hypnotized almost into believing that no other world existed.

"The last ones who came through—that is one of my memories. We never knew by what chance they were sent through our town. One day we looked, and there in our street were half a dozen French soldiers, with bloody heads and arms, limping along between Boche guards on their way to the hospital. All our people rose like a great wave and swept towards them. The guards reversed their rifles and began clubbing with their butt ends—clubbing the old women who tried to toss food to the prisoners, clubbing the little children who stretched out handfuls of chocolate, clubbing the white-haired men who thrust cigarettes into the pockets of the torn, stained French uniforms.

"We were beginning to practise some of the humiliating arts of a captive people then; we remembered that shouting in the streets is not allowed, that no French voice must be heard in that French town, and in all that straining, pressing, yearning crowd there was not a sound, not even a murmur of joy, when the Boche guards occasionally relaxed their vigilance for a moment and some of our presents reached the prisoners.

"Then they came to the hospital—it was a great mansion before the war—and went limping painfully through the broad doors and up the long stone staircase. Outside the doors stood the military car which was to take them to the station—stood the Boche guards—and the crowd, silent, motionless, waiting for the moment when those

soldiers who stood for France should reappear. All
demonstrations of feeling were forbidden by the invaders, yes, but there was no demonstration—only a great
silent crowd waiting. The Boche guards looked about
them uneasily, but there was no violation of any order
to report. Every one waited silently. Twilight fell,
darkness fell, the crowd grew larger and larger, filled
the street, but gave no further sign of life. Not one of
'their' rules was broken, but as far as we could see there
were upturned faces, white in the dusk. An hour passed,
two hours passed, and then the moment was there. The
lights flared up in the great hall of the hospital—all the
lights at once, as if to do justice to a grand fête, an
occasion of supreme honor. At the top of the stairway,
very pale in that great light, with bandaged heads
and arms, appeared those soldiers who stood for
France.

"From all that silent, rigidly self-controlled crowd
went up a sigh like a great stir of the ocean. The prisoners came limping down the stairway. France was
passing there before our eyes, perhaps for the last time.
A thousand handkerchiefs fluttered as silent salute to
France, a thousand heads were bared to her. The weary
soldiers stood very erect and returned a silent military
salute. In their prison car they passed slowly along between the dense ranks of their fellow-countrymen, looking deeply, as though they too thought it might be for
the last time, into those French eyes. Then they were
gone. We had not broken one of 'their' rules—not one.

But 'they' never allowed another French soldier to pass through our town.

" Once after that we had a passing glimpse of English soldiers, a group of wretchedly ill men, with their wounds uncared for, stumbling along to the station. They were not taken to the hospital to be cared for; 'they' are always much harder on the English prisoners than on any others. Those were the days early in the war, when there were still things to buy in the shops, when we still had money to spend. How we all rushed to buy good chocolate, cigarettes! How desperately we tried to throw them to the prisoners! But there was no relaxation, that time, of the guard. Not once did we succeed. There was a double line of guards that day, and they held us far, far at a distance with their rifle butts. It was horrible—the silence of the crowd, rigorously observing the rule against demonstrations of any sort; not a sound except the thud of rifle butts on human flesh. Old M. B—— had his arm broken that day.

" With my hands full of cigarettes and chocolate, I followed them all the way to the station, my heart burning with pity for the poor men who looked at us with such sick, tired, despairing, hungry eyes. We threw them what we dared. Nothing reached them—nothing. At the station they waited, fainting with fatigue, with loss of blood, with hunger, with thirst, ringed around with soldiers, bayonets fixed. There we stood, we women and children and old men, our hands full of food and comforts—no, you never know how sickeningly your heart can throb and still go on beating. I had never thought I could hate as I did in that hour, a helpless spectator of that unnecessary cruelty. Since then I have had many lessons in how deeply even a modern woman can be forced to hate.

"The train came, the wounded men were driven aboard their cattle car. The train disappeared. They were gone. I walked home smiling—we never let 'them' see how 'their' tortures make us suffer. Later Julien, my little Julien—he was twelve then—found me still weeping furiously. He bent over me, his little body all tense and fierce. 'Don't cry so, auntie! Don't cry so! It won't last. It will soon be over.'

"That was two years ago.

"None of us Frenchwomen were allowed to stay long in hospital work. For one reason or another, we were all forbidden to go on caring for the wounded. I had the honor of being the very first to be put out of the door.

"One of the officers in charge said to me one day, some four or five months after the beginning, 'Ah, madame, we shall soon be good friends now.'

"The idea made me fall a step backward. 'What, monsieur? What do you mean?'

"'Yes, France and Germany will soon be friends. I know with absolute certainty that Germany has offered a third of Belgium to France and that France is more than satisfied to accept and end the war.'

"That is always one of the horrors up there. 'They'

can tell you any news they please as ' absolute certainties.'
Since we know nothing of what is going on except what
they choose to tell us, we have no proofs to fling back at
them; no proofs but moral ones, and ' they ' find moral
proofs ridiculous, of course.

" I stiffened and said, ' No, monsieur. No; France
will never do that, never! You cannot understand why
France will never do it, nor why I am sure that she never
will. But it is true.'

" He laughed a little, as you would laugh at a child's
impractical notions, and said: ' Oh, but France *has* done
it, madame! You will see the announcement in a few
days.'

" That cool assumption, my helplessness to refute him
with facts, made me for an instant beside myself. I
said, very hotly: ' Monsieur, if France ever does that, I
will renounce my French blood. I will make myself an
American.' He was still smiling indulgently at my heat.
' Oh, why, madame? Why? '

" ' Because if France should do that, it would be as
much a disgrace for an honest person to be French as now
to be German.'

" He all but struck me with his whip.

" And five minutes later, still in my nurse's uniform,
I was standing in the street, with the door of the hospital closed behind me. I can't say I was particularly
regretful, either."

She looked down at her skirt of threadbare, coarse
black stuff. " Do you know where I got this skirt?

After a year of war I had nothing, nothing left in my wardrobe. We gave away to the poorer ones every garment we could possibly spare. And there was nothing, nothing left in any of the shops to buy. And I had no money to buy if there had been. How was I going to get an overcoat for Julien and a skirt for myself? The scrubwoman in Uncle Henri's office noticed the patches and darns on my last skirt, and said the American Committee had some clothes to distribute. I went there— yes, I—holding out my hand like any beggar. Bless Americans! There is no shame in being helped by them! They gave me there an overcoat that I made over for Julien and enough of this cloth for a skirt. It is the only one I have had for two years. Do you know what I saw all the time I sat sewing on that charity garment, come from so far? Across the street from our house is the great warehouse where the cloth from the ―――― woolen mills was stored. All day long German automobile trucks stood in front of that building, while from the windows German soldiers threw down bale after bale of cloth. As soon as a truck was full it would start forward on its journey to the station, where the cloth was loaded on trains and sent to Germany. An empty one immediately took its place. Heavy woolens, light woolens, blankets, cashmeres, flannels, serges, twill, black, brown, blue, white, figured—hundreds and hundreds of bales. I never knew there were so many kinds of woolen cloth. I never had seen so much all together in my life as I saw tossed down from the windows of that four-story building during those three days. For it took three days of incessant work to steal all that cloth—three long days—just the time it took me to prepare those two charity garments sent from America."

She held up a thick, square, brownish cracker, and said: " Look well at that. You have never seen anything more important to human lives. That is the free American biscuit. It is distributed at ten every morning to every school-child, to every teacher, in the region under German rule. None have had enough to eat. There are no biscuits distributed on Sundays and vacation days. Those are hard days for the children to live through. They beg desperately to go to school, even when they are sick, so they may not miss their biscuit. It is by far the best thing they have to eat all day, the most palatable, the only complete food. The change in the school-children since they have had this added to their diet—it is miraculous! The experts say the biscuits are a carefully compounded product of many grains, which make it a complete aliment. We know better than that. It is manna from heaven.

" And here," she held up a red woolen knitted cap, such as American school-children wear in small towns during the winter. " Somehow the American Committees managed so that there was such a cap for every one of us. They have become the national head-dress. Hundreds and hundreds of them—and every one knit in America and sent to us. Bless America!

" Our lights? There was soon, of course, no kerosene for us, no fats to make candles. And you know the long, long, dark winters in the north of France? Do you know what we did, praying that the American Committee would forgive us and realize that blackness is too dreadful to people whose nerves are almost worn through? We set aside a part of the lard and bacon the Committee provided for us; we melted it, put home-made cotton wicks in it, and— there we had a light, a little glimmering taper, but enough to save our reason in the long evenings. Bless America!

" The schools have kept on, you know; every teacher at her post, not a day missed (even when the town was bombarded). Every year the examinations have been set—they use old examination papers sent from Paris before the war—and diplomas have been given. And besides that, at home we have tried our best to keep the life of our children what the life of French children ought to be. I remember last year, during the summer, Aunt Louise taught a group of children in our part of the town to sing the ' Marseillaise.' The studio of my cousin Jean is at the back of the house and high up, so that she thought the children's voices could not be heard from the street. The Mayor heard of what she was doing, and sent word that he would like to hear them sing. The news spread around rapidly. When he arrived with the city council, coming in one by one, as though merely to make a call, they found the big studio full to overflowing with their fellow-citizens—the old

men and women who are all the fellow-citizens left there.
There must have been two or three hundred of them, the
most representative people of the town, all in black, all
so silent, so old and sad. The children were quite abashed
by such an audience, and filed up on the little platform
shyly—our poor, thin, shabby, white-faced children, fifty
or sixty of them.

"There was a pause, the children half afraid to begin, the rest of us thinking uneasily that we were running
a great risk. Suppose the children's voices should be
heard in the street, after all. Suppose the German police
should enter and find us assembled thus. It would mean
horrors and miseries for every family represented. The
Mayor stood near the children to give them the signal to
begin—and dared not. We were silent, our hearts beating fast.

"Then all at once the littlest ones began in their
high, sweet treble those words that mean France, that
mean liberty, that mean life itself to us:

"'Allons, enfants de la Patrie!' they sang, tilting their
heads back like little birds; and all the other children
followed:

"'Against us floats the red flag of tyranny!'

"We were on our feet in an instant. It was the first
time any of us had heard it sung since—since our men
marched away.

"I began to tremble all over, so that I could hardly
stand. Every one there stared up at the children; every
one's face was deadly white to his lips.

"The children sang on—sang the chorus, sang the second stanza.

"When they began the third, 'Sacred love of our fatherland, sustain our avenging arms!' the Mayor's old face grew livid. He whirled about to the audience, his white hair like a lion's mane, and with a gesture swept us all into the song.

"'Liberty, our adored liberty, fight for thy defenders!' There were three hundred voices shouting it out, the tears streaming down our cheeks. If a regiment of German guards had marched into the room, we would not have turned our heads. Nothing could have stopped us then. We were only a crowd of old men and defenseless women and children, but we were all that was left of France in our French town.

"Letters? You know 'their' rule is that none are allowed, that we may neither write nor receive news from our dear ones. But that rule, like all their rules, is broken as often as we can. There are numbers of secret letter-carriers, who risk their lives to bring and take news. But it is horribly risky. If a letter is found on you, you are liable to a crushing fine, or, worse yet, to imprisonment, and, if you have children or old people dependent on you, you dare not risk leaving them. You might as well cut their throats at once and spare them the long suffering. Even if the letter is not found on you, there is risk if you try to send or receive one. They are not, of course, addressed, so that if the letter-carrier is discovered all those to whom he is bringing mail may not be incriminated. But if he is caught 'they' always threaten him with atrocious punishments which will be remitted if he will disclose the names of those who have employed him. Generally the poor letter-carriers are loyal even to death, suffering everything rather than betray their trust. But some of them are only young boys, physically undermined by hardship and insufficient food, like all our people, and they have not the physical strength to hold out against days of starvation, or floggings, or exposure—naked—to intense cold. They give way, reveal the names of the people who are receiving letters—and then there are a dozen more homes desolate, a dozen more mothers imprisoned, a dozen more groups of children left.

"And yet we all used to get letters before the rules became so terribly strict as at present. I have had six in the three years—just six. They were from my mother —I could not live without knowing whether my old *maman* was alive or not. Curious, isn't it, to think that I would have been imprisoned at hard labor if any one had known that I had received a letter from my old mother?

"Of course you must never carry them on you, if out of doors, for there is always a chance that you may be searched. On the trolley line between our town and the suburb, ——, which I used to take once a week to go to see Pauline when she was so ill, it often happened. The car would stop at a sudden cry of '*Halte!*' and soldiers with bayonets would herd us into a nearby house.

Women—German women, brought from Germany especially for such work—were waiting for us women
passengers. We were forced to undress entirely, not a
garment left on our poor humiliated old bodies, and
everything was searched, our purses opened, our shoes
examined, our stockings turned inside out. If anything
which seemed remotely incriminating was found—an old
clipping from a French newspaper, a poem which might
be considered patriotic—a scrap of a letter, we were taken
away to prison; if not, we were allowed to dress and go
on our way."

We gazed at her, pale with incredulity. It was
as though Americans had heard that such treatment
had been accorded Jane Addams or Margaret De-
land. "Were *you* ever searched in that way?" we
faltered.

She had an instant of burning impatience with our
ignorance. "Good Heavens, yes; many and many times!
How absolutely little idea you have of what is going on
up there under their rule! That was nothing compared
to many, many things they do—their domiciliary visits,
for instance. At any hour of the day or night a squad
of soldiers knock at your door suddenly, with no warning. They search your house from top to bottom, often
spending three hours over the undertaking. They look
into every drawer, take down all the clothes from the
hooks in the closets, look under the carpets, behind the
bookcases, shake out all the soiled clothes in the laundry
bag, pull out everything from under the kitchen sink,

read every scrap of paper in your drawer and in your waste-paper basket—it's incredible. You watch them, with perfect stupefaction at the energy and ingenuity they put into their shameful business. And what they find as 'evidence' against you! It is as stupefying. They always read every page of the children's school copy-books, for instance, and if they find a 'composition' on patriotism, even expressed in the most general terms, they tear out those pages and take them away to be filed as 'evidence.'

"You must know that they can and do often enter for these searching visits at night when every one is in bed; perhaps you can guess how tensely the mothers of young girls endeavor not to offend against the least of 'their' innumerable rules, lest they be sent away into exile and leave their children defenseless. But it is almost impossible to avoid offending against some rule or other. Anything serves as ground for accusation—a liberal book, a harmless pamphlet found in the bookcase, the possession of a copper object forgotten after the summons to give up all copper has gone out, a piece of red, white, and blue ribbon, a copy of the 'Marseillaise,' a book of patriotic poems; but, above all, the possession of anything that serves to point to communication, ever so remote, with the outside world. That is the supreme crime in their eyes. A page of a French or English newspaper is as dangerous to have in the house as a stick of dynamite.

"Many men, women, and young girls are now in a

German prison somewhere for the crime of having circulated little pamphlets intended to keep up the courage of the inhabitants. These little sheets no longer exist, but what exists in spite of all these repressive measures is the unshaken faith in our future, the most utter confidence that the Allies will rescue us out of the hand of our enemies."

What she told us about the deportations I may not repeat for fear of bringing down worse horrors on the heads of those she left behind. You may be thankful that you have not to read that story.

Only two incidents am I permitted to transcribe for you—two incidents which, perhaps, sum up the whole vast and unimaginable tragedy.

"We have tried, you know, to keep the children as busy as possible with their studies, so that they would not have leisure to brood over what they see and hear every day. I've had little Marguerite go on with her English lessons steadily and read as much English as possible. One of the books her teacher gave her was 'Uncle Tom's Cabin.' She looked up from it one day, with a pale face, and said, in a sad, wondering voice: 'Why, auntie, this might have been written about us, mightn't it? It tells about things that happen to us all the time—that we have seen. The men who are flogged and starved and killed, the mothers trying in vain to follow their daughters into captivity, the young girls dragged out of their fathers' arms—it's all just like what the Germans do to us, isn't it?'"

And the other is that last hour at the railway station, when she stood beside the railway tracks, with her little Julien beside her (he was fourteen then), and told him in a fierce, choked voice, "Look, Julien! Look, remember! Never forget what you are seeing to-day," as they watched the soldiers drive into the cattle cars the old men, women, and adolescents torn from their homes in such haste that they had no change of clothing, no food, often not even their hats and wraps. "We stood there, those who were not 'taken,' the great helpless crowd of women and children, agonizing in that dreadful silence which is the last refuge of our poor battered human dignity up there. I was suffocating, literally unable to breathe. You do not know what hate and pity and horror you can feel and still live!

"The wheels of the train began grindingly to turn, the train advanced—it could not have been more unendurable to us if it had gone over our own bodies.

"And then some miraculous wind of high-hearted courage swept through that train-load of weak, doomed, and defenseless human beings. From every crevice, from every crack, waved a hand, fluttered a handkerchief, and from the train with one voice, the 'Marseillaise' went up in an indomitable shout.

"'Allons, enfants de la Patrie.'

"The sound of the singing and the sound of the train died away in the distance.

"We did not weep—no, we have never shown them how they can torture us. Not a tear was shed.

"But the next day our insane asylum at L—— was filled to overflowing with new cases of madness."

A LITTLE KANSAS LEAVEN

BETWEEN 1620 and 1630 Giles Boardman, an honest, sober, well-to-do English master-builder found himself hindered in the exercise of his religion. He prayed a great deal and groaned a great deal more (which was perhaps the Puritan equivalent of swearing), but in the end he left his old home and his prosperous business and took his wife and young children the long, difficult, dangerous ocean voyage to the New World. There, to the end of his homesick days, he fought a hand-to-hand battle with wild nature to wring a living from the soil. He died at fifty-four, an exhausted old man, but his last words were, " Praise God that I was allowed to escape out of the pit digged for me."

His family and descendants, condemned irrevocably to an obscure struggle for existence, did little more than keep themselves alive for about a hundred and thirty years, during which time Giles' spirit slept.

In 1775 one of his great-great-grandsons, Elmer Boardman by name, learned that the British soldiers were coming to take by force a stock of gunpowder concealed in a barn for the use of the barely beginning American army. He went very white, but he kissed his wife and little boy good-bye, took down from its pegs

his musket, and went out to join his neighbors in re-
pelling the well-disciplined English forces. He lost a
leg that day and clumped about on a wooden substitute
all his hard-working life; but, although he was never
anything more than a poor farmer, he always stood very
straight with a smile on his plain face whenever the new
flag of the new country was carried past him on the
Fourth of July. He died, and his spirit slept.

In 1854 one of his grandsons, Peter Boardman, had
managed to pull himself up from the family tradition of
hard-working poverty, and was a prosperous grocer in
Lawrence, Massachusetts. The struggle for the possession of Kansas between the Slave States and the North
announced itself. It became known in Massachusetts
that sufficiently numerous settlements of Northerners
voting for a Free State would carry the day against
slavery in the new Territory. For about a month Peter
Boardman looked very sick and yellow, had repeated
violent attacks of indigestion, and lost more than fifteen
pounds. At the end of that time he sold out his grocery
(at the usual loss when a business is sold out) and took
his family by the slow, laborious caravan route out to
the little new, raw settlement on the banks of the Kaw,
which was called Lawrence for the city in the East
which so many of its inhabitants had left. Here he
recovered his health rapidly, and the look of distress left
his face; indeed, he had a singular expression of secret
happiness. He was caught by the Quantrell raid and

was one of those hiding in the cornfield when Quantrell's men rode in and cut them down like rabbits. He died there of his wounds. And his spirit slept.

His granddaughter, Ellen, plain, rather sallow, very serious, was a sort of office manager in the firm of Walker and Pennypacker, the big wholesale hardware merchants of Marshallton, Kansas. She had passed through the public schools, had graduated from the High School, and had planned to go to the State University; but the death of the uncle who had brought her up after the death of her parents made that plan impossible. She learned as quickly as possible the trade which would bring in the most money immediately, became a good stenographer, though never a rapid one, and at eighteen entered the employ of the hardware firm.

She was still there at twenty-seven, on the day in August, 1914, when she opened the paper and saw that Belgium had been invaded by the Germans. She read with attention what was printed about the treaty obligation involved, although she found it hard to understand. At noon she stopped before the desk of Mr. Pennypacker, the senior member of the firm, for whom she had a great respect, and asked him if she had made out correctly the import of the editorial. "*Had* the Germans promised they wouldn't ever go into Belgium in war?"

"Looks that way," said Mr. Pennypacker, nodding, and searching for a lost paper. The moment after, he had forgotten the question and the questioner.

Ellen had always rather regretted not having been able to " go on with her education," and this gave her certain little habits of mind which differentiated her somewhat from the other stenographers and typewriters in the office with her, and from her cousin, with whom she shared the small bedroom in Mrs. Wilson's boarding-house. For instance, she looked up words in the diction-ary when she did not understand them, and she had kept all her old schoolbooks on the shelf of the boarding-house bedroom. Finding that she had only a dim recol-lection of where Belgium was, she took down her old geography and located it. This was in the wait for lunch, which meal was always late at Mrs. Wilson's. The relation between the size of the little country and the bulk of Germany made an impression on her. " My! it looks as though they could just make one mouthful of it," she remarked. " It's *awfully* little."

" Who? " asked Maggie. " What? "

" Belgium and Germany."

Maggie was blank for a moment. Then she remem-bered. " Oh, the war. Yes, I know. Mr. Went-worth's fine sermon was about it yesterday. War is the wickedest thing in the world. Anything is better than to go killing each other. They ought to settle it by arbi-tration. Mr. Wentworth said so."

" They oughtn't to have done it if they'd promised not to," said Ellen. The bell rang for the belated lunch and she went down to the dining-room even more se-rious than was her habit.

She read the paper very closely for the next few days, and one morning surprised Maggie by the loudness of her exclamation as she glanced at the headlines.

" What's the matter? " asked her cousin. " Have they found the man who killed that old woman? " She herself was deeply interested in a murder case in Chicago.

Ellen did not hear her. " Well, thank *goodness!* " she exclaimed. " England is going to help France and Belgium! "

Maggie looked over her shoulder disapprovingly. " Oh, I think it's awful! Another country going to war! England a Christian nation, too! I don't see how Christians *can* go to war. And I don't see what call the Belgians had, anyhow, to fight Germany. They might have known they couldn't stand up against such a big country. All the Germans wanted to do was just to walk along the roads. They wouldn't have done any harm. Mr. Schnitzler was explaining it to me down at the office."

" They'd promised they wouldn't," repeated Ellen. " And the Belgians had promised everybody that they wouldn't let anybody go across their land to pick on France that way. They kept their promise and the Germans didn't. It makes me *mad!* I wish to goodness our country would help them! "

Maggie was horrified. " *Ellen Boardman,* would you want *Americans* to commit murder? You'd better go to church with me next Sunday and hear Mr. Wentworth preach one of his fine sermons."

Ellen did this, and heard a sermon on passive resist-ance as the best answer to violence. She was accus-tomed to accepting without question any statement she found in a printed book, or what any speaker said in any lecture. Also her mind, having been uniquely devoted for many years to the problems of office administration, moved with more readiness among letter-files and card-catalogues of customers than among the abstract ideas where now, rather to her dismay, she began to find her thoughts centering. More than a week passed after hearing that sermon before she said, one night as she was brushing her hair: "About the Belgians—if a robber wanted us to let him go through this room so he could get into Mrs. Wilson's room and take all her money and maybe kill her, would you feel all right just to snuggle down in bed and let him? Especially if you had told Mrs. Wilson that she needn't ever lock the door that leads into our room, because you'd see to it that nobody came through?"

"Oh, but," said Maggie, "Mr. Wentworth says it is only the German *Government* that wanted to invade Belgium, that the German soldiers just hated to do it. If you could fight the German Kaiser, it'd be all right."

Ellen jumped at this admission. "Oh, Mr. Went-worth does think there are *some* cases where it isn't enough just to stand by, and say you don't like it?"

Maggie ignored this. "He says the people who really get killed are only the poor soldiers that aren't to blame."

Ellen stood for a moment by the gas, her hair up in curl-papers, the light full on her plain, serious face, sallow above the crude white of her straight, unornamented nightgown. She said, and to her own surprise her voice shook as she spoke: "Well, suppose the real robber stayed down in the street and only sent up here to rob and kill Mrs. Wilson some men who just hated to do it, but were too afraid of him not to. Would you think it was all right for us to open our door and let them go through without trying to stop them?"

Maggie did not follow this reasoning, but she received a disagreeable, rather daunting impression from the eyes which looked at her so hard, from the stern, quivering voice. She flounced back on her pillow, saying impatiently: "I don't know what's got into you, Ellen Boardman. You look actually *queer,* these days! What do *you* care so much about the Belgians for? You never heard of them before all this began! And everybody knows how immoral French people are."

Ellen turned out the gas and got into bed silently.

Maggie felt uncomfortable and aggrieved. The next time she saw Mr. Wentworth she repeated the conversation to him. She hoped and expected that the young minister would immediately furnish her with a crushing argument to lay Ellen low, but instead he was silent for a moment, and then said: "That's rather an interesting illustration, about the burglars going through your room. Where does she get such ideas?"

Maggie disavowed with some heat any knowledge of

the source of her cousin's eccentricities. " I don't *know*
where! She's a stenographer downtown."

Mr. Wentworth looked thoughtful and walked away,
evidently having forgotten Maggie.

In the days which followed, the office-manager of the
wholesale hardware house more and more justified the
accusation of looking " queer." It came to be so notice-
able that one day her employer, Mr. Pennypacker, asked
her if she didn't feel well. " You've been looking sort
of under the weather," he said.

She answered, " I'm just *sick* because the United
States won't do anything to help Belgium and France."

Mr. Pennypacker had never received a more violent
shock of pure astonishment. " Great Scotland ! " he
ejaculated, " what's that to *you?* "

" Well, I live in the United States," she advanced, as
though it were an argument.

Mr. Pennypacker looked at her hard. It was the
same plain, serious, rather sallow face he had seen for
years bent over his typewriter and his letter-files. But
the eyes were different—anxious, troubled.

" It makes me sick," she repeated, " to see a great big
nation picking on a little one that was only keeping its
promise."

Her employer cast about for a conceivable reason for
the aberration. " Any of your folks come here from
there? " he ventured.

" Gracious, *no!* " cried Ellen, almost as much shocked
as Maggie would have been at the idea that there might

be " foreigners " in her family. She added : " But you
don't have to be related to a little boy, do you, to get mad
at a man that's beating him up, especially if the boy
hasn't done anything he oughtn't to ? "

Mr. Pennypacker stared. " I don't know that I ever
looked at it that way." He added : " I've been so taken
up with that lost shipment of nails, to tell the truth, that
I haven't read much about the war. There's always
some sort of a war going on over there in Europe, seems
to me." He stared for a moment into space, and came
back with a jerk to the letter he was dictating.

That evening, over the supper-table, he repeated to his
wife what his stenographer had said. His wife asked,
" That little sallow Miss Boardman that never has a word
to say for herself ? " and upon being told that it was the
same, said wonderingly, " Well, what ever started *her*
up, I wonder ? " After a time she said : " *Is* Germany so
much bigger than Belgium as all that ? Pete, go get your
geography." She and her husband and their High School
son gazed at the map. " It looks that way," said the
father. " Gee ! They must have had their nerve with
them ! Gimme the paper." He read with care the war-
news and the editorial which he had skipped in the
morning, and as he read he looked very grave, and rather
cross. When he laid the paper down he said, impatiently : " Oh, damn the war ! Damn Europe, anyhow ! " His wife took the paper out of his hand and
read in her turn the news of the advance into Northern
France.

Just before they fell asleep his wife remarked out of the darkness, " Mr. Scheidemann, down at the grocery, said to-day the war was because the other nations were jealous of Germany."

" Well, I don't know," said Mr. Pennypacker heavily, " that I'd have any call to take an ax to a man because I thought he was jealous of me."

" That's so," admitted his wife.

During that autumn Ellen read the papers, and from time to time broke her silence and unburdened her mind to the people in the boarding-house. They considered her unbalanced on the subject. The young reporter on the Marshallton *Herald* liked to lead her on to " get her going," as he said—but the others dodged whenever the war was mentioned and looked apprehensively in her direction.

The law of association of ideas works, naturally enough, in Marshallton, Kansas, quite as much at its ease as in any psychological laboratory. In fact Marshallton was a psychological laboratory with Ellen Boardman, an undefined element of transmutation. Without knowing why, scarcely realizing that the little drab figure had crossed his field of vision, Mr. Pennypacker found the war recurring to his thoughts every time he saw her. He did not at all enjoy this, and each time that it happened he thrust the disagreeable subject out of his mind with impatience. The constant recurrence of the necessity for this effort brought upon his usually alert, good-humored face an occasional clouded expression like that which darkened his stenographer's eyes. When Ellen came into the dining-room of the boarding-house, even though she did not say a word, every one there was aware of an unpleasant interruption to the habitual, pleasant current of their thoughts directed upon their own affairs. In self-defense some of the women took to knitting polo-caps for Belgian children. With those in their hands they could listen, with more reassuring certainty that she was " queer," to Miss Boardman's comments on what she read in the newspaper. Every time Mr. Wentworth, preaching one of his excellent, civic-minded sermons on caring for the babies of the poor, or organizing a playground for the children of the factory workers, or extending the work of the Ladies' Guild to neighborhood visits, caught sight of that plain, very serious face looking up at him searchingly, expectantly, he wondered if he had been right in announcing that he would not speak on the war because it would certainly cause dissension among his congregation.

One day, in the middle of winter, he found Miss Boardman waiting for him in the church vestibule after every one else had gone. She said, with her usual directness: "Mr. Wentworth, do you think the French ought to have just let the Germans walk right in and take Paris? Would you let them walk right in and take Washington?"

The minister was a young man, with a good deal of natural heat in his composition, and he found himself

answering this bald question with a simplicity as bald:
"No, I wouldn't."

"Well, if they did right, why don't we help them?"
Ellen's homely, monosyllabic words had a ring of despairing sincerity.

Mr. Wentworth dodged them hastily. "We *are* helping them. The charitable effort of the United States
in the war is something astounding. The statistics show
that we have helped . . ." He was going on to repeat
some statistics of American war-relief just then current,
when Mr. Scheidemann, the prosperous German grocer,
a most influential member of the First Congregational
Church, came back into the vestibule to look for his
umbrella, which he had forgotten after the service. By
a reflex action beyond his control, the minister stopped
talking about the war. He and Miss Boardman had, for
just long enough so that he realized it, the appearance
of people "caught" discussing something they ought
not to mention. The instant after, when Ellen had
turned away, he felt the liveliest astonishment and an-
noyance at having done this. He feared that Miss
Boardman might have the preposterous notion that he
was *afraid* to talk about the war before a German. This
idea nettled him intolerably. Just before he fell asleep
that night he had a most disagreeable moment, half
awake, half asleep, when he himself entertained the preposterous idea which he had attributed to Miss Boardman. It woke him up, broad awake, and very much
vexed. The little wound he had inflicted on his own

vanity smarted.   Thereafter at any mention of the war he straightened his back to a conscious stiffness, and raised his voice if a German were within hearing.   And every time he saw that plain, dull face of the stenographer, he winced.

On the 8th of May, 1915, when Ellen went down to breakfast, the boarding-house dining-room was excited. Ellen heard the sinking of the *Lusitania* read out aloud by the young reporter. To every one's surprise, she added nothing to the exclamations of horror with which the others greeted the news. She looked very white and left the room without touching her breakfast. She went directly down to the office and when Mr. Pennypacker came in at nine o'clock she asked him for a leave of absence, "maybe three months, maybe more," depending on how long her money held out. She explained that she had in the savings-bank five hundred dollars, the entire savings of a lifetime, which she intended to use now.

It was the first time in eleven years that she had ever asked for more than her regular yearly fortnight, but Mr. Pennypacker was not surprised. "You've been looking awfully run-down lately. It'll do you good to get a real rest. But it won't cost you all *that!* Where are you going? To Battle Creek?"

"I'm not going to rest," said Miss Boardman, in a queer voice. "I'm going to work, in France."

The first among the clashing and violent ideas which this announcement aroused in Mr. Pennypacker's mind was the instant certainty that she could not have seen the morning paper. " Great Scotland—not much you're not! This is no time to be taking ocean trips. The submarines have just got one of the big ocean ships, hundreds of women and children drowned."

" I heard about that," she said, looking at him very earnestly, with a dumb emotion struggling in her eyes. " That's why I'm going."

Something about the look in her eyes silenced the business man for a moment. He thought uneasily that she had certainly gone a little dippy over the war. Then he drew a long breath and started in confidently to dissuade her.

At ten o'clock, informed that if she went she need not expect to come back, she went out to the savings-bank, drew out her five hundred dollars, went down to the station and bought a ticket to Washington, one of Mr. Pennypacker's arguments having been the great difficulty of getting a passport.

Then she went back to the boarding-house and began to pack two-thirds of her things into her trunk, and put the other third into her satchel, all she intended to take with her.

At noon Maggie came back from her work, found her thus, and burst into shocked and horrified tears. At two o'clock Maggie went to find the young reporter, and, her eyes swollen, her face between anger and alarm, she begged him to come and " talk to Ellen. She's gone off her head."

The reporter asked what form her mania took.

"She's going to France to work for the French and Belgians as long as her money holds out . . . all the money she's saved in all her life!"

The first among the clashing ideas which this awakened in the reporter's mind was the most heartfelt and gorgeous amusement. The idea of that dumb, backwoods, pie-faced stenographer carrying her valuable services to the war in Europe seemed to him the richest thing that had happened in years! He burst into laughter. "Yes, sure I'll come and talk to her," he agreed. He found her lifting a tray into her trunk. "See here, Miss Boardman," he remarked reasonably, "do you know what you need? You need a sense of humor! You take things too much in dead earnest. The sense of humor keeps you from doing ridiculous things, don't you know it does?"

Ellen faced him, seriously considering this. "Do you think all ridiculous things are bad?" she asked him, not as an argument, but as a genuine question.

He evaded this and went on. "Just look at yourself now . . . just look at what you're planning to do. Here is the biggest war in the history of the world; all the great nations involved; millions and millions of dollars being poured out; the United States sending hundreds and thousands of packages and hospital supplies by the million; and nurses and doctors and Lord knows how many trained people . . . and, look! who comes here?—a stenographer from Walker and

Pennypacker's, in Marshallton, Kansas, setting out to the war!"

Ellen looked long at this picture of herself, and while she considered it the young man looked long at her. As he looked, he stopped laughing. She said finally, very simply, in a declarative sentence devoid of any but its obvious meaning, " No, I can't see that that is so very funny."

At six o'clock that evening she was boarding the train for Washington, her cousin Maggie weeping by her side, Mrs. Wilson herself escorting her, very much excited by the momentousness of the event taking place under her roof, her satchel carried by none other than the young reporter, who, oddly enough, was not laughing at all. He bought her a box of chocolates and a magazine, and shook hands with her vigorously as the train started to pull out of the station. He heard himself saying, " Say, Miss Boardman, if you see anything for me to do over there, you might let me know," and found that he must run to get himself off the train before it carried him away from Marshallton altogether.

A fortnight from that day (passports were not so difficult to get in those distant days when war-relief work was the eccentricity of only an occasional individual) she was lying in her second-class cabin, as the steamer rolled in the Atlantic swells beyond Sandy Hook. She was horribly seasick, but her plans were all quite clear. Of course she belonged to the Young Women's Christian Association in Marshallton, so she knew all about it. At Washington she had found shelter at the Y.W.C.A. quarters. In New York she had done the same thing, and when she arrived in Paris (if she ever did) she could of course go there to stay. Her room-mate, a very sophisticated, much-traveled art student, was immensely amused by the artlessness of this plan. "I've got the *dernier cri* in greenhorns in my cabin," she told her group on deck. "She's expecting to find a Y.W.C.A. in *Paris!*"

But the wisdom of the simple was justified once more. There was a Y.W.C.A. in Paris, run by an energetic, well-informed American spinster. Ellen crawled into the rather hard bed in the very small room (the cheapest offered her) and slept twelve hours at a stretch, utterly worn out with the devastating excitement of her first travels in a foreign land. Then she rose up, compara-tively refreshed, and with her foolish, ignorant simplicity inquired where in Paris her services could be of use. The energetic woman managing the Y.W.C.A. looked at her very dubiously.

"Well, there might be something for you over on the rue Pharaon, number 27. I hear there's a bunch of so-ciety dames trying to get up a *vestiaire* for refugees, there."

As Ellen noted down the address she said warningly, her eyes running over Ellen's worn blue serge suit: "They don't pay anything. It's work for volunteers, you know."

Ellen was astonished that any one should think of getting pay for work done in France. "Oh, gracious, no!" she said, turning away.

The directress of the Y.W.C.A. murmured to herself: "Well, you certainly never can tell by *looks!*"

At the rue Pharaon, number 27, Ellen was motioned across a stony gray courtyard littered with wooden packing-cases, into an immense, draughty dark room, that looked as though it might have been originally the coach and harness-room of a big stable. This also was strewed and heaped with packing-cases in indescribable confusion, some opened and disgorging innumerable garments of all colors and materials, others still tightly nailed up. A couple of elderly workmen in blouses were opening one of these. Before others knelt or stood distracted-looking, elegantly dressed women, their arms full of parti-colored bundles, their eyes full of confusion. In one corner, on a bench, sat a row of wretchedly poor women and white-faced, silent children, the latter shod more miserably than the poorest negro child in Marshallton. Against a packing-case near the entrance leaned a beautifully dressed, handsome, middle-aged woman, a hammer in one hand. Before her at ease stood a pretty girl, the fineness of whose tightly drawn silk stockings, the perfection of whose gleaming coiffure, the exquisite hang and fit of whose silken dress filled Ellen Boardman with awe. In an instant her own stout cotton hose hung wrinkled about her ankles, she felt on her neck every stringy wisp of her badly dressed hair, the dip of her skirt at the back was a physical discomfort. The older woman was speaking. Ellen could not help overhearing. She said forcibly: " No, Miss Parton, you will not come in contact with a single heroic poilu here. We have nothing to offer you but hard, uninteresting work for the benefit of ungrateful, uninteresting refugee women, many of whom will try to cheat and get double their share. You will not lay your hand on a single fevered masculine brow . . ." She broke off, made an effort for self-control and went on with a resolutely reasonable air: " You'd better go out to the hospital at Neuilly. You can wear a uniform there from the first day, and be in contact with the men. I wouldn't have bothered you to come here, except that you wrote from Detroit that you would be willing to do *anything*, scrub floors or wash dishes."

The other received all this with the indestructible good humor of a girl who knows herself very pretty and as well dressed as any one in the world. " I know I did, Mrs. Putnam," she said, amused at her own absurdity. " But now I'm here I'd be *too* disappointed to go back if I hadn't been working for the soldiers. All the girls expect me to have stories about the work, you know. And I can't stay very long, only four months, because my coming-out party is in October. I guess I *will* go to Neuilly. They take you for three months there, you know." She smiled pleasantly, turned with athletic grace and picked her way among the packing-cases back to the door.

Ellen advanced in her turn.

"Well?" said the middle-aged woman, rather grimly. Her intelligent eyes took in relentlessly every detail of Ellen's costume and Ellen felt them at their work.

"I came to see if I couldn't help," said Ellen.

"Don't you want direct contact with the wounded soldiers?" asked the older woman ironically.

"No," said Ellen with her habitual simplicity. "I wouldn't know how to do anything for them. I'm not a nurse."

"You don't suppose *that's* any obstacle!" ejaculated the other woman.

"But I never had *anything* to do with sick people," said Ellen. "I'm the office-manager of a big hardware firm in Kansas."

Mrs. Putnam gasped like a drowning person coming to the surface. "You *are!*" she cried. "You don't happen to know short-hand, do you?"

"Gracious! of course I know short-hand!" cried Ellen, her astonishment proving her competence.

Mrs. Putnam laid down her hammer and drew another long breath. "How much time can you give us?" she asked. "Two afternoons a week? Three?"

"Oh, *my!*" said Ellen, "I can give you all my time, from eight in the morning till six at night. That's what I came for."

Mrs. Putnam looked at her a moment as though to assure herself that she was not dreaming, and then, seizing her by the arm, she propelled her rapidly towards the back of the room, and through a small door into a dingy

little room with two desks in it. Among the heaped-up
papers on one of these a blond young woman with inky
fingers sought wildly something which she did not find.
She said without looking up: "Oh, Aunt Maria, I've
just discovered that that shipment of clothes from Louis-
ville got acknowledged to the people in Seattle! And I
can't find that letter from the woman in Indianapolis who
offered to send children's shirts from her husband's factory. You said you laid it on your desk, last night, but
I *cannot* find it. And do you remember what you wrote
Mrs. Worthington? Did you say anything about the
shoes?"

Ellen heard this but dimly, her gaze fixed on the confusion of the desks which made her physically dizzy to
contemplate. Never had she dreamed that papers, sacred
records of fact, could be so maltreated. In a reflex
response to the last question of the lovely, distressed
young lady she said: "Why don't you look at the car-
bon copy of the letter to Mrs. Worthington?"

"*Copy!*" cried the young lady, aghast. "Why, we
don't begin to have time to write the letters *once*, let
alone *copy* them!"

Ellen gazed horrified into an abyss of ignorance which
went beyond her utmost imaginings. She said feebly,
"If you kept your letters in a letter-file, you wouldn't
ever lose them."

"There," said Mrs. Putnam, in the tone of one unexpectedly upheld in a rather bizarre opinion, "I've been
saying all the time we ought to have a letter-file. But

do you suppose you could *buy* one in Paris? " She spoke
dubiously from the point of view of one who had bought
nothing but gloves and laces and old prints in Paris.

Ellen answered with the certainty of one who had
found the Y.W.C.A. in Paris: " I'm sure you can. Why,
they could not do business a *minute* without letter-files."

Mrs. Putnam sank into a chair with a sigh of bewil-
derment and fatigue, and showed herself to be as truly
a superior person as she looked by making the following
speech to the newcomer: " The truth is, Miss . . ."

" Boardman," supplied Ellen.

" Miss Boardman, the fact is that we are trying to do
something which is beyond us, something we ought never
to have undertaken. But we didn't know we were undertaking it, you see. And now that it is begun, it must
not fail. All the wonderful American good-will which
has materialized in that room full of packing-cases must
not be wasted, must get to the people who need it so
direly. It began this way. We had no notion that we
would have so great an affair to direct. My niece and
I were living here when the war broke out. Of course
we gave all our own clothes we could spare and all the
money we could for the refugees. Then we wrote home
to our American friends. One of my letters was published by chance in a New York paper and copied in a
number of others. Everybody who happened to know
my name "—(Ellen heard afterwards that she was of
the holy of holies of New England families)—" began
sending me money and boxes of clothing. It all arrived

so suddenly, so unexpectedly. We had to rent this place to put the things in. The refugees came in swarms. We found ourselves overwhelmed. It is impossible to find a single English-speaking stenographer who is not already more than overworked. The only help we get is from volunteers, a good many of them American society girls like that one you . . ." she paused to invent a sufficiently savage characterization and hesitated to pronounce it. "Well, most of them are not quite so absurd as that. But none of them know any more than we do about keeping accounts, letters . . ."

Ellen broke in: "How do you keep your accounts, anyhow? Bound ledger, or the loose-leaf system?"

They stared. "I have been careful to set down everything I could *remember* in a little note-book," said Mrs. Putnam.

Ellen looked about for a chair and sat down on it hastily. When she could speak again, after a moment of silent collecting of her forces she said: "Well, I guess the first thing to do is to get a letter-file. I don't know any French, so I probably couldn't get it. If one of you could go . . ."

The pretty young lady sprang for her hat. "I'll go! I'll go, Auntie."

"And," continued Ellen, "you can't do anything till you keep copies of your letters and you can't make copies unless you have a typewriter. Don't you suppose you could rent one?"

"I'll rent one before I come back," said Eleanor, who

evidently lacked neither energy nor good-will. She said to Mrs. Putnam: "I'm going, instead of you, so that you can superintend opening those boxes. They are making a most horrible mess of it, I know."

"Before a single one is opened, you ought to take down the name and address of the sender, and then note the contents," said Ellen, speaking with authority. "A card-catalogue would be a good system for keeping that record, I should think, with dates of the arrival of the cases. And why couldn't you keep track of your refugees that way, too? A card for each family, with a record on it of the number in the family and of everything given. You could refer to it in a moment, and carry it out to the room where the refugees are received."

They gazed at her plain, sallow countenance in rapt admiration.

"Eleanor," said Mrs. Putnam, "bring back cards for a card-catalogue, hundreds of cards, thousands of cards." She addressed Ellen with a respect which did honor to her native intelligence. "Miss Boardman, wouldn't you better take off your hat? Couldn't you work more at your ease? You could hang your things here." With one sweep of her white, well-cared-for hand she snatched her own Parisian habiliments from the hanger and hook, and installed there the Marshallton wraps of Ellen Boardman. She set her down in front of the desk; she put in her hands the ridiculous little Russia leather-covered note-book of the "accounts"; she opened drawer after drawer crammed with letters; and with a happy sigh she went out to the room of the packing-cases, closing the door gently behind her, that she might not disturb the high-priestess of business-management who already bent over those abominably mis-used records, her eyes gleaming with the sacred fire of system.

There is practically nothing more to record about the four months spent by Ellen Boardman as far as her work at the *vestiaire* was concerned. Every day she arrived at number 27 rue Pharaon at eight o'clock and put in a good hour of quiet work before any of the more or less irregular volunteer ladies appeared. She worked there till noon, returned to the Y.W.C.A., lunched, was in the office again by one o'clock, had another hour of forceful concentration before any of the cosmopolitan great ladies finished their lengthy *déjeuners,* and she stayed there until six in the evening, when every one else had gone. She realized that her effort must be not only to create a rational system of records and accounts and correspondence which she herself could manage, but a fool-proof one which could be left in the hands of the elegant ladies who would remain in Paris after she had returned to Kansas.

And yet, not so fool-proof as she had thought at first. She was agreeably surprised to find both Mrs. Putnam and her pretty niece perfectly capable of understanding a system once it was invented, set in working order, and explained to them. She came to understand that what, on her first encounter with them, she had naturally enough taken for congenital imbecility, was merely the result of an ignorance and an inexperience which remained to the end astounding to her. Their good-will was as great as their native capacity. Eleanor set herself resolutely, if very awkwardly, to learn the use of the typewriter. Mrs. Putnam even developed the greatest interest in the ingenious methods of corraling and marshaling information and facts which were second nature to the business-woman. "I never saw anything more fascinating!" she cried the day when Ellen explained to her the workings of a system for cross-indexing the card-catalogues of refugees already aided. "How *do* you think of such things?"

Ellen did not explain that she generally thought of them in the two or three extra hours of work she put in every day, while Mrs. Putnam ate elaborate food.

It soon became apparent that there had been much " repeating " among the refugees. The number possible to clothe grew rapidly, far beyond what the " office force " could manage to investigate. Ellen set her face against miscellaneous giving without knowledge of conditions. She devised a system of visiting inspectors which kept track of all the families in their rapidly growing list. She even made out a sort of time-card for the visiting ladies which enabled the office to keep some track of what they did, and yet did not ruffle their leisure-class dignity . . . and this was really an achievement. She suggested, made out, and had printed an orderly report of what they had done, what money had

come in, how it had been spent, what clothes had been
given and how distributed, the number of people aided,
the most pressing needs. This she had put in every
letter sent to America. The result was enough to justify
Mrs. Putnam's naïve astonishment and admiration of
her brilliant idea. Packing-cases and checks flowed in
by every American steamer.

Ellen's various accounting systems and card-catalogues responded with elastic ease to the increased volume of facts, as she of course expected them to; but Mrs.
Putnam could never be done marveling at the cool certainty with which all this immense increase was handled.
She had a shudder as she thought of what would have
happened if Miss Boardman had not dropped down from
heaven upon them. Dining out, of an evening, she spent
much time expatiating on the astonishing virtues of one
of her volunteers.

Ellen conceived a considerable regard for Mrs. Putnam, but she did not talk of her in dining out, because
she never dined anywhere. She left the "office" at six
o'clock and proceeded to a nearby bakery where she
bought four sizable rolls. An apple cart supplied a
couple of apples, and even her ignorance of French was
not too great an obstacle to the purchase of some cakes of
sweet chocolate. With these decently hidden in a small
black hand-bag, she proceeded to the waiting-room of
the Gare de l'Est where, like any traveler waiting for
his train she ate her frugal meal; ate as much of it, that
is, as a painful tightness in her throat would let her.

For the Gare de l'Est was where the majority of French soldiers took their trains to go back to the front after their occasional week's furlough with their families.

No words of mine can convey any impression of what she saw there. No one who has not seen the Gare de l'Est night after night can ever imagine the sum of stifled human sorrow which filled it thickly, like a dreadful incense of pain going up before some cruel god. It was there that the mothers, the wives, the sweethearts, the sisters, the children brought their priceless all and once more laid it on the altar. It was there that those horrible silent farewells were said, the more unendurable because they were repeated and repeated till human nature reeled under the burden laid on it by the will. The great court outside, the noisy echoing waiting-room, the inner platform which was the uttermost limit for those accompanying the soldiers returning to hell,—they were not only always filled with living hearts broken on the wheel, but they were thronged with ghosts, ghosts of those whose farewell kiss had really been the last, with ghosts of those who had watched the dear face out of sight and who were never to see it again. Those last straining, wordless embraces, those last, hot, silent kisses, the last touch of the little child's hand on the father's cheek which it was never to touch again . . . the nightmare place reeked of them!

The stenographer from Kansas had found it as simply as she had done everything else. " Which station do the families go to say good-bye to their soldiers?" she had asked, explaining apologetically that she thought maybe if she went there too she could help sometimes; there might be a heavy baby to carry, or somebody who had lost his ticket, or somebody who hadn't any lunch for the train.

After the first evening spent there, she had shivered and wept all night in her bed; but she had gone back the next evening, with the money she saved by eating bread and apples for her dinner; for of course the sweet chocolate was for the soldiers. She sat there, armed with nothing but her immense ignorance, her immense sympathy. On that second evening she summoned enough courage to give some chocolate to an elderly shabby soldier, taking the train sadly, quite alone; and again to a white-faced young lad accompanied by his bent, poorly dressed grandmother. What happened in both those cases sent her back to the Y.W.C.A. to make up laboriously from her little pocket French dictionary and to learn by heart this sentence: " I am sorry that I cannot understand French. I am an American." Thereafter the surprised and extremely articulate Gallic gratitude which greeted her timid overtures, did not leave her so helplessly swamped in confusion. She stammered out her little phrase with a shy, embarrassed smile and withdrew as soon as possible from the hearty handshake which was nearly always the substitute offered for the unintelligible thanks. How many such handshakes she had! Sometimes as she watched her right hand, tapping on the typewriter, she thought: "Those hands which it has touched, they may be dead now. They were heroes' hands." She looked at her own with awe, because it had touched them.

Once her little phrase brought out an unexpected response from a rough-looking man who sat beside her on the bench waiting for his train, his eyes fixed gloomily on his great soldier's shoes. She offered him, shame-facedly, a little sewing-kit which she herself had manufactured, a pad of writing-paper and some envelopes. He started, came out of his bitter brooding, looked at her astonished, and, as they all did without exception, read in her plain, earnest face what she was. He touched his battered trench helmet in a sketched salute and thanked her. She answered as usual that she was sorry she could not understand French, being an American. To her amazement he answered in fluent English, with an unmistakable New York twang: "Oh, you are, are you? Well, so'm I. Brought up there from the time I was a kid. But all my folks are French and my wife's French and I couldn't give the old country the go-by when trouble came."

In the conversation which followed Ellen learned that his wife was expecting their first child in a few weeks . . . "that's why she didn't come to see me off. She said it would just about kill her to watch me getting on the train . . . and anyhow she's not fit to walk. Maybe you think it's easy to leave her all alone . . . the poor kid!" The tears rose frankly to his eyes. He blew his nose.

"Maybe I could do something for her," suggested Ellen, her heart beating fast at the idea.

"Gee! Yes! If you'd go to see her! She talks a little English!" he cried. He gave her the name and address, and when that poilu went back to the front it was Ellen Boardman from Marshallton, Kansas, who walked with him to the gate, who shook hands with him, who waved him a last salute as he boarded his train.

The next night she did not go to the station. She went to see the wife. The night after that she was sewing on a baby's wrapper as she sat in the Gare de l'Est, turning her eyes away in shame from the intolerable sorrow of those with families, watching for those occasional solitary or very poor ones whom alone she ventured to approach with her timidly proffered tokens of sympathy.

At the Y.W.C.A. opinions varied about her. She was patently to every eye respectable to her last drop of pale blood. And yet *was* it quite respectable to go offering chocolate and writing-paper to soldiers you'd never seen before? Everybody knew what soldiers were! Some one finally decided smartly that her hat was a sufficient protection. It is true that her hat was not becoming, but I do not think it was what saved her from misunderstanding.

She did not always go to the Gare de l'Est every evening now. Sometimes she spent them in the little dormer-windowed room where the wife of the New York poilu waited for her baby. Several evenings she spent chasing elusive information from the American Ambulance Corps as to exactly the conditions in which a young man without money could come to drive an ambulance in France . . . the young man without money being of course the reporter on the Marshallton *Herald*.

It chanced to be on one of the evenings when she was with the young wife that the need came, that she went flying to get the mid-wife. She sat on the stairs outside, after this, till nearly morning, shaken to her soul by the cries within. When it was quiet, when the midwife let her in to see the baby, she took the little new citizen of the Republic in her arms, tears of mingled thanksgiving and dreadful fear raining down her face, because another man-child had been born into the world. Would *he* grow up only to say farewell at the Gare de l'Est? Oh, she was not sorry that she had come to France to help in that war. She understood now, she understood.

It was Ellen who wrote to the father the letter announcing the birth of a child which gave him the right to another precious short furlough. It was Ellen who went down to the Gare de l'Est, this time to the joyful wait on the muddy street outside the side door from which the returning *permissionnaires* issued forth, caked with mud to their eyes. It was Ellen who had never before " been kissed by a man " who was caught in a pair of dingy, horizon-blue arms and soundly saluted on each sallow cheek by the exultant father. It was Ellen who was made as much of a godmother as her Protestant affiliations permitted . . . and oh, it was Ellen who made the fourth at the end of the furlough when (the first time the new mother had left her room) they went back to the Gare de l'Est. At the last it was Ellen who held the sleeping baby when the husband took his wife in that long, bitter embrace; it was Ellen who was not surprised or hurt that he turned away without a word to her . . . she understood that . . . it was Ellen whose arm was around the trembling young wife as they stood, their faces pressed against the barrier to see him for the last time; it was Ellen who went back with her to the silent desolation of the little room, who put the baby into the slackly hanging arms, and watched, her eyes burning with unshed tears, those arms close about the little new inheritor of humanity's woes. . . .

Four months from the time she landed in Paris her money was almost gone and she was quitting the city with barely enough in her pocket to take her back to Marshallton. As simply as she had come to Paris, she now went home. She *belonged* to Marshallton. It was a very good thing for Marshallton that she did.

She gave fifty dollars to the mother of baby Jacques (that was why she had so very little left) and she promised to send her ten dollars every month as soon as she herself should be again a wage-earner. Mrs. Putnam and her niece, inconsolable at her loss, went down to the Gare du Quai d'Orsay to see her off, looking more in keeping with the elegant travelers starting for the Midi, than Ellen did. Her place, after all, had been at the Gare de l'Est. As they shook hands warmly with her, they gave her a beautiful bouquet, the evident cost of which stabbed her to the heart. What she could have done with that money!

"You have simply transformed the *vestiaire*, Miss Boardman," said Mrs. Putnam with generous but by no means exaggerating ardor. "It would certainly have sunk under the waves if you hadn't come to the rescue. I wish you *could* have stayed, but thanks to your teaching we'll be able to manage anything now."

After the train had moved off, Mrs. Putnam said to her niece in a shocked voice: "Third class! That long trip to Bordeaux! She'll die of fatigue. You don't suppose she is going back because she didn't have *money* enough to stay! Why, I would have paid anything to keep her." The belated nature of this reflection shows that Ellen's teachings had never gone more than skin deep and that there was still something lacking in Mrs. Putnam's grasp on the realities of contemporary life.

Ellen was again too horribly seasick to suffer much apprehension about submarines. This time she had as cabin-mate in the unventilated second-class cabin the "companion" of a great lady traveling of course in a suite in first-class. This great personage, when informed by her satellites' nimble and malicious tongues of Ellen's personality and recent errand in France, remarked with authority to the group of people about her at dinner, embarking upon the game which was the seventh course of the meal: "I disapprove wholly of these foolish American volunteers . . . ignorant, awkward, provincial boors, for the most part, knowing nothing of all the exquisite old traditions of France, who thrust themselves forward. They make America a laughing-stock."

Luckily, Ellen, pecking feebly at the chilly boiled potato brought her by an impatient stewardess, could not know this characterization.

She arrived in Marshallton, and was astonished to find herself a personage. Her departure had made her much more a figure in the town life than she had ever been when she was still walking its streets. The day after her departure the young reporter had written her up in the *Herald* in a lengthy paragraph, and not a humorous one either. The Sunday which she passed on the ocean after she left New York Mr. Wentworth in one of his prayers implored the Divine blessing on "one of our number who has left home and safety to fulfil a high moral obligation and who even now is risking death in the pursuance of her duty as she conceives it." Every one knew that he meant Ellen Boardman, about whom they had all read in the *Herald*. Mr. Pennypacker took, then and there, a decision which inexplicably lightened his heart. Being a good business-man, he did not keep it to himself, but allowed it to leak out the next time the reporter from the *Herald* dropped around for chance items of news. The reporter made the most of it, and Marshallton, already spending much of its time in discussing Ellen, read that "Mr. John S. Pennypacker, in view of the high humanitarian principles animating Miss Boardman in quitting his employ, has decided not to fill her position but to keep it open for her on her return from her errand of mercy to those in foreign parts stricken by the awful war now devastating Europe."

Then Ellen's letters began to arrive, mostly to Maggie, who read them aloud to the deeply interested boarding-house circle. The members of this, basking in reflected importance, repeated their contents to every one who would listen. In addition the young reporter published extracts from them in the *Herald,* editing them artfully, choosing the rare plums of anecdote or description in Ellen's arid epistolary style. When her letter to him came, he was plunged into despair because she had learned that he would have to pay part of his expenses if he drove an ambulance on the French front. By that time his sense of humor was in such total eclipse that he saw nothing ridiculous in the fact that he could not breathe freely another hour in the easy good-cheer of his carefree life. He revolved one scheme after another for getting money; and in the meantime let no week go by without giving some news from their "heroic fellow-townswoman in France." Highland Springs, the traditional rival and enemy of Marshallton, felt outraged by the tone of proprietorship with which

Marshallton people bragged of their delegate in France.

So it happened that when Ellen, fearfully tired, fearfully dusty after the long ride in the day-coach, and fearfully shabby in exactly the same clothes she had worn away, stepped wearily off the train at the well-remembered little wooden station, she found not only Maggie, to whom she had telegraphed from New York, but a large group of other people advancing upon her with outstretched hands, crowding around her with more respectful consideration than she had ever dreamed of seeing addressed to her obscure person. She was too tired, too deeply moved to find herself at home again, too confused, to recognize them all. Indeed a number of them knew her only by her fame since her departure. Ellen made out Maggie, who embraced her, weeping as loudly as when she had gone away; she saw Mrs. Wilson who kissed her very hard and said she was proud to know her; she saw with astonishment that Mr. Pennypacker himself had left business in office hours! He shook her hand with energy and said: " Well, Miss Boardman, very glad to see you safe back. We'll be expecting you back at the old stand just as soon as you've rested up from the trip." The intention of the poilu who had taken her in his arms and kissed her, had not been more cordial. Ellen knew this and was touched to tears.

There was the reporter from the *Herald*, too, she saw him dimly through the mist before her eyes, as he carried the satchel, the same he had carried five months before with the same things in it. And as they put her in the "hack" (she had never ridden in the hack before) there was Mr. Wentworth, the young minister, who leaned through the window and said earnestly: "I am counting on you to speak to our people in the church parlors. You must tell us about things over there."

Well, she did speak to them! She was not the same person, you see, she had been before she had spent those evenings in the Gare de l'Est. She wanted them to know about what she had seen, and because there was no one else to tell them, she rose up in her shabby suit and told them herself. The first thing that came into her mind as she stood before them, her heart suffocating her, her knees shaking under her, was the strangeness of seeing so many able-bodied men not in uniform, and so many women not in mourning. She told them this as a beginning and got their startled attention at once, the men vaguely uneasy, the women divining with frightened sympathy what it meant to see all women in black.

Then she went on to tell them about the work for the refugees . . . not for nothing had she made out the card-catalogue accounts of those life-histories. "There was one old woman we helped . . . she looked some like Mrs. Wilson's mother. She had lost three sons and two sons-in-law in the war. Both of her daughters, widows, had been sent off into Germany to do forced labor. One of them had been a music-teacher and the other a dressmaker. She had three of the grandchildren with her. Two of them had disappeared . . . just lost somewhere. She didn't have a cent left, the Germans had taken everything. She was sixty-seven years old and she was earning the children's living by doing scrub-woman's work in a slaughter-house. She had been a school-teacher when she was young.

" There were five little children in one family. The mother was sort of out of her mind, though the doctors said maybe she would get over it. They had been under shell-fire for five days, and she had seen three members of her family die there. After that they wandered around in the woods for ten days, living on grass and roots. The youngest child died then. The oldest girl was only ten years old, but she took care of them all somehow and used to get up nights when her mother got crazy thinking the shells were falling again."

Ellen spoke badly, awkwardly, haltingly. She told nothing which they might not have read, perhaps had read in some American magazine. But it was a different matter to hear such stories from the lips of Ellen Boardman, born and brought up among them. Ellen Boardman had *seen* those people, and through her eyes Marshallton looked aghast and for the first time believed that what it saw was real, that such things were happening to real men and women like themselves.

When she began to tell them about the Gare de l'Est she began helplessly to cry, but she would not stop for that. She smeared away the tears with her handkerchief wadded into a ball, she was obliged to stop frequently to blow her nose and catch her breath, but she had so much to say that she struggled on, saying it in a shaking, uncertain voice, quite out of her control. Standing there before those well-fed, well-meaning, prosperous, *safe* countrymen of hers, it all rose before her with burning vividness, and burningly she strove to set it before them. It had all been said far better than she said it, eloquently described in many highly paid newspaper articles, but it had never before been said so that Marshallton understood it. Ellen Boardman, graceless, stammering, inarticulate, yet spoke to them with the tongues of men and angels because she spoke their own language. In the very real, very literal and wholly miraculous sense of the words, she brought the war—*home*—to them.

When she sat down no one applauded. The women were pale. Some of them had been crying. The men's faces were set and inexpressive. Mr. Wentworth stood up and cleared his throat. He said that a young citizen of their town (he named him, the young reporter) desired greatly to go to the French front as an ambulance driver, but being obliged to earn his living, he could not go unless helped out on his expenses. Miss Boardman had been able to get exact information about that. Four hundred dollars would keep him at the front for a year. He proposed that a contribution should be taken up to that end.

He himself went among them, gathering the contributions which were given in silence. While he counted them afterwards, the young reporter, waiting with an anxious face, swallowed repeatedly and crossed and uncrossed his legs a great many times. Before he had finished counting the minister stopped, reached over and gave the other young man a handclasp. "I envy you," he said.

He turned to the audience and announced that he had counted almost enough for their purpose when he had come upon a note from Mr. Pennypacker saying that he would make up any deficit. Hence they could consider the matter settled. "Very soon, therefore, our town will again be represented on the French front."

The audience stirred, drew a long breath, and broke into applause.

Whatever the rest of the Union might decide to do, Marshallton, Kansas, had come into the war.

EYES FOR THE BLIND

She woke in the morning to the sound of her alarm clock, an instrument of torture which, before the war, she had never heard. At once there descended upon her two overpowering sensations, one an intense desire to stay in bed and rest, the other the realization that she had no time to lose if she was to be at her office on time. She was up at once, and began making a hasty toilet with cold water. It was so hasty that she had no time to think, even in passing, of the old days when waking up meant ringing for some one to open shutters, close windows and bring hot water, breakfast, and the mails. By the time she had finished her Spartan toilet, her *concierge,* very sleepy-eyed and frowsy, rang at the door and handed in a bowl of *café au lait* and a piece of bread, with the morning paper folded across the tray. The Directrice sat down in her cheerless dining-room and ate her breakfast, reading, eagerly at first, and then grimly, the communiqué of the day. " No advance anywhere along the lines; a few *coups-de-main* here and there—indecisive results." Another day like all the others had begun, a day when hope was forbidden, when the only thing left was to endure and do the task at hand. For her, personally, there was nothing to fear in the lists of the dead, because she had found there, two long years before, the name which alone gave meaning to her life.

She put on her hat without looking in the mirror. This is a strange action in a Frenchwoman, but the Directrice was already preoccupied by the work awaiting her in her office. As she walked rapidly along through the rain, she was turning over in her mind the possibilities for one of her charges, Philippe, the childlike one who was perfectly willing to sit down there in the comfortable home provided for him and allow himself to be forever supported. It was not, Heaven knows, that our Directrice would not have liked forever and ever to have him supported and cared for like any child. But she had the instinctive grasp on the exigencies of human nature which is characteristic of her nation, and she knew that if he were to be again a normal human being, he must be roused to a sense of responsibility for his own life, in spite of the dreadful calamity which war had brought him. But how could he *be* aroused? He had shown no interest in learning how to be a professional knitter; he had only dabbled in clay-modeling; his typewriting continued indifferent—what could there be which she had not yet tried?

Never before, until the war took away not only the meaning of her life but all her goods, had she known what it was to walk at that dismally early hour in the morning through a dismally rainy street. But now she was so absorbed with the needs of another that she did not at all feel the rain in her face or see the mud on her shoes, and had not even the most passing pang of pity for herself, losing her youth from one day to another, with very little to hope for and,—alas!—nothing left to fear.

As she turned into the door of her institution, she had an inspiration. The only thing to do for Philippe was to turn to account the inimitable charm of his personality, since that was about all the equipment he seemed to have. Why could not he be a traveling salesman? But how *could* a blind man be a traveling salesman? Ah, that was the thing for the Directrice to contrive! That was why she was there!

She was, as usual, the first person to arrive at her office, although the blind men, just coming out from breakfast, were already standing idling about the hall before going to their classes, lighting cigarettes and chatting. They recognized her quick, light, steady step, and all their blind and mutilated faces lit up with welcome. Hers also. Although they could not see it, she gave to every one the smile, the animated look, the pretty, sideways toss of her head, the coquettish poise of her upright little figure, which she would have given to him seeing. It was strange to see her there, all those blind faces turned towards her, and hers irradiating a light and warmth— Well, perhaps, they saw it, after all. . . . Then she dismissed them to their work, with peremptory affection. " Off with you now, boys; don't stand fooling around here. There isn't a minute to lose, with all you have to do." They nodded, saluted, and dispersed like obedient children.

She went into her office to begin the day's work. The light which had transformed her face died out into fatigue, as she sat opening one after another of the innumerable letters which lay on her desk, most of them pitiful, some of them very foolish, all from people who were clamoring for help. The stenographers came in; the professors began to arrive; the telephone bell rang tyrannically over and over; one of the men came groping his way back from his class to complain fretfully that his teacher had treated him with insufficient respect; another arrived, his cane tapping in front of him, beaming with pride, and held out a perfectly typewritten page to show his progress; a third one limped to the door to say he had a sore throat, and please would the Directrice take care of it herself and not turn him over to the nurse, who did not understand him? The minutes passed,—an hour, a precious hour was gone, and nothing yet accomplished!

The telephone rang again, the Directrice was called and received over the wire a communication from a lady who announced herself as the Marquise de Rabat-Sigur, *née* Elizabeth Watkins. That considerable personage said she would like to do something for the war-blind ("everybody in my set has an *aveugle de guerre*") and on being questioned as to her competence, stated squarely that all she could do was to take them out for walks, and please, if she did, she would like a good-looking one, not one of those with the dreadfully mutilated faces.

The Directrice turned away from the telephone, a hard line of scorn at the corner of her lips, her eyes very tired and old. She had not as yet been able to attend to any of her letters.

She now began dictating rapidly the answer to one of them when the bare-kneed boy-scout page came hurriedly to say that Pigier, the one who had the bad face-wounds, was worse, was in one of his " spells," and the nurse could do nothing with him. Blindness always comes of course from head-wounds, and head-wounds mean the disorganization of all the nervous centers. The Directrice left her work and went upstairs into the sick man's room and sat down by his bed. The great-shouldered, massively muscled fellow clutched at her like a scared child, and began in a rapid, hysteric whisper to tell her of the awful things he saw in his eternity of blackness. For he was not really blind, he told her, he saw, yes he saw, but only not what was really there . . . dreadful things, horrible things, dead men in the trenches after an attack, corpses rotting in the rain, artillery wagons driving headlong over men only half-dead—he told all these visions to her, all, and as he spoke he felt them grow faded, harmless, unreal. But she grew pale as she listened, and turned rather sick.

When he had poured out all his terrors and she had assured him—as she had forty times before—that they were all imaginary, just the result of his nerves not being settled yet; that as soon as he got back his appetite and could take more exercise out of doors, and learn to roller skate in the gymnasium, he would find they would all disappear. Having transferred to her all his horrors, he felt himself immensely lightened and comforted. He promised her that if she went with him to the gymnasium, he would get up and dress and see if he could learn to stand up on the roller skates. She left him, her imagination full of new nightmare images to beset her next sleepless night, and hurried down to her office again, making a hopeful calculation that while he was dressing —this is a lengthy process with a newly blinded man— she could certainly have time to answer some letters.

As she entered her office, a pretty young girl, richly dressed, with a sweet, child's face, flushed with emotion, sprang up, grasped her arm and said, in a trembling voice of nervous determination: " Madame, you do not know me, but I have come to you at a critical moment in my life. I have decided that I will either go into a convent, or marry a blind man. I have plenty of money, I can support a blind man." At the expression which came into the face of the Directrice, her voice rose hysterically. " Don't laugh at me! Don't try to dissuade me. I detest the life at home. My family do not understand me. I have run away from home this morning to tell you this. My decision is irrevocable."

The Directrice, feeling herself a thousand years old in worldly wisdom, summoned all her patience and sat down to tell her what she had told all the other pretty, child-faced young ladies who had come with such fixed determination. She said clearly and firmly that it was not to be thought of; that her visitor was far too young to make any such decision; that it would be unfair to any blind man to put him in a position where he would certainly soon feel himself a terrible drag on a young life; that she would not go into a convent, either, but would stay at home with her parents, like a sensible girl, until she married a man like herself. These were the words she pronounced, very simple, common-sense, conversational words, which would have had no effect in any one's else mouth. But what she was spoke more loudly than what she said. The Directrice did not wear the black and penitential garb of a Mother Superior, but she had acquired, through intensive experience, all of a Mother Superior's firm, penetrating authority and calm manner. Not a trace of the amused scorn she felt for the silly child penetrated to the surface of her quiet manner. In ten minutes, the girl was crying, quite relieved that her visit had come to nothing, and the Directrice was calling for a cab to take her home. She herself put the weeping child into the carriage, and stood looking after it with a tolerant smile on her firm lips. " Was I ever as young as that?" she asked herself as she went back to her office.

As she turned again to the letter from the important members of the American colony who wanted to be put on the Governing Committee of the institution because of the other distinguished names there, her blind man, the one who had had the horrors, appeared at the door, dressed, still animated with the new energy given him by his Directrice, and held out his hand to her. She

jumped up laughing—how could she manage that laugh!
—and told him he looked as though he were leading her
out to dance. By this device she managed so that, while
in reality leading him, he seemed to be leading her down
the steps and across the courtyard, to the gymnasium.

While the instructor put on his roller skates and he
started on his first round, she stayed, her face all
a-sparkle with fun and interest, calling out joking encour-
agements to him, and making such merry fun of his
awkwardness that he laughed back at her. One quite
forgot for the moment that he had not only no eyes,
but very little face left.

Then, seeing him well started, already taking an interest in the new sport, she turned back across the courtyard. Now that it was no longer needed, the sparkle
and animation had all gone from her face again. She
looked very old and tired, and cross and severe; and one
of the volunteer teachers (a wealthy woman, coming in
to give a half-hour of English in the intervals of her
shopping and dressmaking expeditions) thought what a
disagreeable-looking woman the Directrice was.

Then, for half an hour, she was, by some extraordinary chance, left uninterrupted in her office, and dic-
tated rapidly the answers to her morning mail. In order
to accomplish as much as possible in this unheard-of
period of quiet, she became a sort of living flame of attention. The real meaning of each letter was sucked out
of it by a moment's intense scrutiny. She had but a moment, in each case, to make the decision, sometimes a

very important one. The wealthy American lady who wanted to be on the Committee was referred vaguely to some far-distant authority, who would in turn refer her to some one else, and so put her off without offending her; because if it is possible, wealthy people, no matter how preposterous or self-seeking, must not be offended. The money which Providence has so curiously placed in their hands means too much to the needy charges in the care of the Directrice. She who, before the earthquake changes in her life, had been so scornful of self-seeking and pretentiousness, had now learnt a hundred adroit ways of setting those evil forces to turn the wheels of her mill. This was the part of her work she hated the most. . . .

Another letter was from a blinded soldier in one of the hospitals, sent by one of his friends, since the authorities of the hospital would not permit him to write. He wanted to come to the Directrice's institution, and a clique in the hospital, who were jealous of it, were combining in a thousand subterranean ways to prevent his going there. It is very easy for two or three seeing people to circumvent a blind man. The Directrice did not answer this letter—she put it aside with a bright light of battle in her eyes and a slightly distended nostril.

Four begging letters from people who had no claim on her or the institution; two from inventors—one of whom had quite simply discovered the secret of perpetual motion, which, he thought, would be of especial benefit to blind people,—the other had invented a typewriter

wonderfully adapted for the blind, a detailed description
of which he forwarded. In her lightning survey the
Directrice perceived that the machine weighed seventy
pounds, threw the letter violently in the waste-paper
basket, and turned to the next. Over this one she lin-
gered a moment, her face softening again. It was from
one of her graduates, who had come into the institution
with the horrors, who had clung to her like a dead weight
for the first month of his stay, but who, before the end
of his six months' sojourn there, had become perfect
master of the knitting machine. Just before leaving, he
had married the nurse who had taken care of him in the
hospital, the Directrice being, of course, chief witness
at the wedding. And now, after a year, he wrote her to
make a report. They earned their living well, he and
his wife, he had bought three other knitting machines and
had a little workroom in his house, where he, his wife
and two employees carried on a lucrative business; that
is, his wife did until the arrival of a baby—such a
healthy, hearty little boy whom they had called Victor,
because the Directrice's name is Victorine; and please,
will she be his godmother? . . . Yes, there are good
moments in the life of the Directrice, moments when
there is no mask on her face, either of courageous smiling or of bitter fatigue; when she is, for just a moment,
a very happy woman, happy in a curious, impersonal
way which was as little within her capacities before the
war as all the rest of her laborious, surcharged life.

And then, somehow, it was lunch time. Where had

the morning gone? She must needs go in now and sit down at one of the long tables, looking up and down the line of blind faces, watching the fumbling hands trying so hard to learn the lesson of self-reliance in the new blackness. She had acquired an almost automatic dexterity in turning a cup so that the handle will be in the right place for the groping hand, in cutting up a morsel of meat on the plate of the man beside her, while engaging him in lively conversation so that he shall not notice it, in slipping the glass under the water carafe which is being awkwardly tilted by one of those dreadful searching hands. Through some last prodigy of dexterity she ate her own lunch while she did this. There were four of the long tables, and every day she must sit at a different one, or the others will be jealous.

After lunch she stood for a few minutes in the big hall, laughing and talking with the men, helping them light their cigarettes, listening to their complaints or their accounts of the triumphs of the morning. As she went back into her office, she saw that one of them was following her, and her experienced eye saw by his shambling gait, by the listless way in which he handled his little bamboo cane, by every slack line of his body, what the trouble was. He had the " *cafard* "—the blues —and nobody could do anything for him but the Directrice. She was very tired herself, and for just a moment she reflected that if she had an instant's time, she would probably have the worst fit of " *cafard* " ever known to man. But she had *not* an instant's time, so,

without seeming to note the cloud on his face, she pulled
open the drawer where she always kept some device
against these evil hours. This time it was a new invention for writing Braille by hand. She told her "pension-
naire" that she was so glad he happened to come, because she had been wanting his opinion on the advisabil-
ity of this. "See, it is intended to be used thus,"—she
put it in his hands,—"and the little bar is made of such
and such an alloy instead of the aluminum that is usually used, with such and such claimed benefits." Did he
think, now, that it would be better than the standard one
they were using, and what did he think about the advis-
ability of giving the inventor a chance to make a few
samples? With that she was launched upon a history of
the inventor's life, what a hard time he had had, how
eager he was to do something for the blind, and she
wondered if perhaps her blind men there would be willing to give him an interview. The inventor would consider it such an honor. But in the meantime, of course,
let him look carefully at the little invention, so that he
can have the best judgment possible to give the inventor.
The west wind of this new interest in another's life, this
new importance for himself, blew away visibly before
her eyes the black clouds of disheartenment. Her blind
man was only a boy, after all. He took the little Braille
plaque under his arm and, tapping briskly before him,
felt his way to the door, saying, over his shoulder im-
portantly, that he would try to find half an hour's time
to give the inventor, although his days were really very

much occupied. The Directrice looked after him with speculative eyes. "Now I have used up that device, what shall I do for the next one?"

Suddenly she realized that this was the visiting hour for the hospital where the blind man was being held in durance by the little plot against him. The fighting light came into her eyes again, she clapped on her hat—you will note it is the second time this day she has put on her hat without looking at herself in the glass—and swept out to do combat, all her firm, small, erect person animated by the same joy in battle which had sent her crusading forefathers into the fight singing and tossing their swords up into the air. She was gone an hour and a half, and when she came back, although she looked several degrees more tired even than before, a grim satisfaction sat upon her hard, small mouth. She had won her point. The blind man was to be allowed to come.

But there was Philippe, the man with whom she had begun the day. By looking out of the window, she could see him idling, as usual, in the garden, ostensibly taking a lesson in English from a volunteer professor, and in reality doing his best mildly to flirt with her. The Directrice frowned and smiled at the same time. What an absurd, lovable fellow he was! Thank Heaven, there was one of her "pensionnaires" whom it was impossible to take tragically. She gave a few orders for the disposition of the office work, wondered when she would ever have time really to go over her accounts thoroughly, and went out again to interview the head of a big whole-

sale groceries firm. In the old days, when she and hers
lived in a château, they bought *en gros* their supplies
from this firm, and the head of it still had a respectful
attention for any one of her name. This time she looked
at herself when she put on her hat, looked very intently,
rearranged her hair, noticed with impatience, quite im-
personally, that the gray was beginning to show more
every day, put on a little touch of powder and bit her lips
to make them red. Then she took a fresh pair of gloves
and put on a crisp veil. Thus accoutered, looking inimi-
tably chic, the grande dame entirely in spite of her few
inches, she went forth to triumph. After a long conversation with the big grocer, she extracted from him a
promise to try Philippe as a traveling salesman. She
felt very young and almost gay, as she brought back
this news. "If Philippe cannot sell anything to anybody, whether he wants it or not, I am much mistaken,"
she thought, watching him out of the window, wheedle
a would-be stern professor of typewriting into lounging
there instead of going back for the lesson. Somehow, in
the intervals of this day, which you will see to have been
reasonably full, she had worked out all the details with
what device in Braille Philippe could take down his orders, what kind of a typewriter he could carry about
him to copy them, how he could be met at the station by
such a volunteer to settle him in his hotel, and at the
other station by another—our Directrice had a network
of acquaintances all over France. Philippe came stroll-
ing into the room, very handsome, showing only by the

unmoving brightness of his clear dark eyes that he was blind. " See here, Philippe," she said, pulling him into a chair beside her as though he were a child.

" Yes, yes." Philippe agreed to the new plan. " *There* is something really sensible! That's a life that amounts to something! That is something that a man can do and take an interest in! Thank Heaven, I never need to take another English lesson as long as I live. I will go at once and work hard at my typewriter! How soon before I can begin? You know that I am engaged. I must earn enough to be married as soon as possible." Yes, she knew, although she knew also that it was the third time that Philippe had been engaged to be married since he was blinded! She reflected how curiously little a temperament like his is changed by any outward event.

Just at this moment of amused relaxation, when the Directrice was looking young and carefree, she glanced out of her window and saw a very handsomely dressed, tall woman descend from a very handsome limousine and make ready to enter. Have I said that our Directrice can look very cross and tired? She can also look terrifying, in spite of her small stature.

She went rapidly down the steps and across the courtyard, giving the impression of a very much determined mother-hen bristling in every feather to defend her brood. On her side, the woman who came to meet her gave the impression of a hawk, with a thin, white face, whitened to pallor by powder, and with shallow, black eyes.

" Madame," said the Directrice, " you are not to enter here to-day, nor any other day."

" You have no right to keep me out," said the other.

The Directrice did not deny this; but she repeated sternly: " You are not to enter here, nor to see Auguste Leveau anywhere at all. He has a wife and two children. He is not only blind, but as weak as water. But I am not. You are not to enter."

The woman in the sables broke out into a storm of vulgar language, at which the Directrice advanced upon her with so threatening an air that she literally turned tail and ran back to her car, although she was shouting over her shoulder as she fled. The small, erect figure stood tense and straight like a sentry on guard until the car moved away, the occupant shouting out of the window the direst threats of revenge.

A gleaming car came up from another direction, and another handsomely dressed woman descended, greeting the Directrice in an affectionate, confidential manner. She said: "Oh, my dear, I am so glad to find you here. I always come to you, you know, when I am in difficulties! What would happen to me without your good advice! A friend of mine from the provinces, an engineer by profession, wants so much to come and see your weaving workroom, because he is interested in machinery and thinks perhaps he may do something for the blind in that part of France—not *here,* you know, not the slightest idea of stealing your ideas and duplicating your work here. When will you allow us to come, when he can really look at the machinery without bothering the men?" That was what she said, but this was what the Directrice understood very distinctly: "My search for the Légion d'Honneur is getting on famously. If I can only just add a weaving-room to my outfit before the Minister of the Interior comes for his visit, I am sure I'll get the red ribbon, and then I won't have to bother any more about these tiresome war-blind."

The Directrice answered guardedly: "Why, yes; come into my office, and I will see what will be the best time."

As she walked across the courtyard with her visitor, chatting about the difficulties of war-time housekeeping in Paris, she was thinking: "Yes, she only wants it to make a temporary show in order to get the Legion of Honor. But what of that! Let her have it. But if she opens a weaving-room, she must have blind there to operate the looms, and if she takes them up only to drop them, what will become of them? Let me see what I can do about that. Perhaps this is the way to get her to pay for the installation of a new weaving-room. As soon as she gets what she wants out of it, we could perhaps take it over and add the men to the number we care for here. I wonder if the American Committee would be willing to send more money for that. Yes, it's worth taking the risk."

But nothing of this elaborate calculation appeared in her smooth, affable manner as, having come to her decision, she announced, after gravely looking through a card catalogue, that Thursday afternoon at a certain hour would be the best time to see the looms. "And if you don't mind, Mrs. Wangton," she said, "I am just going to treat you like an old friend of the institution and let you and your engineer wander about at your pleasure, without anybody bothering to escort you." That was what she said. What she thought was: "There, that will give them a chance to steal the names of the makers and the dimensions of the looms as much as they please."

Her visitor confounded herself in effusive expressions of gratitude and friendliness, which the Directrice received with a smile. She went away, sweeping her velvet gown over the stone steps and looking down with antici-patory eyes on that spot of her well-filled bosom where she hoped to pin the coveted red ribbon. The Directrice let her go with almost an audible sniff of contempt, and turned again to work.

This time it was a plan to be worked out whereby the blind could learn certain phases of the pottery trade at Sèvres. It involved a number of formalities and ad-ministrative difficulties which only one who has been in contact with French bureaucratic methods can faintly imagine. Our Directrice plunged into it headlong, and did not stir from her desk until she saw with a start that it was dinner time. And she had not yet looked over her accounts, the complicated accounts of a big, expensive, many-arteried institution. However, long ago, all her friends had stopped asking her to go to din-ner or to go to hear music. They had learned that she rarely spent the evening in any other way than finishing up what work she had not found time to do during the day. She was assured of several hours more of quiet.

She went out to dinner (one meal a day in the company of many mutilated and blinded men is as much as one woman can stand) and had a solitary meal in a quiet restaurant, turning her glass about meditatively between the courses and wondering if she dared ask enough from the philanthropic American manufacturer to settle Benoit in the country. With his tendency to tuberculosis, that was the only safe life for him and his family. She made a mental calculation of what his pension would come to, and how much he could earn by his trade. Then, if he kept chickens, and a garden, and rabbits, and if he could get a house for six thousand francs . . . by the time she had finished her dinner she had thought out a plan and a definite and businesslike proposition to put to the well-disposed American. Out of the depth of her experience with philanthropic people, she said to herself as she walked out: " I think I'd better tell him that we will put a bronze plaque on the house announcing that it is his gift to one of the war-blind. *That* ought to settle him."

At her office the evening passed very rapidly, between her account books and the sauntering in and out of one and another of the blind men. At ten o'clock, tired to the marrow of her bones, she stood up, dreading the effort to get home and get to bed, and yet looking forward to sleep as the one certain blessing of life. As she went out of the door she saw two shadowy forms standing in

the summer starlight, and recognized two of her charges.
" Come, come, children," she said; " it is bedtime. You
must get to bed and sleep and get back your strength."

" But we *can't* sleep," one of them told her. " We go
to bed and lie awake and get the ' *cafard* ' worse and
worse." The other one suggested timidly: " We thought
that perhaps, before you went home, you might take us
for a little turn about the lake in the park? " Our Directrice accomplished the last violent action of her violent
day. There was not an instant's hesitation before she
said cordially: " That's an excellent idea! Just what I
would like to do myself. One always sleeps so much better for a bit of a walk in the fresh air."

Taking one on one arm and the other on the other,
she set off, the two men towering above her little upright
figure. At first they talked as they strolled beside the
little lake. Then, as the Directrice had hoped, the en-
chantment of the hot, still night fell on them all. The
men walked silently, breathing in the good smell of the
stirred earth and watered paths. Their blind eyes looked
steadily into the blackness, no blacker than their every
day; their scarred, disfigured faces were hidden by the
darkness.

The Directrice looked up at the stars, and, for the first
time in all that long day, thought for an instant of herself. The night brought to her a sudden stabbing recol-
lection of another night, before the war, before the end
of the world, when the starlight had fallen white on the
clear road leading her straight and sure to her heart's

desire. The road before her feet now seemed as black as that before her blind men. But she stepped out bravely and held her head high.

The blind men leaned on her more and more. She could feel by the touch of their hands on her arms, that they were relaxing, that the softness of the night air had undone the bitter tension of their nerves. Now was the time to take them back. Now they would sleep well.

"Come, my friends," she said, and led them back to their door, through which, the next morning, she would enter early to another such day as the one she had just passed. And after that another, and then another. . . .

In her bed, that hot night, in the stuffy little Paris bedroom, she was quite too tired to sleep, and so, knitting her forehead in the blackness, she wondered how she could best place Brousseau, he who had a weak heart, and three little children dependent on him.

THE FIRST TIME AFTER

THE little newspaper in his home town put the matter thus: " Our young fellow-citizen Louis Vassard has returned from the hospital to his home. He received a bad head-wound in the battle of Verdun and unfortunately has lost his eyesight."

Of course the family meant to keep from him this casual method of announcing the end of his world, as they meant to keep everything from the newly blinded man, but he overheard the item being read aloud in the kitchen, and took a savage pleasure in its curt brevity. He liked it better, he told himself disdainfully, than the " sympathy " which had surrounded him since his return home. He cast about for an adjective hateful enough, and found it: " snivelling sympathy "—that was the word. He rejoiced in its ugliness, all his old sensitive responsiveness curdled into rage.

The hospital had been hell, nothing less, intolerable physical agony constantly renewed; and of course home, where he was petted and made much of and treated like a sick child, home was not hell; but sickened and embittered, resenting with a silent ferocity the commiserations of those about him, he felt sometimes that hell was the better place of the two.

The most galling of all his new humiliations was that

he was never allowed to be alone. His ears, sharpened like all his other senses by the loss of his sight, heard the silly whispering voices at the door. "I can't stay any longer," whispered his aunt, who for an hour had been stupefying him with her dreary gabble; "come, it's your turn," and he heard the dragging step of his old cousin advancing with a stifled sigh to do his duty by their martyred hero. Or it was the light irregular step of his little sister, irritated at being forced to do what would have been a pleasure if she had been left free.

He dared not protest against this as hotly as he felt, because, his self-control hanging by a thread, he knew that if he let himself go at any point he would be lost, would be raving and shrieking to be killed like the man in the bed next him at the hospital. He swallowed down his rage and his humiliation and only said coldly: "You don't need to mount guard on me like that, all the time. I'm blind, I know, but I'm not an imbecile . . . yet!" He shocked them by his brutal, outspoken use of the word, and they drove him frantic by beating about the bush to avoid it, always saying to others that he "had had a bad head-wound and his eyes were affected." He said once sternly: "Why should you think I'm ashamed to hear the word? You don't suppose it's any doings of mine, being blind!"

But no matter how brusquely or roughly he spoke he could never anger them. He felt often and often that if only he could hurt them, startle them into irritability, he would be relieved. But they never varied from the condescending amiability one shows to children and sick people. He sickened and shivered at the thought of the glances of pitying comprehension with which they probably accompanied those never-varying soft answers.

And always they stayed with him! Even when for a few moments they pretended to go away and leave him, he heard the breathing and the imperceptible stirrings of some one left on guard. Or he imagined that he heard them, and scorned to grope his way to see. Instead he sat motionless, his mask of pride grimmer and harder than ever.

Next after their always being there, he hated their efforts to cheer him up. That had been the phrase of the doctor at the hospital, when they went there to take him away: "Now he must be cheered up. He mustn't be left to brood. He needs cheerful company about him." Of course there was his mother . . . and he was so young that only a few years of intense growth separated him from the time when he ran to his mother for consolation. Certainly his mother could not be accused of attempting too much to cheer him up, the poor mother who, try as she might, had not yet mastered herself so that she could command her voice when she looked into the tragic sightless face of her son. Himself poised on the brink of hysteria, he dreaded more than anything in the world the sound of that break in his mother's voice. Oh yes, he realized it perfectly, it was not their fault, it was not that they did the wrong things, it was only that he hated everything they did, if they spoke cheerfully or wept, were silent or laughed. He was like a man all one raw sore, to whom every touch is torture.

He often woke up in the morning feeling that he could not go on another day, that he *could* not. . . . Every one about him commented on his remarkable quiet. "He never complains, he talks about all kinds of things, he has the newspaper read to him every morning," they reported to visitors. They did not see the sweat on his forehead as he listened.

One day they had taken him out of doors, on the bench at the end of the garden. It was his little sister's turn to "be with poor Louis," the little sister who would have been so unconsciously droll and diverting if she could have been natural. He said to her: "Oh, go and play, Celia! Why don't you bring your hoop out here? Or your jumping-rope?" But the conscientious, sensitive child, drugged by the thick fumes of self-sacrifice which filled the house, was incapable of being herself. She sat on the bench beside her big brother, holding his hand, talking affectedly, with an artificial vivacity, in as close an imitation as possible of her elders. The man to whom she chattered, winced, shrugged his shoulders, and fell into a morose silence.

But Celia, after all, was only eight years old, and at that age honest human nature is hard to stifle. Over across the road in the meadow was Jacques with his new net, hunting butterflies. And . . . she stood on tiptoe to see . . . yes, he seemed to have caught . . . oh, could it be that blue and black variety they hadn't yet found? She darted away, ran back, caught her brother's hand: " Louis, just a minute! I won't be gone but just a moment! " she cried, and was off, her little feet pattering down the path to the road.

Why, he was alone! It was the very first time since · . . . he did not finish the sentence, shrinking away in terror from the word, now that there was no need for bravado.

He stood up wildly. He must get away at once, to find some hidden spot, to be more and yet more alone. He knew that from the house they could not see the bench . . . oh, he knew every inch of the ground around the house from having played all over it from his childhood. He knew too that on the other side of the hedge there was an open field with a big clump of chestnut-trees, further along, opposite the hole in the hedge where you could scramble through.

He started down the path. It was the first time he had taken a step without having some one rush to lead him. His heart beat fast.

He followed the path, feeling his way with his cane. There was the hole in the hedge. Somehow, he was through, and walking on sod, soft, soft, under his feet; no, something round and hard was there. He fumbled, picked it up; a chestnut. He must be near the clump of trees. Alone he had found the way!

He turned to the left. In the old days there was a little hollow where the brook ran, a little hollow all thickly overgrown with ferns just large enough to hide a boy who was playing robbers. If he could only find that place and lie down in the ferns again! Scorning to put out his hands to grope, he stepped forward slowly into the black infinity about him. After a few steps, something brushed lightly against his hanging hand. He stooped and felt in his fingers the lace-like grace of a fern-stalk. The sensation brought back to him with shocking vividness all his boyhood, sun-flooded, gone forever.

He flung himself down in the midst of the ferns, the breaking-point come at last, beating his forehead on the ground. . . . It was the first time that he could throw aside the racking burden of his stoicism. At last he was alone, entirely alone in the abyss where henceforth he was to pass his days and nights. Dreadful tears ran down from his blind eyes upon the ferns. He was alone at last, he could weep. At last this was not rage, this was black, black sorrow.

Now they were shed, the tears, the great scalding flood of them had fallen. The man lay on his face in the ferns like a dead body on a battlefield, broken, drained dry of everything, of strength, of stoicism, of suffering, even of bitterness. For the moment there was nothing left . . . nothing but the consciousness of being alone, empty and alone in the blackness.

And yet was he alone, quite alone? Something in the black gulf stirred and made a rustle of leaves high over his head. The little sound came clear to his ears. Then three clear whistling notes dropped down to him, a thrush trying his voice wistfully, dreaming of the summer past. The angel-pure perfection of those notes sounded across the black gulf with ineffable radiance. The prostrate man at the foot of the tree heard them ringing out in the echoing, empty rooms of his heart. They seemed the first sounds he had ever heard, the presage of something new, of everything new. He did not stir, but he held his breath to listen.

The bird did not sing again. And yet there was no silence as he had thought. Listening for the bird's note, he heard the delicate murmur of the leaves, light arpeggios accompanying the singing voice of the little brook, now suddenly quite loud in his ears. He felt the fern-stalks stirring against his cheek and divined their supple submission to the wind. The chestnut was still in his hand, unimaginably smooth, polished, flawless. The breeze lifted his hair in a movement gentler than anything human . . . his blackened house was no longer empty of all things.

Presently his young body wearied of immobility. He found himself on his back, stretched out on the good earth, his arms crossed under his head, his eyes turned toward the sky he would never see again. His muscles were all relaxed as they had not been for months, every taut nerve was loosened. The wind blew softly among the leaves, across his forehead. On a sudden caprice, the thrush again sent down its three perfect notes, like an enchanted flute. . . .

They ushered him into the moment he had inexpressibly longed for, inexpressibly feared, the moment when he must stop hating and raging, must stop pretending to be hard, when he must at last be honest with himself, must face what there was to face, must say out the word he had never dared to say in his heart, although his proud lips had brought it out so many times, when he must announce to his terrified heart: " I am a blind man. What does it mean to be blind? "

Above his body, infinitely tired, infinitely reposed by his paroxysm of sorrow, his mind soared, imperious, eagle-like, searching. What was the meaning of it? He looked squarely at it like a brave man, and knew that he had the courage to look at it. With an effort of all his being, he began to think; with all his force, with all his will, with all his energy, to think. With the action he felt a stirring of life in all those empty chambers of his being.

The moments passed. The thrush sang once, stirred in the trees, flew to another, sang again, and was not heard. The blind eyes staring up at the sky saw nothing material, and yet began to see. A dim ray glowed in the blackness.

After a time he said hurriedly to himself, nervously anxious lest he should let the clue out of his hand: " Our

senses are not ourselves; we are not our senses.   No;
they are the instruments of our understanding.   To be
blind means that I have one less instrument than other
men.   But a man with a telescope has one more than
other men, and is life worthless to them because of
that?"

He paused breathless with the effort of the first thought
of his own since, since . . .   "And our senses, even
the best of them are like an earthworm's vague intuitions
beside scientific instruments, a thermometer, a microscope, a photographic plate.   And yet with what they
give us, poor, imperfect as it is, we make our life, we
make our life."

He took one more poor stumbling step along the path
he divined open to him: "A man with understanding,
without a telescope, without a microscope can see more
than a fool with both instruments."   Aloud he said
gravely, as though it were a statement of great value:
"The use one makes of what one has, that is the formula.
That is my formula."

There was a pause, for him luminous.   He told himself quietly, without despair: "And as for understanding,
for really seeing what is, aren't we all groping our way
in the dark?   Am I blinder than before?"   It seemed
to him that something within him righted itself, balanced,
poised.   His sickness left him.   He knew an instant's
certainty . . . of what?   Of himself?   Of life?   If
so it was the first he had ever known in all his life.
Strange that it should come now, when. . . .

Then all this fell away from him. He thought no more. He lay on the earth now, not like a dead man on a battlefield, but like a child on its mother's knees. He felt the earth take him in her arms, and he closed his eyes, abandoning himself to her embrace.

The sound of distant voices roused him from his dreaming doze. He turned on his elbow to listen. The old aunt, the old cousin were talking together: " Oh, the naughty little girl, off there in the meadow chasing but-terflies! How heartless children are! To leave her poor brother all alone, when he needs so to be cheered!"

The blind man lying in the ferns broke out into a laugh, a ringing young laugh, without irony, without bitterness.

It was the first time he had laughed since . . . since his blindness.

HATS

My attention was first attracted to him by the ring of his voice as he answered the question a woman near me put to him, amiably trying to start a conversation: "And may I ask, Mr. Williams, what are you in France for, Red Cross, or Y.M.C.A., or perhaps reconstruction work? I'm refugees, myself. It's always interesting to know other people's specialties. You often have so much in common. The only branches I *don't* know anything about are orphans and the blind."

To this the distinguished-looking, gray-haired man responded gravely, "Madame, I am in France for hats."

"*Hats!*" exclaimed the war-worker.

"Hats," he reaffirmed quietly.

She looked at him wildly and moved to another part of the room towards a recognizably tagged young woman in a gray uniform.

The timbre of his voice struck curiously on my ear. I cannot express its quality other than to say it made the voices of the rest of us sound like those of college professors and school-teachers; and I don't pretend to know exactly what I mean by that.

He aroused my curiosity. I wanted to investigate, so I began looking vague, letting my eyes wander, and answering at random. Presently the earnest talker holding forth to me grew indignant at my lack of attention, broke off abruptly, and went away. I turned to the man with the different voice and asked, "What in the world makes you come to France for hats, *just now* in the midst of the war?"

He answered with instant decision, "Because the only hats worth buying are made in Paris."

"*Now?* with France bleeding to death, how *can* they make hats, invent new fashions!"

His eye kindled. "Madame, a good French modiste on her deathbed could make a better hat than any one in New York ever could."

I pondered this. His accent was indubitably American, not to say New York. But there are cases of French people who have spent part of their childhood in the States who speak perfectly. "You must be at least partly of French extraction to be able so to understand and admire France," I ventured.

He opposed a rather startled and very emphatic negative. "Me? Not much! I'm as American as they make 'em. Born on lower Broadway and brought up in the New York public schools. I don't know anything about France, except that we have to come here to get the right styles in hats. I don't even speak any French except to say '*combien*' and enough to count."

I was put off the scent entirely. "Oh, I thought from the way you spoke that you knew France well. This is your first visit, then?"

He was silent a moment, making a mental calculation.

Then he said: "This is my fifty-first visit to Paris. I have come twice a year for a little more than twenty-five years."

"Always for hats?" I queried, my imagination reeling at this vista.

"Always for hats," he said seriously.

I tried to be facetious. "Dear me! You must know all there is to know about hats."

He shook his head. "Nobody knows anything about hats." He added, very much in earnest, "Style is one of the great obscure mysteries of life."

This had always been one of my observations, but one I have petulantly and impatiently deplored. I had never thought to hear it expressed with such heartfelt gravity and weight by a man of such evident vigor of personality.

I said, laughing uneasily, "It makes one very self-conscious about one's own hat, to know oneself in the presence of such a connoisseur."

He reassured me: "Oh, I never look at hats except in the way of business." In his turn he looked vague, and let his eyes wander, evidently much bored with my remarks. In another moment he would have turned away, but just then an acquaintance came up to me, addressing me by name, and my new interlocutor broke in with a quite human eagerness, "Oh, are you Mr. John P. Hulme's niece?"

"Why, do you know my Uncle John?" I cried astonished.

" He's one of the best business friends I have," he assured me, " and I have often seen the picture of you and the children he has on his desk. You must let me go to see them. I've got grown-up children of my own. It will be a real treat to me to know some American children here."

In this casual manner, slipping in on the good graces of my little son and daughter, I entered a world the very existence of which I had never suspected, long and frequent as had been my sojourns in Paris; the world of hat-buyers. And I had for guide the very dean and master of the guild, to whom the younger aspirants looked up, whose sure, trained instinct was their despair and inspiration.

It was perhaps his influence, dominating that circle, which made them all so serious and intent on mastering their profession, so respectful of their chosen occupation, so willing to give it the very best of their judgment and taste. This was the more remarkable as, with the exception of my new friend, they were quite the opposite of serious-minded men and women, and, in the intervals of the exercise of their profession, enjoyed rather more than was good for their health, morals, and pocketbooks, the multiple occasions offered by a great city to damage those possessions. I was not at all in sympathy with what seemed to me the indifference of their relaxations in a country so stricken as France; but I could not withhold my astonished admiration for the excellent seriousness with which they approached their business. I would

have blushed to disclose to them the light shallow femin-
ity of my careless, rather slighting attitude towards "la
mode." Also I was amazed at the prodigious financial
importance of their operations. The sums which, without a blink, they paid out for hats, and the number of
hats they thus secured and the further sums which they
looked forward to paying into the coffers of the United
States Customs, sounded to me as unbelievable as those
nightmare calculations as to the distance of the stars
from the earth or how much it has cost to build the
Panama Canal.

"All that for *hats!*" I cried, "and every year, twice
a year!"

"Oh, this is only the smallest part of what goes into
hats," the expert assured me. "What I'm buying now
are only single models, you understand; the successful
ones, the well-chosen ones, will be copied by the hundred
dozen in the States and in Canada. That chenille toque
you saw me buy the other day . . ."

"That little, plain, ugly scrap of a thing you paid a
hundred dollars for?" I asked, giddy again with the
remembered shock of that price.

"Yes. Well, probably that will be very widely copied,
at first in New York and then everywhere. It's a fair
guess to say, that being a model that's sure to be popular,
there will be at least twenty thousand toques like it
sold in different places in the States for five dollars
apiece."

I was staggered. "A hundred thousand dollars spent

in *one* season, just for *one* out of all the different models of women's hats!" My old superficial scorn for "the style" disappeared in an alarmed dismay at its unsuspected scope. "Why, that's *terrible!* It's appalling! When there isn't enough money to make the schools what they ought to be, nor to take care of the sick, nor to keep up the . . ."

He showed an unexpected humanity. "Yes, it is awful," he agreed gravely—"very, very awful. And still more awful is the way we live right along beside such an awful force and never have the slightest idea that it rules our lives and not what we wish or decide."

For all my consternation I found this excessive. "Oh, come, it's not so bad as *that!*" I cried.

"Yes, it is," he assured me with his formidable quiet certainty. "Yes, it is. It goes beyond anything we can imagine. It's the greatest force in the world, this desire, this absolute necessity to be in the style. Nothing else can stand up against it for a moment, not hunger, not fear, not love, not religion. They only exist so far as they don't get in the way of being in the style. The minute they interfere with that, over they go like a pack of cards in a tornado! What do you think a man is doing when he works all his life for his family? Is he earning their livings? Not much. He's enabling them to keep in style, and if he doesn't he is a failure. What do you really want for your children? That they may grow up to develop all the best they have in them . . . yes, *if* that doesn't prevent their being in style."

I found all this so outrageous that I could only stare a silent protest.

" I don't mean just my small part of it, hats," he explained, " although hats are always, so to speak, the crest of the tidal wave. It's everything. Style rules everything. Of course all material things, furniture, clothes, the way houses are built and gardens laid out and parks made and pictures painted. Everybody can *see* with his own eyes how *they* are all determined by whatever the style happens to be in that century or year, and not by anything we want or need. But more than that, too. Everything goes together. We talk and eat and act according to the kind of furniture we have; for instance, when rough-hewn Morris furniture was the rage and we all had to have it or dry up and blow away with envy, don't you remember how the athletic blowsy styles in clothes and manners came in too, and it was all the thing to go to a funeral in a striped shirt and yellow shoes and the girls' shirtwaists bloused over in front as though they had forgotten to tuck them in, and how bulging pompadours straggled down in every woman's eyes? "

" Do you mean," I was ready to laugh at him, " that you think that our Morris furniture influenced us so deeply as all that? Even Morris would be surprised to hear so much claimed for it."

He was scornful of my incapacity to grasp the scope of his idea. " No, Lord no! The Morris furniture hadn't anything more to do with it than a tree bent double with the storm has to do with making the wind blow. I mean that the same thing that *made* us mortgage our souls to have Morris furniture just then, made us also talk slang and wear yellow shoes ·to funerals."

" Well, what *did* make us? " I challenged him.

He answered monosyllabically, solemnly, with his redoubtable, arresting conviction, " The style did."

We were both silent a moment as if in the presence of Niagara or the ocean.

Then I said, in a feebler challenge, " Well, what *is* ' the style ' ? "

He professed the admirable ignorance of a wise man in the face of mystery.

" I wish I knew. It looks to me like a big current that takes in everything, that is so big we don't know it's there, just the way people didn't use to know the world was round, because it is too big to see. And it carries us along like dry leaves and where it's going to, nobody knows. We know just as much about it, as we do about where water runs underground; which is to say, nothing. But when it comes to that part of style that makes hats and dresses, there are a few people who can hold a hazel-rod and have it point downwards, and they are oftener right than the rest of us. And every one of those few is French and lives in Paris. Don't ask me why! That's the way it is. And it would be enough sight more convenient for *me*, let me tell you, if it were otherwise."

I understood this exclamation, having learned by this time how great an affliction to Mr. Williams personally were these semi-annual trips to France. He knew nothing of Paris outside of the great modistes' shops, and he cared less. Since he knew no French the theaters were closed to him. Since he was mildly musical (he played the violin a little) concerts helped a little to allay his ennui; but only a little. Being a family man of very domestic tastes, he took slight part in the very cheerful proceedings with which the other buyers whiled away the hours between business operations, and although he was invited to their gay suppers in expensive restaurants, he struck an austere note there, drinking only water, not smoking, and eating sparingly of simple dishes, quite evidently counting the hours till he could get back to America and to his garden in Westchester County.

In spite of this lack of appreciation of what was offered him, he was very frequently invited to the nightly feasts of his young confrères, and they hung about him eagerly because of their superstitious reverence for what they called his " hunch." " Whatever Grandpa says is going to go, goes," was their expressed belief. They tried by ingenious devices to exploit his scent for the style, to be within earshot when he was making selections, to suborn the milliners into showing them the models he had selected. Such crude, outright efforts at getting the better of him he defeated with a wary dexterity, getting up and leaving a shop abruptly if one of his rivals began to loiter too near him, and letting it be known that he would buy no more from any milliner who reproduced " his " models for one of the other

American buyers. This last precaution was not necessary, for the sense of professional honor and jealousy is not keener among doctors themselves than among Paris fashion-makers, nor was the capacity for darkly guarding secrets more developed in Renaissance Italian poisoners than in a twentieth-century modiste's shop on the Place Vendôme. Also Mr. Williams, who had seen a whole generation of modistes grow up and disappear into old age, enjoyed the very high esteem of those quick-eyed, quick-fingered, quick-witted ladies with the wonderful simple coiffures and the wonderful simple hats. This was not solely because of the very large sums of money which were at his disposition and which he spent with Napoleonic decision and despatch. They respected his competence also. "There is one who can appreciate our work!" they said of him. "He always picks out the best. There is one who could have made hats, himself!" A characterization which the American would have repudiated with energy if he could have understood a word they were saying.

But although, as a matter of business acuteness, he refused to allow himself to be exploited in small ways by his young competitors, he was always ready to expound his philosophy to them and to lay down the general lines along which they might develop as he had. Not infrequently their elaborate dinners, where too much had been eaten and drunk by the elaborately dressed women and smooth-shaven, young-old men, ended by the question flung despairingly at Mr. Williams' impassive respectability, "Grandpa, how the dickens *do* you *do* it? Tell us!"

He always told them, at length, in detail, as long as they would listen, although they never understood one word of what he said. Hoping to catch him off his guard and to cull some valuable short-cut tip to success, they lent ears as attentive as their somewhat bemused condition would let them, as long as their patience held out.

"The trouble with most of you young people," he was wont to say, presenting as he went on the abhorrent spectacle of a man at the Café Riche taking occasional sips from a glass of water, "is that you don't realize that you are up against a *big thing,* the biggest thing there is. You think you can just josh along somehow, pick out what looks good to you, what you think would be pretty for your best girl to wear, and have it go. Nothing like that! What *you* like, what *you* think is pretty, hasn't a thing to do with what's going to happen. What's going to happen, *happens,* whether anybody likes it or not, and the only thing for us to do is to keep our ears to the ground *hard* and try to guess three or four months sooner than most people. Nobody can guess further ahead than that and mighty few people even as far as that. Most people don't know what style is coming till it hits them in the eye. Now, to make a good guess you've got to keep your eyes open to everything, everything, and then sort of gather yourself together and listen, hold your breath and listen, as if you were eavesdropping folks who were trying to keep a secret from you; as if you had to catch a very faint A sounded way off that you could tune your own fiddle to. And you've got to get passive all over, the way the hypnotizers tell you to do, let yourself go, don't try to have any ideas of your own, don't try to swim against the current, don't try to hurry things up by swimming faster than the current. No power on earth can hurry that current, nor make it bring anything but what it's going to bring! And it's up to us, let me tell you, to take what it does bring! I've seen lots of styles that nobody liked, not the modistes who made them, not the buyers who took them to the States, not the hundreds of thousands of American women who paid out their husbands' good money to buy them. And yet those styles had just as big a vogue and lasted just as long as any others, and the buyers who tried to dodge them and who chose what looked prettier to them got everlastingly stung. And aren't there styles that everybody just hates to see disappear, comfortable, decent, becoming styles? But do they stay in, just because we'd like to have them? You know they don't.

"And it's no use trying to do anything on your own hook. There was old man Blackmar, head of the Blackmar and Jennings Ribbon Company; he could manufacture ribbons to beat any French factory going, *if* he got the designs from France. Every time he tried to have one designed by a perfectly good American designer, the ribbon didn't sell. It didn't look so very different, but

it wouldn't sell. You'd have thought he'd have learned
something out of seeing that happen every time he tried
it, wouldn't you? But he never did. Why, I was honestly sorry for him, five or six years ago when all of a
sudden the styles went dead against ribbons or any other
trimming for hats. It pretty near ruined him, coming
after the modistes had been piling everything they could
buy on top of their hats. But he didn't know enough to
take his medicine without making a face. He couldn't get
it through his head that he was up against a bigger proposition than *he* was, than anybody is. He came to me and
he said: ' Williams, I'll give you fifteen thousand dollars,
cash, in your hand, if you'll steer things over in Paris so's
to bring hat-trimmings back into style; ribbons of course
if you can, but if not, most any kind of trimmings. I
can alter our machines to do braids and such. This
craze for just the naked hat-shapes with one little rag
of an ornament, I tell you, it'll send me into the bank-
ruptcy court.'

" I was very sorry for him and I said so, and I said
I'd do anything to help him out except try to slap back
the Hudson river with the flat of my hand. He said he
was sick of hearing me always get off that same old guff,
and if I really wanted to, I could. ' Why, they tell me
every modiste in Paris calls you " uncle." With plenty
of money you could get on the right side of them and
get them to launch trimmed styles.'

" I just threw up my hands at that. I saw he didn't
know any more about the innerds of his business than a

babe unborn. I said to him: 'Why, old man, you don't suppose for a minute that the modistes in Paris *invent* the styles, make 'em up out of their heads? They haven't got any more to say about what it's to be than you or me. All they can do is to take the style that's going to arrive in six months, and put it into silk and felt and straw. They can't have it the way they *want* it any more than the priestess of something-or-other could say what she wanted, when they put her over the oracle-hole, filled her up with gas, and told her to make an oracle.'

"Blackmar was sore as a boil at me, and said if I wouldn't do it he'd give the job to Pierce. Pierce was buying for Condit and Vergary in those days. I said he could throw away all the money he wanted to, but *I* wouldn't help him spill it.

"Well, Pierce tried to swing the deal, bucking the universe all alone, and so proud to have the chance to. He went to all the best modistes in Paris and said he'd give—well, I'm ashamed to tell you what he gave— if they would make him models all trimmed up, heavy and expensive with handsome trimmings. Of course, at first they said they couldn't do it, the hats wouldn't be in style. And he said if they made the hats that way and sent them out with their names in gilt letters in the lining, they would be in style, would *be* the style. Didn't everything they made set the fashion? They tried to explain to him that that was because they took the greatest pains to make things that were in fashion, but Lord! he couldn't talk their language. He just kept on insisting and holding out those banknotes, and by and by they said, well, to get rid of him they *would*. And he came to my hotel and bragged all over me like a man who's cornered the wheat-market.

"They did make him trimmed models: and as they were the best modistes in the world they were as pretty hats as ever you saw. They were all trimmed up as per agreement with ribbons that would make a dead woman sit up and reach out her hand. Pierce took me into his office before they were packed, to show them to me, and he said, '*Now,* Grandpa, what you got to say?' And I said, 'You let me know four months from now how much money you've made on them.'

"About six weeks after that, back in New York, I went into his office and there, by George, were all but two of his fifteen models. None of the American manufacturers would have them, not at any price. They'd send their head milliner to see them and she'd say, 'Oh, what perfectly lovely ribbon,'—but no, thanks, she didn't want to buy the model, because they wouldn't sell. They weren't what were being worn that season. Pierce said: 'Great Scott! look at the labels. They come from all the best modistes in Paris'; and she'd say she couldn't help that; if they weren't what was being worn they wouldn't sell. And before three months were up he'd given them to the janitor's little girl for dolls' clothes. There you are."

There were evident signs of inattention from his audience by this time, but he went on: "And young Hammond, he tried to tear the teeth off the buzz-saw with his fingers, too. And *he* got what was coming to him. He had a great idea, regular perpetual motion scheme for economy, of how he could beat the game and he hypnotized old John Harbine into standing for it. It was as simple as bread and milk. Hammond would take up a Paris modiste, somebody on a back-street somewhere, get her under contract to be ' Harbine's,' and Harbine's alone. Then they'd put her name in the hands of the best advertising agency in New York and let things rip. Well, they started out as though they were going to a fire. You couldn't see the spokes, the wheels went around so fast. The advertising people delivered the goods, put the best people on their force on the job. I remember they had one college-graduate woman that could write ads that would make you pay five dollars for a strawberry basket—*once!* She wrote up their great find in Paris, wrote it up like a magazine short-story—modiste who up to the time Hammond had spotted her had been so exclusive you couldn't find her with a microscope, had only worked for the pure-bloods among the French aristocracy, no mere Americans had ever known her name (you can bet your life they hadn't)—you can imagine the kind of patter, the sort of thing women suck up by the barrelful. And then, owing to unheard-of prices offered by Harbine's out of that disinterested devotion to American womanhood which is Harbine's great quality, she had finally consented to send a few hats, never more than a dozen a season, to Harbine's, where the first collection would be on exhibition March 21st, and which would be exactly copied to order in imported materials with all the inimitable *chic* of the original models, for such low prices as from fifteen dollars up.

"It was well done. I'm bound to admit that ad.-writer got just the right esthetic, superior tone into it. And as for Hammond, he ought to have been a stage-manager. He got some of the people back of me sort of worried. They came to me, 'Look-y here, Grandpa, sure you're not missing a point in the game? How *about* this Suzette Rellot person?'

"I said: 'Her real name is Marie Duval and she used to sew in linings at Reboux', that's who *she* is. If she *could* have trimmed hats you can bet your life Reboux would have developed her years ago. Reboux has candles burning in every church in Paris, praying Heaven to send her apprentices that she can do something with! And if she *can't* trim hats you can bet your life old man Harbine is going to lose some money, a lot of it in one clip, and he and Jimmy Hammond will part company with a bang.'

"Well, I was over here in Paris when their great opening came off. But I heard about it. Nothing lacked. They all but served free champagne. But when I went back only a month later, the talk was already going around among folks on the ins, that there was something the matter with the Rellot collection. The women weren't just crazy about the hats and the modistes wouldn't look at them. Later on, what was left of them

were sent down to South America—Colombia, I think.
Women just hatching out from mantillas will stand for
anything with a French label on it! And that summer
Jimmy Hammond decided he'd go in for life-insurance."

When he had talked as long as this I was usually the
only person left listening, the rest having yawned,
turned to each other, or melted away. But I listened,
always, open-mouthed with astonishment and wonder.
Before putting on my hats in those days I used to look
at them hard, with respect, almost with alarm, feeling
heavy on my head the weight of their unsuspected significance. Wondering what the great expert's opinion
would be about the plain, everyday hats of ordinary
women I asked him one day: "Tell me, can you descend
to small beer? What do you think of the hats you see,
not in those wonderful, silk-hung studios, but those you
see on the heads of the women in the streets, on mine?
Is this hat I have on stylish? I warn you I bought it
off a counter for less than four dollars."

He answered instantly, without giving a glance at my
headgear: "You are a healthy, normal woman and
you're wearing it. Of course it's in style. If it weren't,
and you had to wear it, you'd be sick abed."

"You exaggerate, you are always exaggerating," I
protested. "You only know women who *care* about the
styles. I never bother my head about my hats! I just
walk into almost any shop and buy the first hat that
doesn't make me look too queer."

"You don't have to bother yourself about it," he told

me, his accent tinged with weary bitterness. "*We* do the bothering! Months beforehand. An army of us, able-bodied men, smart women, pretty young girls, we all of us give up our lives to fixing things so you can walk into most any shop and pick up most any hat and find it doesn't make you look too 'queer,' which is your way of saying that it doesn't make you look out of style."

"There are moments," I told him, in a half-serious indignation, "when I find you too absurd for words, the victim of the most absurd hallucinations! All this portentous talk about the world-wide conspiracy to make people keep up with the style. As if the style had any importance for sensible people!"

"If you knew more about the capital and brains that are invested in that conspiracy, you'd take it seriously, all right," he assured me with melancholy, "and as for not taking the styles seriously, how many thousand dollars would it take to pay you to go around in the street one day, just one day, in the big bustle your mother used to be ashamed to go outdoors without?"

I lost myself in horrified contemplation of the grotesque vision he had conjured up and forgot to refute him. Perhaps I couldn't.

Towards the end of his stay he was very much troubled by persistent rumors that the boat on which he was to sail would be torpedoed on the way to New York. He acknowledged, with the fatigued frankness of his sixty years past, that he was mortally afraid of the passage and that his fear would deprive him of

sleep all the way over. " No sane man likes to be killed,"
he complained, " let alone be blown up and burned to
death and drowned into the bargain! I'm a family man!
I want to go on earning a living for my wife and children!"

The evening before he went away he was so fretful
about this and so outspoken about his dread, that I asked
him, " Why don't you wait over a boat?"

" Oh, what's the use? One boat's as likely to go
down as another. And, anyhow, I've got to get home.
And then come over again for the next season, curse the
luck!"

I thought him again a little absurd. " Oh, come, the
heavens wouldn't fall if you missed one or two sea-
sons!"

He turned grave, and after a moment's hesitation,
opened a door which I had thought locked and nailed
up, and showed me that the room in his heart which I
had thought was certainly empty and vacant was a queer,
dimly lighted little chapel, with queer, dim little candles
burning before what was recognizably an ideal.

" Oh, it's no time for anybody to lie down on the
job," he said offhand. I did not dream that he was
referring to the war. I had become convinced that his
curious, specialized world held no place for the horror
and apprehension which filled the lives of the rest of us.
Nor had I ever seen him give any signs of the shocked
pity which most people feel at the sight of the war-
maimed men, the black-clad, white-faced war-orphans

and the widows with blurred eyes. I had thought he saw in France, only and uniquely, hats. So I asked in genuine ignorance of his meaning: " How do you mean, this being no time to lie down on the job? What job? "

He sat back in his chair and looked at the ceiling; thereafter, as he talked, transferring his gaze to his finger-tips, joined with nicety. " Well, I guess I mean something about like this. If we humans are to get on at all, get any further away from having tails and living in trees, we've got to knock down the partitions and make one big room of the world, the same way each nation is one big room, with the blacksmith trading his horseshoes for clothes and not trying to be a tailor himself. Take farmers. Maybe you can't remember, but *I* can, when old farmers in Connecticut raised nearly every single thing they used all the year around, and were proud of being such idiots. Nowadays the Connecticut farmer don't waste his time trying to grow corn in a climate where you're liable to get frosts in early September; he leaves the farmer in Iowa to do that, and he raises the best apples in the world and with the money he makes that way, he buys him oranges that a Florida farmer has raised. It's my opinion that we've got to come to that on a big, big scale. And if we do come to it there won't be any more wars. Now, I don't know anything about anything but hats, and so I don't try to have an opinion about the League of Nations, nor how the trick is going to be turned by the statesmen—if there are any such—but if it *is* going to be turned, it's going to take everybody's shoulder to the wheel, you can be sure. And I've got a shoulder. What's got to be done is to get it through everybody's head that every nation ought not to learn to produce anything but what it can produce best, and that self-defense ought not to force it to make a botch of trying to do what another nation could do better. Now, *one* of the things that France can produce better than other people (and it happens to be the thing that I know about) is hats. I don't know whether it's because she's been at the business of running the styles so long, so much longer than anybody else so that she's got all her fibers settled together, just right to catch the note, the way the wood in an old violin trembles all over at sounds that leave the wood in the leg of a chair perfectly calm. Mind, I don't say the violin is any more important than a chair. As far as I'm concerned personally, if I had to choose I'd rather have the chair. What I'm trying to say is that they are *different*. And we've got to get used to the idea that *because things are different it doesn't mean one is better than the other and they ought both to be like the best one.* Now, maybe it's the other way around, that France has been at this business of setting styles so long because she's had the gift to begin with. Anyhow, what's sure is that they do it better, everything along that line, ribbons, braids, straws, hats, dresses, furniture, houses, parks—original designs don't come from anywhere but France. But France is at war and pretty nearly gone under. She's got to make her designs with one hand and fight for her life with the other."

He paused. " Well, I don't feel just like picking out that time to stop coming to France to get her designs and to do my part to keep up the taste for them, at home."

I found no sufficiently admiring comment to make on this, and kept a respectful silence.

He went on, rubbing his hand back and forth over his gray hair: " But all that is only my guess at it. What's my guess worth? Nothing. But it's all I've got to go by, and so I *do* go by it. I don't *know* anything about anything but hats, and I can't but just make a guess at them."

He folded his hands before him and sighed. " There is a lot too much in hats for any one man to understand."

A HONEYMOON . . . VIVE L'AMERIQUE!

I NEVER knew many of the mere facts of their existence; where all their money came from, nor the extraordinary romance which must have lain back of them. Nor did I care to. They were too epic a pair for realism to touch. I find on thinking them over that I never quite came to believe in their actual existence; and yet, whatever value this slight sketch of them may have will be due to its literal truthfulness to fact.

My first sight of them was on a very cold day in the second year of the war when they suddenly filled with their resplendent presence the dreary room which was known as my " office." For several difficult months, against all the obstacles which made up everyday life in war-time France, I had been laboring to organize and get into shape a Braille printing establishment which would provide books for those most tragic of war-victims, the blind. Together with a crew of devoted volunteers I had tugged at the task, struggling like everybody else in France with a universal shortage of supplies, which began with able-bodied men and ran down to tacks and cheesecloth. There was also the difficulty of getting the " Authorization from the Government " before draw-

ing your breath; but unless you have experienced this
potent brake on enterprise, there is no use trying to describe it to you.

And yet, somehow, we had managed to get along, had
added to our two plaque-making machines a couple of
presses (very poor, both of them), had scrambled together a home-made device for wetting and drying the
paper, had hunted down enough men to run the machines, had trained enough proof-readers and assembled
enough voluntary editors, so that after a fashion we
were really printing. The magazine, liberally bedewed
with our blood and sweat, came out once a month; and
although the two presses broke down with great fre-
quency, we managed, by dint of incessant repairing, to
keep at least one in shape to do tolerable work. We
really had something patched-up, ungainly, but reasonably valid to show the sightseers who came through on
the weekly visiting day, when all the rest of the institution was open to visitors.

I took my two Olympian guests for the usual idle,
visiting-day couple. I went the rounds with them, point-
ing out with a weary satisfaction our various makeshifts.
When I found that they listened receptively, I indulged
in considerable self-pity over our difficulties, past and
present. On their part they asked a good many pointed
questions about the business end of our enterprise, about
the financial status of the institution, about the prob-
ability of permanence for the venture. They came back
to the " office " with me, the goddess in sables taking

the solitary chair, while her mate sat down on the edge of my little table, stretching out before him legs clad in cloth of a fineness I had forgotten could exist. Quite casually, like the diamonds and pearls of the fairy-tales, amazing words now issued from their lips. " See here," said he of the broadcloth overcoat, " this is no way to do business. You can't get good work done with any such junk as those two presses! Why, I wouldn't take them as a gift, not for old iron! And turned by hand-power! Isn't that Europe for you? Why, for twenty-five cents a day of electric current, you could do ten times the work you are doing now, and have women run the presses! Go find a modern electric press that a man can look at and not think he's Benjamin Franklin come to life again, and let us know how much it costs."

He handed me his card as he spoke.

The goddess quitted my rickety, cane-bottomed chair and from her superb height dropped down on me, " You know, the kind that opens and shuts its jaws like a whale; perhaps you've seen them in printing establishments at home." She tempered her assumption of my ignorance by a smile out of the loveliest eyes imaginable and added: " My father was a printer out West. I used to play 'round in his shop. That's how I happen to know."

Gazing up at her fascinated, I noted how deep the little lines of kindliness were at the corners of her smiling gray eyes, and how, beyond the usual conventional coating of powder, no effort had been made to hide the fact that

the beautiful face was not in its first youth. The conse-
quent effect of honesty and good faith was ineffable,
and had its perfect counterpart in the extraordinary simplicity and directness of her gentle manner. She drew
her regal fur up around her long neck and her husband
put his hat back on his thick white hair. " While you're
about it, you'd better get those two plaque-making machines electrified," he remarked. " Any electrician could
do it for you. There's no sense in having your operators
push down that pedal for every letter they make. Man-
power again! Europe!"

I realized that they were moving towards the door and
shook myself out of my entranced silence. " But you
can't buy a press of that kind in Paris!" I called after
them, all the bitterness of my past struggles in my voice.
" You can't buy anything in war-time France. There
hasn't been a press or anything else manufactured in
France for two years! Don't you know that all the factories are making munitions?"

Mr. Robert J. Hall—that was the name on the card
—came back to me and said earnestly: " Money can't *do*
everything, but I tell you that it can buy anything buyable
if you've got enough of it. Now we'll give you money
enough to buy that press. It's up to you to find it."
From the doorway his wife smiled to mitigate his intense seriousness and said again, " It's the kind that opens
and shuts its jaws, you know." The door swung shut
behind them to a last call-to-arms, " Go to it!" from Mr.
Hall.

Five minutes later a proof-reader coming found me still standing, staring at their card.

" What's the matter? " she asked.

I took her by the arm. " Look here," I said, " did I just show two visitors around the place? "

" Do you mean that awfully good-looking man with the white hair and the royal-princess-effect in sables and eyes like Trilby's? "

I nodded, reassured. I had not dreamed them!

Of course I went to it. Of course I found the press. After such a galvanic shock, I could have found, if that had been my need, a featherbed on the Arc de l'Étoile. I have too many other things to tell you about the Halls to describe the hunt after the press, although in its way that was epic, too. Enough to say that after three weeks of impassioned concentration on the subject during which I ate, drank, slept, and lived printing-press, it was located, a second-hand one in excellent condition, in a loft in the remotest corner of a remote industrial region of Paris. It was quite exactly what we needed, a thousand times better than anything we had dreamed of having. I felt almost a reverent admiration to see it opening and shutting its great jaw, and spewing out perfect raised-type pages, at least twelve times faster than our wretched hand press; doing in one day the work of two weeks!

But the price! Like all war prices it was five times what it was worth when new. I hadn't the least idea that my extraordinary visitors would buy it for us.

Why in the world should they? In fact, by that time I had gone back to thinking that I had dreamed them.

However, I betook myself to their hotel, into their private sitting-room, bright with chintz and copper and flowers. I found Mrs. Hall without her hat even lovelier than before, a little gray in her thick soft hair as honestly shown as the faint, fine lines of simple kindness in her clear skin. She wore a dark-blue satin dress richly embroidered, evidently a creation from one of the great Paris houses. She assured me cordially that she was awfully glad to see me.

Sitting on the edge of the Beauvais tapestry chair like the poor relation on a begging expedition which I felt myself to be, I timidly told of my search, trying to be amusing about it. Now that I was there I dared not mention the price. Finally, however, having run out of expedients to put off that dangerous moment, I brought out haltingly the sum needed, and began to say, excusingly, that I thought I might get *part* of that from . . .

Mr. Robert J. Hall moved to the writing-table and took out a check-book. " I'll tack another thousand francs on to that," he said over his shoulder as he wrote, " I haven't been able to sleep nights for thinking of those operators punching down the pedals by main strength and awkwardness."

There was a silence as he wrote. Mrs. Robert J. Hall examined her glistening nails, looked out of the window, and, with a tact for which I was grateful, did not once glance at my face. I fancy that my expression, instead of gratitude, must have been stupefaction. Mr. Hall blotted his check, detached it, and handed it to me—the little bit of blue paper through which I saw as in a vision hundreds of the terribly needed raised-type books put into those terribly empty hands. I could find no words at all. "It's . . . it's just like a miracle!" I was stammering, when some one knocked at the door, a timid, hesitating knock, such as mine had been.

The sound seemed to alarm the Halls. "Good Lord, I bet it's the abbé!" said Mr. Hall.

"You don't happen to speak French, do you?" asked his wife hastily. "Oh, you do? It's all right then. It's the curé of a town in the war-zone and we want to help him with some war-orphans, but we have the most awful time trying to make him understand about business details. It's perfectly terrible, not speaking the languages."

We turned to meet a short, elderly, double-chinned ecclesiastic who carried his bulky body with the impersonal professional dignity of his calling, but was not otherwise in the least impressive. The conversation began.

It consisted of an attempt on the part of Mr. Hall to get the curé to "come to the point," as he expressed it, and name a sum, and of terror-stricken evasions on the part of the curé to do any such thing for fear of losing their interest. This fencing centered about a large house which the curé needed to fit up for the reception of a number of war-orphans. "How much will it cost?" asked Mr. Hall patiently, over and over, evidently seeing no reason for his not receiving a direct answer. Upon my pressing the abbé hard, he finally brought out the sum, miserably, in a faltering voice which made me want to shake his hand. I knew how he felt.

The Halls consulted each other with a look of intimate understanding. "All right," said the husband, "all right, *on condition* that he can get the funds from his diocese to keep the thing going if we set it on foot." To me, he added: "The more we see of this sort of thing, the more we see you've got to go slow at times. These Europeans are so impractical that first thing you know they've used the money you give them to get themselves into some fool scheme, without half seeing their way through. We make it a rule not to give anything to a concern which isn't on a good, sound, business basis. What's the use?"

I turned to the waiting priest, who had been wildly trying to guess from our faces what we were saying, and translated Mr. Hall's philosophy of philanthropy. I found a little difficulty in hitting on the exact French phrase to express "a good, sound, business basis" but evidently I made myself understood, because the old man's lips began to tremble eagerly. "Oh yes, yes, madame, tell them that I can bring a letter to-morrow from my bishop guaranteeing the support . . . if only the house can be secured and fitted up."

Mr. Hall sent back through me: "Well, you tell him

that the minute he shows me that letter from his bishop, I'll give him a check for the house, and some over for extras."

I translated this exactly as it was said.

For an instant the curé kept a solemn silence, his eyes looking through us and beyond. I knew what he was seeing, a big sheltering house with happy, rescued children playing in the garden. The graceless, stout old man looked very touching to me.

Then he came back to a sense of the inherent probabilities of things, and appealed to me in a trembling voice, as to one who at least spoke his language and to this degree was more of the real world than these amazing strangers: "Are you sure you told them correctly? It is such a great sum! And nobody else has been willing to . . . Madame, do you . . . *do you really think they will do it?*"

I showed him the check still in my hand. "They have just given me this for the war-blind," I said. I found my own voice not entirely steady.

Then it was my turn to look out of the window while he took his agitated departure. I tried not to listen, but I could not help hearing that he gave them his blessing. I wondered how he managed it, being but half their height.

I was still at the window when he emerged from the hotel entrance into the open square below. He stood looking up and down wildly, forgetting to put his broad-brimmed, flat-crowned hat on his head although it was raining. Then, as though at random, he crossed the wet asphalt and vanished down a side street. He staggered a little as he walked. I knew just how he felt.

When I turned back from the window, the Halls asked, offhand and as though it would be doing them a favor, to accompany them on an automobile trip out to the front, near St. Quentin. (I had been trying vainly for three months to get a *sauf-conduit* which would let me get to the front.) "We want to take some money out to the villages the Germans blew up when they retreated last month; and seeing how quick we got the curé fixed up with somebody to talk French, we thought it would be nice if you could go with us." This from Mrs. Hall. Her husband continued, as if in explanation of a slightly eccentric taste: "You see, we like to dodge the committee-and-report effect in war-relief. It takes so long for those big shebangs to get into action, don't you think?

"And we like to manage so that the spending of the money we give isn't in the hands of one of these self-satisfied young women in uniform who know all about Elmira, New York, but do they about the Department of the Aisne? It's unscientific, I know, but in such cases as these people who have been cleaned out by the Germans, we like to put the money right in the fists of the people who need it; and then go away and leave them to spend it the way they want to. If my house burned down, I don't believe I'd enjoy having a foreigner tell me how to build it over, and you needn't tell me they like our ideas any better."

I was by this time in the state of silent stupor which was the effect not infrequently produced on me by the Halls. I found no words to tell them how precisely their invitation fell in with my wishes, and they took my momentary hesitation for doubt. "We've got a *very* comfortable car," urged Mrs. Hall. "I don't think it would tire you much!"

And Mr. Hall added: "Honestly, it would make me a lot more satisfied if you would. You haven't any idea what a fool you feel just to poke money under people's noses and not be able to say anything to them!"

I thought to myself it was a sort of "foolishness" which I could well endure, but before I could put this idea into words we were deep in a discussion of ways and means, what clothes to wear, whether cameras would be permitted, what to do about food. The date for the expedition was set. My call was over. Dazed, their check still clutched tightly in my hand, I was emerging from the hotel entrance into the street. I think I must have staggered a little as I walked, but the resplendent doorkeeper did not seem to notice. He was probably quite used to this phenomenon as a feature of the departure of visitors to the Halls.

This is not the place to tell you of that phantasmagoric trip to the front, the nightmare of the dynamited villages, the carefully and expertly murdered fruit-trees and vines, the ravaged gardens and fields, the grimly enduring women and old men who toiled feebly with an invincible determination to bring a beginning of order out of the hideous chaos which had been their homes. For me the recollection of all that horror of desolation is shot through with the incredible presence of the Halls, resplendent in health and good looks and wealth and good will, brightly interested in everything, cut off by their untouched prosperity from any grinding comprehension of what they saw, but somehow not needing to be ground into comprehension like the rest of us, somehow not needing to put on the sackcloth of bitterness and passion in order to feel fellowship.

They kept vaguely reminding me of something . . . and on the last night out I learned what it was.

Everywhere the gesture was the same. The car rolled into a new set of ruins, as like the ones we had just left as one part of hell must be like another. Mrs. Hall always began at once to take photographs, methodically noting down the name of the village which had stood there. Mr. Hall got out from his pocket the wallet containing more cash that I had ever seen together in my life, and I went off with the French officer escorting me to find the mayor of the ruined town. For the most part, the real mayor had been carried off by the Germans for forced labor, and we found some substitute, chosen by the remnant of the citizens left. Usually it was a white-haired man, once it was a woman, lean, energetic, stern, who had lost one eye through the explosion of a dynamite petard. Always we found a worker at his work . . . ah, the noble procession of valiant old men we saw in their shirt-sleeves, in worn, faded, patched over-alls, hammer or mason's trowel in their knotted hands, sweating and toiling among the ruins.

The same thing always happened. I explained the Halls' mission. The mayor opposed to my account the prompt defense of a total incredulity. Things didn't happen that way, he always explained to me, as we walked towards the car, he wiping his hands on his over-alls. He told me that nobody gave help at once, that people came and looked and exclaimed and said how awful and said they would write articles, and others came and took notes and said they would report to a committee in Paris, and others said that if a report were written by the mayor and viséed by the *sous-prefet* and signed by the *Deputé* and sent through the Ministry of the Interior . . . by this time we were beside the car, where the mayor's eyes were always instantly fascinated by Mrs. Hall's tall beauty.

Mr. Hall shook him by the hand and left in it big, crisp, crackling French bank-notes, at which the old man gazed hypnotized, while I tried to express to him some-thing of the kindliness in the hearts of the two shining messengers from another world. During this time Mrs. Hall always took our photographs again.

Then we shook hands all around. The mayor tried convulsively to express his thanks, and failed. The auto-mobile moved forward. We were off to a repetition of the scene.

When our time-limit was up, we scurried back towards

Paris in order to reach the city before the hour set in
our *sauf-conduits.* The car rushed forward over the
long, level road, dimly shining in the starlight, the flank-
ing poplars shadowy, the cold, pure air blowing hard in
our faces. Mrs. Hall and I were in the tonneau, looking
up at the stars, incredibly steady above our world of
meaningless misery. Then it was that I learned of what
they had reminded me. Mrs. Hall said to me, evidently
thinking it the simplest and most matter-of-fact explanation of their being in France, of their life there, " You
see, we haven't been married so very long, only three
months ago. And we were awfully happy to be married. Of course all newly married folks are, but we had
special reasons. And we wanted to have a very special
kind of honeymoon, the nicest kind anybody ever had.
It seemed silly to go to Florida, or to the Yellowstone,
or yachting, or to Hawaii, or to Japan for cherry-
blossom time, or any of the things you usually do. We'd
done all those anyhow, but more than that, when you
read the newspapers about the war and think that our
country isn't taking any part in it you don't get much
good out of cherry-blossoms or surf-riding, do you?
We wanted to do what would give us the very best time
we ever had, to celebrate our being married. That's
what honeymoons are for, of course. And we decided
that what we would like best, seeing that our Government
isn't doing anything, would be to come to France and
help out. So we did."

She was silent for a moment, while I slowly took in

the significance of what she had said. Then she went on: "And we like it even better than we thought. We are happier even than we expected. It has been perfectly, perfectly lovely."

Then I knew of what they had reminded me. They had reminded me of America, they *were* America incarnate, one side of her, the dear, tender-hearted, uncomprehending America which did not need to understand the dark old secrets of hate and misery in order to stretch out her generous hand and ease her too happy heart by the making of many gifts.

Of course, such an extraordinary phenomenon did not go unheeded by the sharp eyes of the elegant and cosmopolitan circle in Paris war-relief work. That circle had as well trained a predatory capacity for emptying fat pocketbooks as the prettiest girl who ever sold tencent bouquets for five dollars at a church fair. It was with something of the same smiling security in levying philanthropic blackmail that they began to close in on the Halls. I heard excited talk of them everywhere. Everybody's mouth watered at the stories of their "easiness" and plots to entrap them were laid by every cosmopolitan mondaine who now felt about her own pet "war-work" the same competitive pride she had had (and would have again as soon as the new fad was no longer new) for her collection of pet dogs, or Egyptian rings.

A scouting party from another charitable institution, one of the very "chic" *œuvres,* nosing around our institution to make sure they were losing no points in the game, stumbled on our new press and were as awestruck as I had been by its costliness and speed. After this, all the information which I had about the Halls, scanty and highly improbable as you will see it to have been, was repeatedly pumped from me by one past mistress after another in the art of pumping.

I became so curious as to what the reaction of the Halls to this world would be, and as to what this world would make of the Halls, that one afternoon I took the time off to go to one of those horribly dull afternoon teas in which fashionably disposed charitable ladies made up for the absence of their usual pre-war distractions. I did not see the guests of honor at first, and stood dismally taking my tea, submerged in the talk customary at such affairs, for the most part complaints of war inconveniences . . . the hardship it was to have so few taxis in Paris, how inconsiderate the Government had been to forbid cakes and candy on two days a week, how the tailors and dressmakers were profiting by the high prices to ask preposterous ones, " even of their old clients," how hard it was to get coal enough to have a fire in one's *cabinet de toilette* . . . it was one of the days when we had heard of the failure of a great French offensive, and of the terrible shortage of hospital supplies at the front! My tea and sandwiches were ashes in my mouth! Through the window I saw a one-armed soldier with his head in bandages hobbling by the house, and I found myself bitterly longing for a bolt from heaven to descend and consume the whole worthless lot of us. Then I caught sight of the Halls.

They towered above the crowd and above the very small but very important person who was monopolizing them, none other than the Duchesse de Sazarat-Bégonine, who was obviously engaged in opening upon them, one after another, her redoubtable batteries of persuasion. Do not let this casual mention of so well known a title lead you to the very erroneous idea that I move in the aristocratic society which she adorns. Nothing could be further from the truth. The very fact that I know the Duchesse de Sazarat-Bégonine is a startling proof of the extent to which, in the pursuit of her war-relief work, she has wandered from her original circle! It shows, as nothing else could, what a thorough sport she was in the pursuit of her new game, stopping at nothing, not even at promiscuous mingling with the obscure. She was, if you will allow me the expression, the *as des as* of the fashionable war-relief world in Paris. As in the case of Guynemer, when she mounted her aerial steed in pursuit of big cash donations to her *œuvre,* all lesser lights abandoned hopes for theirs.

She had so many different weapons in her arsenal that she was irresistible; her château full of the memories of those distinguished thieves, intriguers, and murderers, the illustrious ancestors of her husband; her far-renowned collection of historic snuffboxes, her wonderful Paris house with its rigorously select circle, to enter which any woman there would have given her ears;

her astonishing and beautiful jewelry; the reputation of
having been in her youth the *bonne amie* of one of the
best-known of the Bourbon pretenders (or was it a Napoleonic) . . . ah, when the Duchesse started out to
bring down a wealthy philanthropist for her Home for
One-armed and Tubercular Soldiers, she never missed
her aim. It was not to be doubted that people who had
succumbed without a struggle to the snuffy old parish
priest with his war-orphans, would put up no resistance
to this brilliant onslaught.

When I perceived the Halls corraled by this well-
known personage, I shamelessly moved closer so that I
could overhear what was being said. This was little
enough on the part of the two Halls. Mrs. Hall smiled
silently down on her short and majestic interlocutor.
Mr. Hall's strongly marked face was inscrutable. However, the great lady was quite used to respectful attention
from those of her excompatriots with whom she deigned
to converse, and she continued to talk with her habitual
certainty of herself. At the moment when I came within
earshot, she was retailing to them exactly how many
hundreds of wounded heroes had passed through " her "
hands to their eternal benefit; exactly the praises the
Minister of War had given her when her red ribbon
was bestowed; exactly how she had attacked and driven
from the field a Spanish lady of wealth who had had
the presumption also to attempt to aid one-armed and
tubercular soldiers; how imitators had tried to " steal "
her methods of outdoor work for the tubercular,

and how she had defeated their fell purpose by allowing no more visitors to that institution without a card from her personally . . .

At this point my attention was called away by an acquaintance who asked me in a whisper if those people whom the Duchesse had so ruthlessly grabbed were really the extravagantly rich and queer Americans everybody was talking about, attached to no institution, who gave as they pleased, dodging recognition and decorations, mavericks of the fashionable war-relief world, breaking all the time-honored traditions of that society.

When I could resume my eavesdropping, the Duchesse was embarked upon her snuffboxes, graciously dropping down from the pinnacle of her lofty exclusiveness an actual invitation to the two nobodies before her to call on her and see that world-famed collection, comprising snuffboxes used by the Duc de Talleyrand, the Duc de St. Simon, the Marquis de la Rochefoucauld. . . .

About this time I detected an inward glow in Mr. Hall's steady eyes. He said grimly, " I don't happen to be acquainted with any of those gentlemen, but in our country snuff-taking is accounted a rather low form of amusing yourself."

The Duchesse was brought up short, not in the least by any intimation that she might not be extracting her usual due of admiration, but by a great desire to laugh at the unsophistication of the barbarians. For my part I went warm all over with cheerfulness, and stepped forward to present my cordial greetings to the Halls. Mrs.

Hall soon fell back a step or two with me, leaving Mr. Hall looking down severely on the jewel-covered woman before him. There was a shade of anxiety on Mrs. Hall's usually clear face. "You don't suppose," she murmured to me, "that Robert will be taken in by that horrid, common old woman and give some money to her? Men are so blind, even the best of them!"

I must have laughed out at this, for the Duchesse turned and came towards us, carrying off Mrs. Hall the moment thereafter, with her wonderful irresistible assurance of conferring a distinction. I said to Mr. Hall, moved by the most genuine curiosity: "What do you think of the celebrated Duchesse de Sazarat-Bégonine? You know she is accounted perhaps the most chic of all chic Parisiennes. Is there any other city where a woman of her age could set the style for the most exclusive society?"

Mr. Hall did not seem interested in the chic-ness of the great lady. He was silent for a moment, watching over the heads of the crowd his wife listening to the Duchesse, her kind eyes bent attentively downward. Then he said, with decision, "If that bragging old harridan gets a cent out of my wife, I'll . . . I'll spank Margaret."

I thought then that my cup of diverted satisfaction was quite full; but it ran over splashingly when, half an hour later, separated by the crowd from the Halls, I heard the Duchesse near me, announcing confidently to a friend: "Oh, no difficulty whatever. The simplest fish who ever swallowed down the bait in one gulp. Hooked? My dear, they are in my basket already!"

I went away on that, full of threadbare meditations on the little child who had been the only one to see that the Emperor had really nothing on.

Although, after this, our Braille printing establishment continued to benefit by casual visits from the Halls, visits followed usually by some sound suggestion for improvement, accompanied by a check, they were strictly Scriptural as regards the ignorance of the right hands of the doings of the left, and I had little idea of what were their occupations in other directions. Once in a while they carried me off to dinner in some famous restaurant where otherwise I would never have set foot, and where my war-tired and gloomy spirits received a lesson in the art of cheer. There was in those delicate and costly repasts a sort of robust confidence in the ultimate rightness of things . . . or at least I used to have this fancy to explain to myself the renewed courage which came to me after such evenings, and which may have been simply the result of a really hearty meal after a good deal of penitential and meager fare.

I needed all the courage and calmness I could extract from any source during those days, for it was at that time that my old school friend, Marguerite Moysset, was notified that her husband was killed in a skirmish on the Champagne front. Marguerite had already lost, almost at the beginning of the war, her only child, a boy of nineteen. The death of her husband left her desperately poor and inexpressibly alone. She had not wept for her boy's death nor did she shed a tear now for her husband whom she had almost extravagantly adored. She shut herself up in a white, stern horror which frightened us, all her well-meaning friends who hovered about her in those clumsy ministrations which often do more harm than good but which nevertheless one dares not omit.

Paradoxically enough it was the much-dreaded moving out of the old apartment, full of memories of the twenty happy years passed there, and the moving into the two little rooms on the fifth floor of a dingy old tenement house in a poor quarter of the city, which did more for Marguerite than all our foolish efforts. At least it aroused her to a sort of shocked and horrified life, and carried her out of her own misery.

Not long after she had gone there to live I found her with four, pale-faced, dirty little children in one of her two rooms. She was heating water on her charcoal stove. "I'm going to give them a bath," she said to me, pronouncing the commonplace words with a strange wild accent. "Do you know they have never had a bath, all over their bodies, in their lives?" I stayed to help her, wondering at the curious expression on her face. She was, as she had been ever since the blow had fallen, still very white, but now that pallor was like white heat. After the children were clean, Marguerite dressed them in coarse, clean, new clothes, which she told me she had sold her watch to buy, " the church-bell strikes so near that I don't need a watch any more," and gave them each a piece of bread and jam. They took their departure then, stricken into an astonished silence, and Marguerite turned to me with an angry toss of her head, " Do you know what the war is? " she asked me fiercely. " *I* know! It is the punishment we have called down on ourselves. I see now that the war has only intensified everything that existed before, it has *changed* nothing fundamentally. We were living as hideously in a state of war before as now, except that it was not physically bloody. There were children in this awful house then as now, without baths, without food, without decency, while I was giving all my energy that one little boy might have everything, everything that he could wish."

At this I could not repress a protest, calling up the very modest comforts of her simple home. She brushed me aside. " It was luxurious, sinfully, wickedly luxurious to live so while other human beings were living as they were in this house. Oh, I see it so plainly, we were all living with all our might according to the horrible Prussian maxim that you have a right to anything you're strong enough to keep other people from sharing. All the Germans did was to carry it to its logical, murdering conclusion, and show us what we really were."

I could not, Heaven knows, deny this, but I ventured

a palliative murmur. " But at least we are ashamed of it. We tried to hide it. We never gloried in it, as the Prussians do."

" I am ashamed of it *now*," she told me somberly, " now when I have nothing, nothing to use as help but my two hands. I am ashamed of it now when it is too late."

The black misery on her face was such that I brought out the foolish phrase I had been repressing all during the weeks since the news had come: " Marguerite dearest, why do you keep such a dreadful calm? Wouldn't it do you *good* to cry?"

" *I?* " she said bitterly. " I haven't the right to cry! Look at my neighbors!"

The next time I went back I found her two little rooms full of children, three small babies on the bed, and a dozen or more of different ages playing together, while Marguerite, in a long black apron, stirred a soup-pot on the charcoal fire.

" Their mothers are working!" She gave me this as all-sufficient explanation, adding: " But there are so many, many more that I can't help! If only I had more room to take them in . . . and more soup . . . and more bread! But with children it's wicked to start more than you can carry on, and . . . I've made the calculation . . . I can't possibly help any more than there are here!"

I noticed that the feverish, wild look had gone from her eyes, that she looked steadied—infinitely tragic—

but quiet, purposeful.   The children had brought her back into real life again.

On a sudden impulse I left her, and went to telephone the Halls, asking them to meet me near there.   While I waited for them, I found myself very much agitated, my head whirling with possibilities for Marguerite's future, my legs a little unsteady under me.   I revolved the best way to " approach " them, the most tactful manner of presenting the matter to them; I brought to mind all the painfully acquired war-relief lore about " managing " people with money, I tried to recall what I knew of them so that I might guess at some weakness of theirs to exploit.   Perhaps I could promise to get recognition for them from the French Ministry of the Interior . . . what *was* the exact name of that medal they give to foreign philanthropists, of course not the red ribbon, but still . . .

In the midst of these cheap calculations, their taxi drove up to the curb, they stepped out, and I perceived that I had forgotten what they were.   It was not surprising.   I lived in a world where there were few reminders of such as they.   Mr. Hall looked at me out of his honest eyes, and said with his honest American accent, " Well, what's doing? " and I found myself without preamble giving them the facts, naked facts, without an adjective to qualify them, without a single picturesque arrangement.   I did not even make an appeal to them.   I simply told them all that had happened since the death of Marguerite's husband.   I even hid nothing of what

Marguerite had said which might seem a criticism of
their way of life and of mine. I told them all. When I
finished, they glanced at each other, their good look of
deep understanding which, in the cold, ill-smelling city
street was like a gust of warm, country-scented air
across my face. Mrs. Hall said, "I wonder if she'd
mind our going to see her?" Mr. Hall qualified: "Of
course if you think best not to . . . we're not acquainted
with her. We don't want to seem to butt in."

We found her giving those little people their noonday
meal, hot soup and bread. Having only her small kitchen
table and four bowls, the children came in relays. The
fear of those who waited, lest the soup should give
out before their turn, was painful to see. Marguerite
glanced at my companions, surprised, and gave me a
questioning, half-challenging look. The Halls stood
quietly in one corner of the dark little kitchen and
watched the white-faced clean little mites, all their ineffably clear child's eyes turned on the tall, pale foster-
mother, bending over them, serving them, stooping to
catch a timidly murmured request, smoothing a little
cheek, tying and untying their bibs, wiping their lips
. . . every gesture pregnant with passionate motherli-
ness. To me she wore the look of a mother who re-
turns to her brood after an absence and, finding them
ill-cared for and unhappy, strives burningly and remorse-
fully to give them their lost due of love and care.

With the last relay of four occurred a tragedy. Scrape
as she might, Marguerite could not bring out of the

kettle more than enough for three bowls. For a moment, there was silent consternation. Then, sighing, without any suggestion from Marguerite, these children of the poor, began dipping from their portions into the empty bowl. There was on their thin little faces a patient and unsurprised resignation. When all the bowls were equally full, they set to eagerly, a natural childlike greediness coming at last into their eyes. I glanced at Mr. Hall and saw that his lips were moving as though in some exclamation, but I could not catch what it was.

When the last drop had been scraped up from the last bowl and Marguerite's long white fingers were once more immersed in dishwater, I ventured to bring my visitors to her and introduce them. They asked a few questions which Marguerite answered in her careful book-English, astonished and a little nettled, I could see by their directness and lack of ceremony.

Yes, she said, turning a second glance of interrogation on me . . . who *were* these strangers in her house? . . . yes, there were other lodgings to be had in the house where she could care for more children, the whole top floor was a big, deserted factory loft with skylights letting in the sun and with windows opening on a flat-roof terrace where the children could play. But of course that was out of the question. The rent was very high, it would cost a great deal to heat the room, and where could she get money to feed any more? . . . "Even with the number I have, you saw . . ."

"Yes," they said hastily, they had seen! I took it from their accent that they would not soon forget what they had seen.

Mrs. Hall looked at her husband, their serious, eloquent glance. He nodded, cleared his throat, and took out his wallet, that famous wallet! I remember exactly what he said, it being of the most masterly brevity, and I mean to set it down textually as he said it. What I cannot set down is the inimitable, straight, clear gaze out of his eyes, as he looked at Marguerite, everything but their common humanity forgotten. He said: "Madame, my wife and I want to help you help these children. I am going to leave five thousand francs with you to-day, for you to rent anything, buy anything, do anything you think best for the children. And there will always be plenty more where that came from, for you to go on."

Having said all that he had to say, he was silent, laying down on the table with his card, the five big banknotes, and putting on them one of the children's soupbowls. I noted especially the gentleness with which he touched the coarse, yellow earthenware, as though it were of great value. I wondered intensely how Marguerite could thank them. I did not venture to look at her face.

Marguerite did not thank them at all. She stood perfectly motionless for a moment, and then, putting her hands over her face, she broke into a storm of loud sobs. The tears ran down between her thin fingers and fell on the coarse yellow bowl and on the bank-notes. . . .

Mrs. Hall pulled at my arm. Mr. Hall opened the door, and I found myself stumbling down the steep, dark stairs, holding desperately to the greasy railing. We groped our way down, step by step, in darkness and in silence, until, nearly at the bottom, I called back, with a quavering attempt at a jest, " But how about the necessity of a sound business basis? "

From the fetid darkness above me, dropped down Mr. Hall's clarion American accent, " Oh, damn a sound business basis! "

I found myself obliged to wink back the tears which came along with my laughter.

Emerging into the gray light of the narrow street, I turned to wait for my companions, but when I saw the expression of their faces I knew I should not be missed, and while they stood to hail a cab I made hasty fare-wells and betook myself to the nearest Métro station, my ears ringing as though I had been hearing the loud, tri-umphant note of trumpets.

I was about to dive into the anthole of the subway en-trance when I heard my name called and saw Mrs. Hall's chic little toque thrust out of a cab window. " We for-got to tell you," she called across the street to me, " that we are very much obliged to you indeed for telephoning us."

With this inimitable farewell they vanished again from my view until months after this I ran across them, for the last time. I was at the Gare de Lyon, seeing off a blind soldier whom, with his family, we had been able to place in a home in the country. As usual with the poor, to whom journeys are considerable events, we had been fearfully ahead of time because they were in a panic for fear of losing their train. I had settled our protégés with all the innumerable valises, baskets, packages, roll-ups, and wraps which are the accompaniment of a French family, even the humblest, *en voyage,* had bidden them godspeed, and was going back along the platform to the exit when I was confronted by a familiar royal effect in furs, followed by a mountain of magnificent baggage on a truck.

" Hello! " said Mr. Hall. " You on the move too? "

I explained my presence and turned back to walk with them to their train. " We are going to Italy," explained Mrs. Hall, " and for once we are going to try and *take* Italy something, instead of just getting the most out of her the way we have done and everybody else has done all these tourist years."

(I had some reflections of my own about what Italian hotel keepers and guides had taken from me, but I kept them to myself, recognizing that as usual I was on a very different plane from the Golden Age of my companions.)

" You see," explained Mr. Hall in their astonishing, matter-of-fact manner, " you see one of our enterprises at home in the States is making a lot more money than ever before because of the war-manufacturing . . .

LA PHARMACIENNE

WHEN the war broke out, Madeleine Brismantier was the very type and epitome of all which up to that time had been considered "normal" for a modern woman, a *nice,* modern woman. She had been put through the severe and excellent system of French public education in her native town of Amiens, and had done so well with her classes that when she was nineteen her family were thinking of feeding her into the hopper of the system of training for primary teachers. But just then, when on a visit in a smallish Seine-et-Marne town, she met the fine, upstanding young fellow who was to be her husband. He was young too, not then quite through the long formidable course of study for pharmacists, so that it was not until two years later, when Madeleine was twenty-one and he twenty-five, that they were married, and Madeleine left Amiens to live in Mandriné, the town where they had met.

Jules Brismantier's father had been the principal pharmacist there all his life, and Jules stepped comfortably into his father's shoes, his business, and the lodgings over the pharmacy. If this sounds common and "working-class" to your American ears, disabuse yourself; the habitation over the pharmacy was as well ordered and well furnished a little apartment as ever existed in a "strictly residential portion" of any American suburb. The beds were heir-looms, and were of mahogany, there were several bits of excellent furniture in the small, white-paneled salon, and three pretty, brocade-covered chairs which had come down from Madeleine's great-grandmother; there was a piano on which Madeleine, who had received a good substantial musical training, played the best music there is in the world, which is to say, German (Jules, like many modern young Frenchmen, had a special cult for Beethoven); and there was a kitchen—oh, you should have seen that kitchen, white tiles on the walls and red tiles on the floor and all around such an array of copper and enamel utensils as can only be found in well-kept kitchens in the French provinces where one of the main amusements and occupations of the excellent housewives is elaborate cooking. Furthermore, there was in the big oaken chests and tall cupboards a supply of bedding which would have made us open our eyes, used as we are to our (relatively speaking) hand-to-mouth American methods. Madeleine had no more than the usual number of sheets, partly laid aside for her, piece by piece, when the various inheritances from provincial aunts and cousins came in, partly left there in the house, in which her mother-in-law had died the year before Madeleine's marriage, partly bought for her (as if there were not already enough!) to make up the traditional wedding trousseau without which no daughter of a respectable bourgeois provincial family can be married. So that, taking them all together, she had two hundred and twenty sheets, every one linen, varying from the delightfully rough old homespun and home-woven ones, dating from nobody knew when, down to the smooth, fine, glossy ones with deep hemstitching on the top and bottom, and Madeleine's initials set in a delicately embroidered wreath. Of course she had pillow-slips to go with them, and piles of woolen blankets, fluffy, soft and white, and a big puffy eiderdown covered with bright satin as the finishing touch for each well-furnished bed. Madeleine pretended to be modern sometimes, and to say it was absurd to have so many, but in her heart, inherited from long generations of passionately home-keeping women, she took immense satisfaction in all the ample furnishings of her pretty little home. What woman would not?

Now, although all this has a great deal to do with what happened to Madeleine, I am afraid you will think that I am making too long an inventory of her house, so I will not tell you about the shining silver in the buffet drawers, nor even about the beautiful old walled garden, full of flowers and vines and fruit-trees, which lay at the back of the pharmacy. The back windows of the new bride's habitation looked down into the tree-tops of this garden, and along its graveled walks her children were to run and play.

For very soon the new family began to grow: first, a little blue-eyed girl like Madeleine; then, two years later, a dark-eyed boy like Jules—all very suitable and as it should be, like everything else that happened to Made-

leine. She herself, happily absorbed in her happy life
and in the care of all her treasures, reverted rapidly to
type, forgot most of her modern education, and became
a model wife and mother on the pattern of all the other
innumerable model wives and mothers in the history of
her provincial family. She lived well within their rather
small income, and no year passed without their adding
to the modest store of savings which had come down
to them because all their grandmothers had lived well
within *their* incomes. They kept the titles relative to
this little fortune, together with what cash they had, and
all their family papers, in a safe in the pharmacy, sunk
in the wall and ingeniously hidden behind a set of false
shelves. They never passed this hiding-place without
the warm, *sheltered* feeling which a comfortable little
fortune gives,—the feeling which poor people go all
their lives without knowing.

You must not think, because I speak so much of the
comfortableness of the life of this typical French provincial family, that there was the least suspicion of laziness
about them. Indeed, such intelligent comfort as theirs
is only to be had at the price of diligent and well-directed
effort. Jules worked hard all day in the pharmacy, and
made less money than would have contented an American ten years his junior. Madeleine planned her busy
day the evening before, and was up early to begin it.
The house was always immaculate, the meals always on
time (this was difficult to manage with Madeleine cooking everything and only a rattle-headed young girl to

help) and always delicious and varied. Jules mounted the stairs from the pharmacy at noon and in the evening, his mouth literally watering in anticipation. The children were always as exquisitely fresh and well-cared for as only French children of the better classes can be, with their hair curled in shining ringlets and their hands clean, as those of our children are only on Sunday mornings. Madeleine's religion was to keep them spotless and healthful and smiling; to keep Jules' mouth always watering in anticipation; to help him with his accounts in the evenings, and to be on hand during the day to take his place during occasional absences; to know all about the business end of their affairs and to have their success as much at heart as he; to keep her lovely old garden flowering and luxuriant; to keep her lovely old home dainty and well ordered; and, of course, to keep herself invariably neat with the miraculous neatness of French women, her pretty, soft chestnut hair carefully dressed, her hands white and all her attractive person as alluring as in her girlhood.

Madeleine saw nothing lacking in this religion. It seemed to her all that life could demand of one woman.

In the spring of 1914, when Raoul was five years old and Sylvie eight, Madeleine was once more joyfully sorting over the tiny clothes left from their babyhood. All that summer her quick fingers were busy with fine white flannel and finer white nainsook, setting tiny stitches in small garments. Every detail of the great event was provided for in advance. As usual in French families, in all good families everywhere, the mother-to-be was lapped around with tenderness and indulgence. Madeleine was a little queen-regnant whose every whim was law. Of course she wanted her mother to be with her, as she had been for the arrival of Sylvie and Raoul, although her mother was not very well, and detested traveling in hot weather; and she wanted the same nurse she had had before, although that one had now moved away to a distant city. But Madeleine did not like the voice of the nurse who was available in Mandriné, and what French daughter could think of going through her great, dreadful hour without her mother by her to comfort and reassure her and to take the responsibility of everything! So of course the nurse was engaged and her railway fare paid in advance, and of course Madeleine's mother promised to come. She was to arrive considerably in advance of the date, somewhere about the middle of August. All this was not so unreasonable from a money point of view as it sounds, for when they made up the weekly accounts together they found that the business was doing unusually well.

All through the golden July heats Madeleine sewed and waited. Sometimes in the pharmacy near Jules, sometimes in the garden where Raoul and Sylvie, in white dresses, ran and played gently up and down the paths. They played together mostly and had few little friends, because there were not many " nice " families living near them, and a good many that weren't nice. Of course Madeleine kept her children rigorously separated from these children, who were never in white but in the plainest of cheap gingham aprons, changed only once a week, and who never wore shapely, well-cut little shoes, but slumped about heavily in the wooden-soled, leather-topped " galoches " which are the national foot-gear for poor French children. Like many good mothers in France (are there any like that elsewhere?) Madeleine looked at other people's children chiefly to see if they were or were not " desirable " playmates for her own; and Sylvie and Raoul were not three years old before they had also learned the art of telling at a glance whether another child was a nice child or not, the question being settled of course by the kind of clothes he wore.

July was a beautiful month of glorious sun and ripening weather. For hours at a time in her lovely green nest, Madeleine sat happily, resting or embroidering, the peaches pleached against the high stone walls swelling and reddening visibly from one day to the next, the lilies opening flaming petals day by day, the children growing vigorously. Jules told his pretty wife fondly that she looked not a day older than on the day of their marriage, ten years before. This was quite true, but I am not so sure as Jules that it was the highest of compliments to Madeleine.

The last week of July came, the high-tide moment of lush growth. Madeleine was bathed in the golden, dreamy content which comes to happy, much-loved women in her condition. It was the best possible of

worlds, she had the best possible of husbands and children, and she was sure that nobody could say that she
had not cultivated her garden to be the best possible of
its kind. The world seemed to stand still in a sunny
haze, centered about their happiness.

Drenched in sunshine and peace, their little barque
was carried rapidly along by the Niagara river of history over the last stretch of smooth, shining water
which separated them from the abyss.

I dare not tell you a single word about those first four
days in August, of the utter incredulity which swiftly,
from one dreadful hour to the next, changed to black
horror. Their barque had shot over the edge, and in a
wild tumult of ravening waters they were all falling together down into the fathomless gulf. And there are not
words to describe to you the day of mobilization, when
Jules, in his wrinkled uniform, smelling of moth-balls,
said good-bye to his young wife and little children and
marched away to do his best to defend them.

There are many things in real life too horrible to be
spoken of, and that farewell is one.

There was Madeleine in the empty house, heavy with
her time of trial close upon her; with two little children
depending on her for safety and care and cheer; with
only a foolish little young maid to help her; with such a
terrible anxiety about her husband that the mere thought
of him sent her reeling against the nearest support.

Almost at once came the Mayor in person, venerable and white-bearded, to gather up the weapons in all the houses. To Madeleine, wondering at this, he explained that he did it, so that *if* the Germans came to Mandriné he could give his word of honor there were no concealed arms in the town.

It was as though thunder had burst there in the little room. Madeleine stared at him, deathly white. " You don't think . . . you don't think it possible that the Germans will get as far as *this!* " The idea that she and the children might be in danger was inconceivable to her. Monsieur le Maire hastened to reassure her, remembering her condition, and annoyed that he should have spoken out. " No, no, this is only a measure of precaution, to leave nothing undone." He went away, after having taken Jules' shotgun, her little revolver, and even a lockless, flintless old musket which had belonged to some of the kin who had followed Napoleon to Russia. As he left, he said, " Personally I have not the faintest idea they will penetrate as far as Mandriné—not the *faintest!* "

Of course when Jules left, *no* one had the faintest idea that his peaceful home town would see anything of the war. That horror, at least, was spared the young husband and father. But during the fortnight after his departure, although there were no newspapers, practically no trains, and no information except a brief, brief announcement, written by hand, in ink, posted every day on the door of the Town Hall, the air began to be unbreathable, because of rumors, sickening rumors, unbelievable ones . . . that Belgium was invaded, although not in the war at all, and that Belgian cities and villages were being sacked and burned; that the whole north country was one great bonfire of burning villages and farms; then that the Germans were near! Were nearer! And then all at once, quite definitely, that they were within two days' march.

Every one who could, got out of Mandriné, but the only conveyances left were big jolting farm-wagons piled high with household gear; wagons which went rumbling off, drawn by sweating horses lashed into a gallop by panic-stricken boys, wagons which took you, nobody knew where, away! away! which might break down and leave you anywhere, beside the road, in a barn, in a wood, in the hands of the Germans . . . for nobody knew where they were. The frightened neighbors, clutching their belongings into bundles, offered repeatedly to take Madeleine and the children with them. Should she go or not? There was nobody to help her decide. The little fluttering maid was worse than nothing, the children were only babies to be taken care of. After her charges were all in bed, that last night, Madeleine wrung her hands, walking up and down the room, literally sick with indecision. What ought she to do? It was the first great decision she had ever been forced to make alone.

The last of the fleeing carts went without her. During the night she had come to know that the first, the most vital of all the innumerable and tragic needs of the hour was the life of the unborn baby. She was forced to cling to the refuge she had. She did not dare fare forth into the unknown until she had her baby safely in her arms.

And perhaps the Germans would not come to Mandriné.

For two days the few people left in town lived in a sultry suspense, with no news, with every fear. M. le Curé had stayed with his church; M. le Maire stayed with the town records, and his white-haired old wife stayed to be with her husband (they had never been separated during the forty years of their marriage); good fresh-faced Sister Ste. Lucie, the old nun in charge of the little Hospice, stayed with some bed-ridden invalids who could not be moved; and there were poor people who had stayed for the reason which makes poor people do so many other things, because they could not help it, because they did not own a cart, nor a wheelbarrow, nor even a child's perambulator in which to take along the old grandfather or the sick mother who could not walk. Sœur Ste. Lucie promised to come to be with Madeleine whenever she should send the little maid with the summons.

Madeleine sickened and shivered and paled during these two endless days and sleepless nights of suspense. There were times when she felt she must die of sheer horror at the situation in which she found herself, that it was asking too much of her to make her go on living. At such moments she shook as though in a palsy and her voice trembled so that she could not speak aloud. There were other times when she was in an unnatural calm, because she was absolutely certain that she was dreaming and must soon wake up to find Jules beside her.

The children played in the garden. They discovered a toad there, during that time, and Madeleine often heard them shouting with laughter over its antics. The silly little maid came every few moments to tell her mistress a new rumor . . . she had heard the Germans were cannibals and ate little children, was that true? And was it true that they had a special technique for burning down whole towns at once, with kerosene pumps and dynamite petards? One story seemed as foolish as the other to Madeleine, who hushed her angrily and told her not to listen to such lies. Once the little maid began to tell her in a terrified whisper what she had heard the Germans did to women in Madeleine's condition . . . but the recital was cut short by a terrible attack of nausea which lasted for hours and left Madeleine so weak that she could not raise her head from the pillow. She lay there, tasting the bitterness of utter necessity. Weak as she was, she was the strongest of their little band. Presently she rose and resumed the occupations of the day, but she was stooped forward for very feebleness like an old woman.

She told herself that she did not believe a single word the terror-stricken little maid had told her; but the truth was that she was half dead with fear, age-old, terrible, physical fear, which had been as far from her life before as a desire to eat raw meat or to do murder. It was almost like a stroke of paralysis to this modern woman.

For two whole days the town lay silent and helpless, waiting the blow, in an eternity of dread. On the morning of the third day the sound of clumsily clattering hoofs in the deserted street brought Madeleine rushing downstairs to the door of the pharmacy. An old farmer, mounted on a sweating plow horse, drew rein for an instant in the sun and, breathing hard, gave the news to the little cluster of white-faced women and old men who gathered about him. Madeleine pressed in beside her poorer neighbors, closer to them than at any time in her life, straining up to the messenger, like them, to hear the stroke of fate. Its menacing note boomed hollowly in their ears. The Germans were in the next town, Larot-en-Multien, only eight miles away. The vanguard had stopped there to drink and eat, but behind them was an antlike gray horde which pressed steadily forward with incredible haste and would be in Mandriné within two hours.

He gathered up his reins to go on, but paused to add a brief suggestion as to what they might expect. The Germans were too hurried to burn or to destroy houses; they were only taking everything which was easily portable. They had robbed the church, had taken all the flour from the mill, all the contents of all the shops, and when he left (the sight of the shining plate-glass windows of the pharmacy reminded him) they were just in the act of looting systematically the pharmacy of Larot, taking down all the contents of the shelves and packing them carefully into a big camion.

He rode on. The women dispersed, scurrying rapidly each to her dependents, children, or sick women, or old men. The Mayor hurried away to carry a few more of his priceless town records to the hiding-place. The priest went back to his church. For an instant Madeleine was left alone in the empty street, echoing to disaster impending. She looked at the pharmacy, shining, well ordered, well stocked, useful, *as Jules had left it*.

At the call to action her sickness vanished like a mere passing giddiness. Her knees stiffened in anger. They should not carry off everything from the Mandriné pharmacy! What could the town *do* without remedies for its sick? The mere first breath from the approaching tornado annihilating all in its path crashed through the wall which had sheltered her small, comfortably arranged life. Through the breach in the wall she had a passing glimpse of what the pharmacy was; not merely a convenient way for Jules to earn enough for her and the children to live agreeably, but one of the vital necessities of the community life, a very important trust which Jules held.

And now Jules was gone and could not defend it. But she was there.

She ran back into the shop, calling for her little maid,

in a loud, clear voice such as had not issued from her throat since Jules had gone away. " Simone! Simone!"

The maid came running down the stairs and at the first sight of her mistress expected to hear that her master had returned or that the French troops were there, so like herself did Madeleine seem, no longer stooping and shivering and paper-white, but upright, with hard, bright eyes. But it was no good news which she brought out in the new ringing voice. She said: " The Germans will be here in two hours. Help me quickly hide the things in the cellar . . . you know, the further room . . . and we can put the hanging shelves over the door so they won't know there is another part to the cellar. Bring down the two big trays from the kitchen. We can carry more that way. Then light two or three candles up and down the cellar stairs. It won't do for me to fall, these last days."

She was gathering the big jars together as she spoke, and taking out the innumerable big and little drawers.

In a moment the two women, one who had been hardly strong enough to walk, the other scarcely more than a child, were going slowly down the cellar stairs, their arms aching with the weight of the trays and then running back upstairs in feverish haste. Shelf after shelf was cleared of the precious remedies that meant health, that might mean life, in the days to come. The minutes slipped past. An hour had gone.

From her attic windows from where she could see the road leading to Lorat-en-Multien, a neighbor called down shrilly that dust was rising up in thick clouds at the lower end. And even as she called, silently, composedly, there pedaled into the long main street five or six men in gray uniforms on bicycles, quite calm and sure of themselves, evidently knowing very well that the place had no defenders. Madeleine saw the white hair of M. le Curé and the white beard of M. le Maire advance to meet the invaders.

" We can't do any more here," she said. " Down to the cellar now, to mask the door. No, I'll do it alone. Somebody must be here to warn us. We mustn't be caught down there." She turned to go, and came back. " But I can't move the hanging shelves alone!"

Simone ventured, " Mlle. Sylvie? Could she watch and tell us?"

Madeleine hesitated a fraction. Sylvie, like her mother, had been asked to do very little with herself except to be a nice person.

Then, " Sylvie! Sylvie!" called her mother with decision.

The little girl came running docilely, her clear eyes wide in candid wonder.

Madeleine bent on her a white, stern face of command. " The Germans are almost here. Simone and I have been hiding papa's drugs in the cellar and we've not finished. Stay here . . . pretend to be playing . . . and call to us the moment you see the soldiers coming. *Do you understand?*"

Sylvie received her small baptism of fire with courage.

Her chin began to tremble and she grew very white. This was not because she was afraid of the Germans. Madeleine had protected her from all the horrid stories which filled the town, and she had only the vaguest baby notions of what the Germans were. It was her mother's aspect, awful to the child, which terrified her. But it also braced her to effort. She folded her little white lips hard and nodded. Madeleine and the maid went down the cellar stairs for the last time.

When they came back, the troops were still not there, although one could see beyond the river the cloud of white dust raised by their myriad feet. The two women were covered with earth and cobwebs, and were breathing heavily. Their knees shook under them. Taking the child with them, they went up the stairs to the defenseless home. They found five-year-old Raoul just finishing the house-and-farmyard which he and Sylvie were beginning when she was called down. "If only I had three more blocks to do this corner!" he lamented.

Twenty minutes from that time they heard heavy, rapid footsteps enter the shop below and storm up the stairs. There was a loud knocking, and the sound of men's voices in a strange language.

Madeleine went herself to open the door. This was not an act of bravery but of dire necessity. There was no one else to do it. She had already sent the children to the most remote of the rooms, and at the sound of those trampling feet and hoarse voices Simone had run away, screaming. Madeleine's fingers shook as she pushed back the bolt. A queer pulse began to beat very fast in the back of her dry throat.

The first Germans she had ever seen were there before her. Four or five tall, broad, red-faced men, very hot, very dusty, in gray, wrinkled uniforms and big boots, pushed into the room past her. One of them said to her in broken French: "Eat! Eat! Drink! Very thirsty. Quick!" The others had already seized the bottles on the sideboard and were drinking from them.

Madeleine went into the kitchen and brought back on a big tray everything ready-cooked which was there: a dish of stew, cold and unappetizing in its congealed fat, a long loaf of bread, a big piece of cheese, a platter of cooked beans. . . . The men drinking at the sideboard cried aloud hoarsely and fell upon the contents of the tray, clutching, cramming food into their mouths, into their pockets, gulping down the cold stew in huge mouthfuls, shoveling the beans up in their dirty hands and plastering them into their mouths, already full. . . .

Some one called, warningly, from below. The men snatched up what bottles were at hand, thrust them into their pockets, and still tearing off huge mouthfuls from the cheese, the bread, the meat, they held, and masticating them with animal noises, turned and clattered down the stairs again, having paid no more attention to Madeleine than if she had been a piece of the furniture.

They had come and gone so rapidly that she had the impression of a vivid, passing hallucination. For an in-

stant she continued to see them there still, in lightning
flashes. Everywhere she looked, she saw yellow teeth,
gnawing and tearing at food; bulging jaw-muscles straining; dirty foreheads streaked with perspiration, wrinkled
like those of eating dogs; bloodshot eyes glaring in physical greed.

"Oh, les sales bêtes!" she cried out loud. "The dirty
beasts!"

Her fear left her, never to come back, swept away
by a bitter contempt. She went, her lip curling, her
knees quite strong under her, to reassure Simone and
the children.

The house shook, the windows rattled, the glasses
danced on the sideboard to the thunder of the innumerable marching feet outside, to the endless rumble of the
camions and artillery. The volume of this wild din, and
the hurried pulse of straining haste which was its rhythm,
staggered the imagination. Madeleine scorned to look
out of the window, although Simone and the children
called to her from behind the curtains: "There are millions and millions of them! They are like flies! You
couldn't cross the street, not even running fast, they
are so close together! And how they hurry!"

Madeleine heard some one come up the stairs and enter
the hall without knocking. She found there a well-
dressed man with slightly gray hair who informed her
in correct French, pronounced with a strong accent, that
he would return in one hour bringing with him four
other officers and that he would expect to find food and

drink ready for them. Having said this in the detached, casual tone of command of a man giving an
order to a servant, he went away down the stairs, un-
folding a map.

Madeleine had all but cried an angry refusal after
him, but, as brutally as on a gag in her mouth, she
choked on the sense of her absolute defenselessness in the
face of physical force. This is a sensation which mod-
erns have blessedly forgotten, like the old primitive fear
of darkness or of thunder. To feel it again is to be
bitterly shamed. Madeleine was all one crimson flame of
humiliation as she called Simone and went into the
kitchen.

They cooked the meal and served it an hour later to
five excited, elated officers, spreading out maps as they
ate, laughing, drinking prodigiously and eating, with inconceivable rapidity, such vast quantities of food that
Simone was sure she was serving demons and not human
beings and crossed herself repeatedly as she waited on
table. In spite of all their haste they had not time to
finish. Another officer came up the stairs, thrust his
head in through the door, and called a summons to them.
They sprang up, in high feather at what he had said,
snatching at the fruit which Simone had just set on the
table. Madeleine saw one of her guests crowd a whole
peach, as big as an apple, into his mouth at once, and
depart, choking and chewing, leaning over so that the
stream of juice which ran from his mouth should not fall
on his uniform.

Simone shrieked from the kitchen, "Oh, madame! The garden! The garden!"

Madeleine ran to a window, looked down, and saw long rows of horses picketed in the garden. Two German soldiers were throwing down hay from the gable end of the Mandriné livery-stable which overlooked the wall. The horses ate with hungry zest, stamping vigorously in the flowerbeds to keep off the flies. When they had finished on the hay, they began on the vines, the little, carefully tended fruit-trees, the bushes, the flowers. A swarm of locusts could not have done the work more thoroughly.

As she stood there, gazing down on this, there was always in Madeleine's ears the incessant thundering rumble of the passing artillery. . . .

Through the din there reached her ears a summons roared out from below: "Cellar! Cellar! Key!"

She was at white heat. She ran downstairs, forgetting all fear, and, raising her voice to make herself heard above the uproar outside, she shouted with a passionate wrath which knew no prudence: "You low, vile thieves! I will not give you one thing more!"

Her puny defiance to the whirlwind passed unnoticed. The men did not even take the time to strike her, to curse her. With one movement they turned from her to the cellar door, and, all kicking at it together, burst it open, trooped downstairs, returning with their arms full of bottles and ran out into the street.

And all the time the very air shook, in almost visible

waves, to the incessant thundering rumble of the artillery passing.

Madeleine went upstairs, gripping the railing hard, her head whirling. She had scarcely closed the door behind her when it was burst open and five soldiers stormed in, cocked revolvers in their fists. They did not give her a look, but tore through the apartment, searching in every corner, in every closet, pulling out the drawers of the bureaus, tumbling the contents on the floor, sweeping the cupboard shelves clear in one movement of their great hands, with the insane haste which characterized everything done that day. When they had finished they clattered out, chalking up something unintelligible on the door. Raoul and Sylvie began to cry wildly, their nerves undone, and to clutch at their mother's skirts.

Madeleine took them back into their own little room, undressed them and put them to bed, where she gave them each a bowl of bread and milk. All this she did with a quiet air of confidence which comforted the children. They had scarcely finished eating when they fell asleep, worn out. Madeleine heard Simone calling for her and went out in the hall. A German soldier, desperately drunk, held out a note which stated that four Herr-Lieutenants and a Herr-Captain would eat and sleep there that night, dinner to be sharp at seven, and the beds ready.

After delivering this he tried to put his arm around Simone and to drag her into the next room. Simone struggled and screamed, shriek after shriek, horribly.

Madeleine screamed too, and snatching up the poker, flung herself on the man. He released his hold, too uncertain on his feet to resist. Both women threw themselves against him, pushing him to the door and shoving him out on the narrow landing, where he lost his balance and fell heavily, rolling over and over, down the stairs.

Madeleine bolted the door, took a long knife from the kitchen table, and waited, her ear at the keyhole, to see if he tried to come back.

This was the woman, you must remember, who less than a month before had been sitting in the garden sewing on fine linen, safe in an unfathomable security.

The man did not attempt to return. Madeleine relaxed her tense crouching attitude and laid the knife down on the table. The perspiration was streaming down her white cheeks. It came over her with piercing horror that their screams had not received the slightest response from the outside world. No one was responsible for their safety. No one cared what became of them. It made no difference to any one whether they had repelled that man, or whether he had triumphed over their resistance. . . .

And now she must command her shaking knees and trembling hands to prepare food for those who had sent him there. Of all the violent efforts Madeleine had been forced to make none was more racking than to stoop to the servility of this submission. She had an instant of frenzy when she thought of locking the door and defying them to enter, but the recollection of the assault on the thick oaken planks of the cellar door, and of its splintering collapse before those huge hobnailed boots, sent her to the kitchen, her teeth set in her lower lip. "I never will forgive them this, never, never, never!" she said aloud passionately, more passionately than she had ever said anything in her life, and she knew as she spoke that it was not of the slightest consequence to any one whether she would or not.

At seven the meal was ready. At half-past seven the four officers entered, laughing, talking loudly, jubilant. One of them spoke in good French to Madeleine, complimenting her on her soup and on the wine. "I told my friends I knew we would find good cheer and good beds with Madame Brismantier," he told her affably.

Astonished to hear her name, Madeleine looked at him hard, and recognized, in spite of his uniform, a well-to-do man, reputed a Swiss, who had rented a house for the season, several summers back, on a hillside not far from Mandriné. He had professed a great interest in the geology of the region and was always taking long walks and collecting fossils. Jules had an amateur interest in fossils also, and this, together with the admirably trained voice of the Swiss, had afforded several occasions of social contact. The foreigner had spent an evening or two with them, singing to Madeleine's accompaniment. And once, having some valuable papers left on his hands, he had asked the use of the Brismantier safe for a night. He had been very fond of children, and had had always a jolly greeting for little Raoul, who was then only a baby of two. Madeleine looked at him now, too stupefied with wonder to open her lips. A phrase from " An die ferne Geliebte," which he had sung very beautifully, rang in her ears, sounding faint and thin but clear, through the infernal din in the street.

She turned abruptly and went back into the kitchen. Standing there, before the stove, she said suddenly, as though she had but just known it, " Why, he was a spy, all the time! " She had not thought there were such people as spies outside of cheap books.

She was just putting the roast on the table when some one called loudly from the street. The men at the table jumped up, went to the window, leaned out, exchanged noisy exultant words, cursed jovially, and turned back in haste to tighten the belts and fasten the buttons and hooks which they had loosened in anticipation of the feast. The spy said laughingly to Madeleine: " Your French army runs away so fast, madame, that we cannot eat or sleep for chasing it! Our advance guard is always sending back word to hurry faster, faster! "

One of the others swept the roast from the table into a brown sack, all crammed their pockets full of bread and took a bottle under each arm. At the door the spy called over his shoulder: " Sorry to be in such a hurry! I will drop you a card from Paris as soon as the mails begin again."

They clattered down the stairs.

In the morning, when Sylvie and Raoul awoke, they found Simone crouched in a corner of their mother's room, sobbing endlessly tears of sheer nervous exhaustion. But out from their mother's white, white face on the pillow looked triumphant eyes. She drew the covers down a little and lifted her arm. " See, children, a little new brother."

As she spoke she thrust out of her mind, with a violence like that with which she had expelled the ruffian from the door, the thought that the little brother would probably never see his father. It was no moment to allow herself the weakness of a personal sorrow. She must marshal her little forces. " Come, Sylvie dear. Simone is all tired out; you must get us something to eat, and then you and Simone must bring in all you can of what is left in the kitchen and hide it here under mother's bed." She had thought out her plan in the night.

During the next days Madeleine was wholly unable to stand on her feet. From her bed she gave her orders— desperate, last-resort orders to a defeated garrison. The apartment was constantly invaded by ravenously hungry and thirsty men, but her room was not entered. The first morning the door to her room had been opened brusquely, and a gray-haired under-officer entered hastily. He stopped short when he saw Madeleine's drawn white face on the pillow, with the little red, bald head beside her. He went out as abruptly as he had gone in and chalked something on the door. Thereafter no one came in; although not infrequently, as though to see if the chalked notice were true, the door was opened suddenly and a head with a spiked helmet thrust in. This inspection of a sick woman's room could and did continually happen without the slightest warning. Madeleine was buffeted by an angry shame which she put aside sternly, lest it make her unfit to nurse her baby.

They lived during this time on what happened to be left in the kitchen, after that first day of pillage, some packages of macaroni, tapioca, and cornstarch, part of a little cheese, some salt fish, two or three boxes of biscuits, a little sugar, a little flour. They did unsavory cooking over the open fire till their small supply of wood gave out. The children submitted docilely to this régime, cowed by their mother's fierce command not for an instant to go out of her sight. But the little maid, volatile and childish, could not endure life without bread. She begged to be allowed to go out, to slip along the alley to the Hospice and beg a loaf from Sister Ste. Lucie. There must be bread somewhere in town, she argued, unable to conceive of a world without bread. And in the daytime the sentries would let her pass.

Madeleine forbade her to leave the room, but on the third day when her mistress was occupied with the baby she slipped out and was gone. She did not come back that day or the next. They never saw or heard of her from that moment.

Madeleine and the children continued to live in that one room, shaken by the incessant rumble of the passing artillery wagons and by the hurrying tread of booted feet. They heard now and again incursions into the other rooms of their home, and as long as there were loud voices and trampling and clattering dishes, the children crept into bed beside Madeleine and the baby, cowering together under the poor protection of their mother's powerless arms. They never dared speak above a whisper during those days. They heard laughing, shouting, cursing, snoring in the rooms all around them. Once they heard pistol shots, followed by a great splintering crash of glass and shouts of wild mirth.

Madeleine lost all count of the days, of everything but the diminishing stock of food. She tried repeatedly to sit up, she tried to put her feet to the floor, but she felt her head swim and fell back in bed. She had little strength left to struggle now. The food was almost gone, and her courage was almost gone. As though the walls of the room were closing in on her, the approach of the spent, beaten desire to die began to close in on her. What was the use of struggling on? If she could only kill the children and herself . . . there was no hope.

One morning Sylvie said in a loud, startled whisper: "Oh, *maman*, they are going the other way! Back towards Lorat . . . and yet they are still hurrying as fast as ever . . . faster!"

Madeleine felt her hair raise itself on her scalp. She sat up in bed. "Sylvie, *are you sure?*"

And when the child answered, always in her strained

whisper, "Yes, yes, I am sure," her mother sprang out of bed with a bound and ran to the window.

It was true. The dusty-gray tide had turned. They were raging past the house, the horses straining at the heavy artillery wagons, lashed into a clumsy canter by the drivers, leaning far forward, straining, urging; the haggard men, reeling in fatigue, stumbling under their heavy packs, pressing forward in a dog-trot; the officers with red angry faces, barking out incessant commands for more haste . . . and their backs were turned to Paris!

The Frenchwoman, looking down on them, threw her arms up over her head in a wild gesture of exultation. They were going back!

She felt as strong as ever she had in her life. She dressed herself, set the wretched room in some sort of order, and managed to prepare an edible dish out of soaked tapioca and sugar. The children ate it with relish, comforted by their mother's new aspect.

About two o'clock that night Madeleine awoke to an awful sense of impending calamity. Something had happened, some tremendous change had come over the world. She lay still for a long moment, hearing only the beating of her own heart. Then she realized that she heard nothing but that, that the thunder of the trampling feet had stopped. She got out of bed carefully, trying not to waken the children, but Sylvie, her nerves aquiver, heard and called out in a frightened whisper, "*Maman, maman!* What is it?" She caught her mother's arm, and the two went together to the window. They leaned out, looked to right and left, and fell to weeping in each other's arms. Under the quiet stars, the village street was perfectly empty.

The next morning Madeleine made the children swallow a little food before, all together, the baby in his mother's arms, they ventured out from their prison-room. They found their house gutted and sacked and sullied to the remotest corner. The old brocade on the chairs in the salon had been slit to ribbons by sword-slashes, the big plate-glass windows over the mantel-pieces had each been shattered into a million pieces, all the silver was gone from the drawers, every piece of linen had disappeared, the curtains had been torn down and carried away, and every bit of bedding had gone, every sheet, every blanket, every eiderdown quilt. The mattresses had been left, each having been cut open its entire length and sedulously filled with filth.

The kitchen, emptied of all its shining copper and enamel utensils, was one litter of splintered wood, remnants of furniture which had been cut up with the ax for fuel. Madeleine recognized pieces of her mahogany beds there. Through the kitchen window she looked down into the walled space which had been the garden and saw it a bare, trampled stable-yard, with heaps of manure at each end. She looked at all this in perfect silence, the children clinging to her skirts, the baby sleeping on her arm. She looked at it, but days passed before she really believed that what she saw was real.

A woman's voice called quaveringly from the landing: "Madame Brismantier, are you there? Are you alive? The Germans have gone." Madeleine stepped to the landing and saw old Sister Ste. Lucie, her face which had always been so rosy and fresh, as gray as ashes under her black-and-white coif. She leaned against the wall as she stood. At the sight of the sleeping baby in Madeleine's arms, the gray face smiled, the wonderful smile which women, even those vowed to childlessness, give to a new mother. "Oh, your baby came," she said. "Boy or girl?"

"Yes," said Madeleine, "he came. A boy. A nice little boy." For one instant the two women stood there in that abomination of desolation, with death all around them, looking down at the baby, and smiling.

Then Sœur Ste. Lucie said: "There is nothing left in the pharmacy, I see. I thought maybe they might have left something, by chance, but I see everything is smashed to pieces. You don't happen to have any supplies up here, do you? We need bandages horribly at the Hospice, for the wounded. There are forty there."

Madeleine knew the minute size of the little Hospice and exclaimed: "*Forty!* Where do you put them?"

"Oh, everywhere, on the floor, up and down the hall, in the kitchen. But we haven't a thing except hot water to use for them; all the sheets were torn up two days ago, what they hadn't stolen! If I only had a little iodine, or any sort of antiseptic. Their wounds are too awful, all infected, and nothing . . ."

Without knowing it Madeleine took a first step forward into a new life. "There's plenty of everything," she said. "I hid them all in the far room of the cellar."

"God grant 'they' didn't find them!" breathed the nun.

Madeleine lighted a candle, left the sleeping baby in the charge of Sylvie, and went with Sœur Ste. Lucie down into the cellar. They found it littered and blocked with emptied and broken bottles. A strange hoarse breathing from a dark corner frightened them. Lifting her candle, Madeleine brought to view a German soldier, dead-drunk, snoring, his face swollen and red. The women let him lie as an object of no importance and turned to the hanging shelves. They heaved a long sigh; the blind was still there, untouched. Madeleine's device was successful.

As they looked among the heaped-up supplies from the pharmacy for bandages and antiseptics, Sœur Ste. Lucie told Madeleine very briefly what had been happening. Madeleine listened in a terrible silence. Neither she nor the nun had strength to spare for exclamations. Nor could any words of theirs have been adequate. The news needed no comment. M. le Maire was dead, shot in front of the Town Hall, on the ground that there had been weapons found in one of the houses. "You know in the Bouvines' house they had some Malay creeses and a Japanese sword hanging up in M. Bouvines' study, things his sailor uncle brought back. The Mayor never thought to take those down, and they wouldn't give him time to explain. M. le Curé was dead, nobody knew or ever would know why—found dead of starvation, strapped to a bed in an attic room of a house occupied by some German officers. Perhaps he had been forgotten by the person who had tied him there. . . ." The nun's voice died away in sobs. She had been brought up under M. le Curé's protection all her life and loved him like a father.

Madeleine sorted bandages in silence, her throat very dry and harsh. Later Sœur Ste. Lucie went on, trying to speak more collectedly: " The worst of trying to care for these wounded is not being able to understand what they say."

" How so? " asked Madeleine, not understanding in the least.

" Why, I don't speak German."

Madeleine stopped short, her hands full of bandages. " Are they *German* wounded? Are we getting these things for *German soldiers?* "

Sœur Ste. Lucie nodded gravely. " Yes, I felt just so, too, at first. But when I saw them wounded, bleeding, so sick, worn out. . . . How would you like German women to treat your husband if he should be wounded in Germany? We are all nothing but wretched sinners in the sight of God. And are we not taught to do good to our enemies? "

Of all this (which meant in reality simply that Sœur Ste. Lucie was a warm-hearted woman whose professional habit had been for forty years to succor the afflicted) Madeleine took in very little at the time, although it was to come back to her again and again. At the moment she thought that she did not believe a single word of it. She certainly did not at all think that we are the best of us but wretched sinners, and she had as remotely academic a belief as any other twentieth-century dweller in the desirability of doing good to your enemies. The idea of Jules wounded in Germany did indeed bring a flood of confused emotions into her mind. If Germany should be invaded, would Frenchmen be stamping into strangers' houses and taking the food out of the mouths of the owners, would they . . . ?

" Well," said Sœur Ste. Lucie, impatient of her trance-like stare.

It was none of what she had been thinking which now moved Madeleine to say automatically, " Oh, of course we'll have to give them the bandages and the peroxide." She could not have named the blind impulse which drove her to say this, beyond that a sort of angry self-respect was mixed with it. Her head ached furiously, whirling with fatigue and lack of food, her back ached as though it were being beaten with hammers. She renounced any attempt to think.

" Here," said Sœur Ste. Lucie, staggering herself with exhaustion. " The baby is only a few days old. You're not fit to be doing this."

Madeleine, who had lain flat on her back for two weeks after the birth of the other two children, shook her head.

"No, no, I can do it as well as you. You look fearfully tired."

"I haven't had my clothes off for ten days," said the nun. "And I'm sixty-two years old."

In the street door, with her basket of bandages on her arm, Sœur Ste. Lucie stood looking around her at the desolate filth-strewn shop, the million pieces of glass which had been its big windows covering the floor, its counter hacked and broken with axes. She said: "We haven't any mayor and the priest is dead, and we haven't any pharmacy and the baker is mobilized, and there isn't one strong, well man left in town. How are we going to live?"

Madeleine took another step, hesitating, along the new road. She leaned against the counter to ease her aching body and put back her hair to look around her at the wreck and ruin of her husband's business. She said in a faint voice: "I wonder if I could keep the pharmacy open. I used to help Jules with the accounts. I know a little about where he bought and how he kept his records. I wonder if I could—enough for the simpler things?"

"You have already," said the nun, as she went away, "and the first things you have given out are bandages for your enemies. God will not forget that."

Madeleine received this with an impatient shrug. She was not at all glad that her first act had been to help the suffering among her enemies. She had hated doing it, had only done it because of some confused sense of decency. She heartily wished she had not had it to do.

But if it had been necessary, she would have done it again . . . and yet to do it for those men who had murdered M. le Maire, so blameless and M. le Curé—so defenseless! . . . No, these were not the same men who lay bleeding to death in the Hospice to whom she had sent bandages. *They* had not murdered . . . as yet!

Her head throbbed feverishly. She renounced again the effort to think, and thrusting all this ferment down into her subconsciousness she turned to the urgent needs of the moment. It seemed to her that she could not breathe till she had set the pharmacy as far as possible in the order Jules had left it. This feeling, imperious and intense, was her only refuge against her certainty that Jules was killed, that she would never see him again. Without an attempt to set to rights even a corner of the desolated little home, upstairs, she began toiling up and down the cellar stairs carrying back the glass jars, the pots, the boxes, and bottles and drawers. It seemed to her, in her dazed confusion, that somehow she was doing something for Jules in saving his pharmacy which he had so much cared for, that she was almost keeping him from dying by working with all her might for him there. . . .

In the middle of the morning she went upstairs and found that Sylvie, working with Raoul, had cleared the kitchen of the worst of the rubbish. In a pot-closet under the sink there were two old saucepans which had not been stolen. Madeleine made a fire, stoically using her own broken-up furniture, and, putting a few potatoes (the

last of their provisions) on to boil, sat down to nurse
the hungry baby.

"*Maman* dear," said Sylvie, still in the strained whisper of the days of terror. She could not speak aloud for
weeks. "*Maman* dear," she whispered, "in the salon,
in the dining-room, I wanted to try to clean it, but it is
all nasty, like where animals have been."

"Hush!" said her mother firmly. "Don't think about
that. Don't look in there. It'll make you sick if you do.
Stay here, tend the fire, watch the baby, and play with
Raoul." She outlined this program with decision and
hurried back downstairs to go on with the execution of
one conceived in the same spirit. If she could only get
the pharmacy to look a little as it had when Jules had
left it, it seemed to her that Jules would seem less lost
to her.

She shoveled the incredible quantity of broken glass
back through the shop into what had been her garden,
hardening herself against a qualm of horror at the closer
view of the wreckage there. The two big sycamore trees
had been cut down and sawn into lengths to use for fuel
in the open fire, the burned-out embers of which lay in a
black ring where the arbor had stood.

She went back to her work hastily, knowing that if
she stopped for an instant to look, she would be lost.

At noon she went upstairs, and with the children
lunched on potatoes and salt.

She was putting the last of the innumerable drawers
back in its place, after having tried it in all the other

possible places, when a poorly dressed, rough-haired, scrawny little boy came into the shop. Madeleine knew him by sight, the six-year-old grandson of Madame Duguet, a bedridden, old, poor woman on Poulaine Street. The little boy said that he had come to get those powders for his grandmother's asthma. She hadn't slept any for two nights. As he spoke he wound the string about a top and prepared to spin it, nonchalantly. Looking at his cheerful, dirty little face, Madeleine felt herself a thousand years old, separated for always and always from youth which would never know what she had known.

" I don't know anything about your grandmother's asthma powders," she said. The little boy insisted, astonished that a grown person did not know everything. "*He* always kept them. Grandmère used to send me twice a week to get them. Grandmère will scold me awfully if I don't take them back. She's scolding all the time now, because the Germans took our soup-kettle and our frying-pan. We haven't got anything left to cook with."

The memory of her immensely greater losses rose burningly to Madeleine's mind. " They took *all my sheets!* " she cried impulsively,—" every one!"

" Oh," said the little boy indifferently, " we never had any sheets, anyhow." This did not seem an important statement to him, apparently; but to Madeleine, her old world shattered, emerging into new horizons, beaten upon by a thousand new impressions, it rang loudly. The

Germans, then, had only put her in the situation in which a woman, like herself, had always lived . . . and that within a stone's throw of these well-filled linen-closets of hers! There was something strange about that, something which she would like to ponder, if only her head did not ache so terribly. The little boy said, insistently, "*He* always gave me the powders, right away!"

Through obscure complicated mental processes, of which she had only the dimmest perceptions, *Jules* had always given the powders . . . how strange it was that precisely a bedridden woman who had most need of them should have owned no sheets . . . there came to her a great desire to send that old woman the medicine she needed. "You go outside and spin your top for a while," she said to the child; "I'll call you when I'm ready."

She went upstairs. Holding her skirts high to keep them out of the filth, she picked her way to the bookcase. Books were scattered all about the room, torn, cut, trampled on, defiled; but for the most part those with handsome bindings had been chosen for destruction. On the top shelf, sober in their drab, gray-linen binding, stood Jules' big record-books, intact. She carried down an armful of them to the pharmacy, and opened the latest one, the one which Jules had put away with his own hand the day he had left her.

The sight of the pages covered with Jules' neat, clear handwriting brought a rush of scalding tears to her eyes. Her bosom heaved in the beginning of sobs. She laid down the book, and, taking hold of the counter with all her strength, she forced herself to draw one long, regular breath after another, holding her head high.

When her heart was beating quietly again, quietly and heavily, in her breast, she opened the book and began studying the pages. Jules set everything down in writing, it being his idea that a pharmacist had no other defense against making those occasional mistakes inevitable to human nature, but which must not occur in his profession.

Madeleine read: " March 10, sold 100 quinine pills to M. Augier. Stock low. Made 100 more, using quinine from the Cochard Company's laboratories. Filled prescription . . ." Madeleine's eyes leaped over the hieroglyphics of the pharmaceutical terms and ran up and down the pages, filled with such items, looking for the name Duguet. She had almost given up when she saw, dated July 30, 1914, the entry: " Made up fresh supply Mme. Duguet asthma powders, prescription 457. Dr. Millier. Drawer No. 17."

Madeleine ran behind the counter and pulled out No. 17. She found there a little pasteboard box marked, " Duguet."

" Oh, boy, little boy! " she called.

When the child came in she asked, " Did your grandmother ever get any other medicine here? "

" No," said the grandson of the bedridden woman, " she hasn't got anything else the matter with her."

"Well," said the pharmacist's wife, "here is her medicine." She put the box in his hand.

"Oh, we never get more than four at a time," he told her. "She never has the money to pay for more. Here it is. Granny hid it in her hair so the Germans wouldn't get it. She hid all we have. She's got more than *five francs,* all safe."

He put a small silver coin in her hand and departed.

The mention of the meager sum of hidden money made Madeleine think of her own dextrously concealed little fortune. She had noticed at once on entering the shop that the arrangement of false shelves which concealed the safe had not been detected, and was intact. She pushed the spring, the shelves swung back, and disclosed the door of the safe just as usual. She began to turn the knob of the combination lock. It worked smoothly and in a moment the heavy door swung open. The safe was entirely empty, swept clear of all the papers, titles, deeds, bonds which had covered its shelves.

As actually as though he stood there again, Madeleine saw the polite pseudo-Swiss geological gentleman, thanking Jules for the temporary use of his excellent safe.

She was petrified by this new blow, feeling the very ground give way under her feet. A cold, cold wind of necessity and stress blew upon her. The walled and sheltered refuge in which she had lived all her life was utterly cast down and in ruins. The realization came to her, like something intolerable, indecent, that *she,* Madeleine Brismantier, was now as poor as that old bedridden neighbor had been all her life . . . *all her life*. . . .

Somehow, that had something to do with those sheets which she had had and the other woman had not . . . her mind came back with a mortal sickness to the knowledge that she had now nothing, nothing to depend upon except her own strength and labor—just like a *poor* woman. She *was* a poor woman!

Somebody was weeping and tugging at her skirts. She looked down blindly. It was Raoul, her little son. He was sobbing and saying: "Sylvie said not to come, but I couldn't stand it any more. I'm hungry! I'm hungry, and there isn't a thing left upstairs to eat! I'm hungry! I'm hungry!"

Madeleine put her hand to her head and thought. What had happened? Oh yes, all their money had been stolen, all . . . but Raoul was hungry, the children must have something to eat. "Hush, my darling," she said to the little boy, "go back upstairs and tell Sylvie to come here and look out for the shop while I go out and find something to eat."

She went down the silent, empty street, before the silent empty houses staring at her out of their shattered windows, and found not a soul abroad. At the farm, in the outskirts of town, she saw smoke rising from the chimney and went into the courtyard. The young farmer's wife was there, feeding a little cluster of hens, and weeping like a child. She stared at the

newcomer for a moment without recognizing her.
Madeleine looked ten years older than she had a fortnight ago.

"Oh, madame, we had three hundred hens, and they
left us just these eight that they couldn't catch! And they
killed all but two of our thirty cows; we'd raised them
ourselves from calves up. They killed them there before
the very door and cooked them over a fire in the courtyard, and they broke up everything of wood to burn in
the fire, all our hoes and rake handles, and the farm-
wagon and . . . oh, what will my husband say when
he knows!"

Madeleine had a passing glimpse of herself as though
in a convex mirror, distorted but recognizable. She said,
"They didn't hurt you or your husband's mother, did
they?"

"No, they were drunk all the time and they didn't
know what they were doing mostly. We could hide
from them."

"Then your husband will not care at all about the
cows and pigs and farm-wagons," said Madeleine very
firmly, as though she were speaking to Sylvie. The
young farmer's wife responded automatically to the note
of authority in Madeleine's voice. "Don't you think he
will?" she asked simply, reassured somewhat, wiping
away her tears.

"No, and you are very lucky to have so much left,"
said Madeleine. "I have nothing, nothing at all for my
children to eat, and no money to buy anything." She

heard herself saying this with astonishment as though it were the first time she had heard it.

The young wife was horrified, sympathetic, a little elated to have one whom she had always considered her superior come asking her for aid; for Madeleine stood there, her empty basket on her arm, asking for aid, silently, helplessly.

"Oh, we have things left to *eat!*" she said. She put some eggs in Madeleine's basket, several pieces of veal left from the last animal killed which the Germans had not had time entirely to consume, and, priceless treasure, a long loaf of bread. "Yes, the wife of the baker got up at two o'clock last night, when she heard the last of the Germans go by, and started to heat her oven. She had hidden some flour in barrels behind her rabbit hutches, and this morning she baked a batch of bread. It's not so good as the baker's of course, but she says she will do better as she learns."

Madeleine turned back down the empty, silent street before the empty silent houses with their wrecked windows. A child came whistling along behind her, the little grandson of the bedridden Madame Duguet. Madeleine did what she had never done before in her life. She stopped him, made him take off his cap and put into it a part of her loaf of bread and one of the pieces of meat.

"Oh, meat!" cried the child. "We never had meat before!"

He set off at a run and disappeared.

As she passed the butcher-shop, she saw an old man hobbling about on crutches, attempting to sweep up the last of the broken glass. It was the father of the butcher. She stepped in, and stooping, held the dustpan for him. He recognized her, after a moment's surprise at the alteration in her expression, and said, " Merci, madame." They worked together silently a moment, and then he said: " I'm going to try to keep Louis' business open for him. I think I can till he gets back. The war *can't* be long. You, madame, will you be going back to your parents? "

Madeleine walked out without speaking. She could not have answered him if she had tried. In front of the Town Hall she saw a tall old woman in black toiling up the steps with a large package under each arm. She put down her basket and went to help. It was the white-haired wife of the old mayor, who turned a ghastly face on Madeleine to explain: " I am bringing back the papers to put them in place as he always kept them. And then I shall stay here to guard them and to do his work till somebody else can come." She laid the portfolios down on a desk and said in a low, strange voice, looking out of the window: " It was before that wall. I heard the shots."

Madeleine clasped her hands together tightly, convulsively, in a gesture of utter horror, of utter sympathy, and looked wildly at the older woman. The wife of the mayor said: " I must go back to the house now and get more of the papers. Everything must be in order." She added, as they went down the steps together: " What will you do about going on with your husband's business? Will you go back to live with your mother? We need a pharmacy so much in town. There will be no doctor, you know. You would have to be everything in that way."

This time Madeleine answered at once: " Yes, oh yes, I shall keep the pharmacy open. I already know about the accounts and the simple things. And I have thought how I can study my husband's books on pharmacy, at night after the children are in bed. I can learn. Jules learned."

She stooped to pick up her basket. The other woman went her way. Madeleine stepped forward into a new and awful and wonderful world along a new and thorny and danger-beset path into a new and terrifying and pleasureless life.

A wave of something stern and mighty swelled within her. She put down her head and walked forward strongly, as though breasting and conquering a great wind.